Love, Lies
and
Wedding
Cake

ALSO BY SUE WATSON

SUE WATSON

Love, Lies and Wedding Cake

Bookouture

Published by Bookouture in 2018

An imprint of StoryFire Ltd.
Carmelite House,
50 Victoria Embankment,
London EC4Y 0DZ

www.bookouture.com

ISBN: 978-1-78681-401-2
eBook ISBN: 978-1-78681-400-5

For beautiful brides of every age everywhere!

Chapter One

Spicy Rioja and Faulty Ballcocks

'Lie back,' he breathed, sliding his warm hand along my thigh. I did what I was told, and lay back on the sunlounger, the sun beating down under a foreign sky. His fingers were now expertly smoothing fragrant oil onto my warm skin, creating an electric sizzle on contact. I pulled down my shoulder straps provocatively and adjusted myself on the lounger so he could enjoy me in my best possible light. I looked at him from under luxurious eyelashes, my bronzed skin glowing in the sun, now high in the sky, the air laced with Hawaiian Tropic. I closed my eyes and relaxed as the gorgeous man applied factor 20 with the enthusiasm of a sex-starved Swedish masseur.

This is how I like to see it anyway, and the above description is pretty close, except for the bit about my skin being bronzed and my eyelashes being luxurious. My skin was more of a faded orange over mottled pink and my eyelashes were spiky and itchy and didn't belong to me. They'd been glued on by Mandy the beauty therapist, who used me like a bloody guinea pig at the salon where I worked. As soon as a new treatment appeared on the horizon, she'd whisk me into her Heavenly Spa above the salon and 'inflict' it on me.

She'd once vajazzled a cougar onto my private parts (not, I must add, at my request) and I was shocked to discover two very lifelike cougar eyes staring back at me when I'd looked down. Not, it has to be said, as shocked as Dan, my boyfriend who'd come face-to-face with the spectacle in the dark during a passionate encounter. He took it like a man but joked about being traumatised by it for some time after. Mandy had assured me these innovative new lashes I was now batting were all the rage in Hollywood and I'd look like a 'hot film star', but by the time I'd left the salon I looked more like a surprised drag queen.

So there I was in a small hotel in the Spanish hills, lying by a pool, with Dan, the love of my life. We'd been together for three years (with only a small gap in the first year when we'd hit a problem) and I'd never met anyone quite like this rather wonderful Australian Adonis who'd turned up in my local deli when I'd thought my life story was over. Free-spirited, with the spontaneity of a teenager, Dan climbed the highest mountains, dived into the deepest oceans and jumped on planes like other people jumped on buses. He'd seduced me with his tales of new worlds, hot sunshine, different flavours, and amazing people, and now we were sharing that journey together.

When I'd first met Dan, I'd been unhappily married to Craig, a career plumber who loved toilet pipes and flange fittings more than he loved me. Plumbing was his passion and nothing and no one could compete with a dripping valve or a faulty ballcock where Craig was concerned.

'Shall we sit in the shade?' Dan was asking me now, his eyes twinkling, not a murmur of faulty ballcocks, just sunshine and white wine.

I nodded, wordlessly, as he took my hand, his own still warm and slippery from the sun oil, and we lay under a huge palm and gazed into each other's eyes. I still couldn't believe this was my life, that Dan and I were together. I was a grandma now, as well as a university student – how crazy is that? Dan and I lived apart but close by, which is why these lovely snatched weekends were so special. After selling the marital home following my divorce, I was lodging with Emma, my daughter, a single mum. I say, 'lodging', but really I had moved in to help Emma look after Rosie, my gorgeous granddaughter. I was happy, and felt like I was almost having it all, but only too aware of how easy it might be to slip back into a life of domesticity, with no goals, and no dreams, just an endless loop of waking, sleeping and working. I'd been there and done that before, having to abandon my own degree as a teenager when I fell pregnant with Emma. So, the first thing I did after Rosie was born was to enrol on a degree course in English Literature again, some twenty-odd years after the first time.

I loved this new life and now, at the age of forty-five, was enjoying all the challenges thrown at me, and was excited about my future. I wasn't sure exactly what I was going to do with my degree, but I had more options than with my previous job as a hairdresser, which I still did part-time to supplement the student loan.

So here I was, a grandmother with a student loan, a lover and a full and busy life. I had my family, my dream course and my dream man. Freshly divorced, I had no plans to jump into marriage again any time soon, but if and when I did, it would only be with Dan. Neither of us had talked of marriage – I think perhaps for both of us it was way into the future, if at all – but I had that comfortable feeling that even if a ring wasn't involved, we'd always be together. We were just meant to be. Despite being crazy in love (as Beyoncé would say), I didn't want another relationship made up of arguments over the washing-up and heated debates involving which colour bin to put out that week. I wanted to preserve me and Dan, keep us special and our time together precious, so we lived apart, but minutes away – which was lovely. We also went away together whenever we could. From a night in Devon to a weekend in Rome, we were doing it all and enjoying our mutual passions: travel, food – and each other.

This weekend we were sampling the delights of Spain, from the weather to the food to the flamenco, and as I gazed at Dan over a glass of red, I felt like my heart was going to burst. His blue eyes were sparkly in the early evening sun, the dimples in his cheeks appeared as his eyes landed on mine and caught like fire. We didn't speak, we didn't need to; we just sat in silence, happy in each other's company, we had the rest of our lives to talk. For now, we just enjoyed being together.

'Is drinking red wine as the sun sets with a brilliant and handsome Australian on your living list?' Dan asked now, the twinkle never leaving his eyes.

When I'd been unhappily married to Craig, I'd kept a list of things I wanted to do, but I couldn't bear to think of it as my bucket list because it reminded me of dying, and this was a list about living. So that's what I'd called it – my living list.

I giggled. 'Not exactly. The specific wording on my list is drinking spicy Rioja while the sun sets behind a mountain in Spain… followed by amazing sex with a brilliant and handsome Australian.'

'Oh… but we've ordered tapas. Where does that figure in your list?'

'Between the Rioja and the sex, I'm just waiting for the brilliant and handsome Aussie to turn up,' I joked.

He laughed, and before he could retaliate the waitress appeared with our tapas – spicy sausage, salty squid, warm pastries with melt-in-the-mouth cheese filling and sun-dried tomatoes, sweet as caramel, with a savoury tang.

Our first trip together had been early on in our relationship, three years before when we'd spent a summer in Santorini together. While there, Dan had introduced me to all kinds of new dishes – white aubergines in olive oil, with garlic and lemon juice; lamb with herbs; a fresh Greek salad, crunchy and light with the saltiness of feta. He made my mouth water in so many ways. But it hadn't all been plain sailing, and when Emma discovered she was pregnant and abandoned I had to leave Dan on our paradise island and head home to be with her.

We split up, then reunited a year later on a rooftop in New York City, where we ate pastrami on rye and salty pretzels, washed down with bright cocktails. Later, as we lay in my hotel suite, we'd watched the flames of the sun reflecting on glass skyscrapers and Dan had told me he still wanted to see the world, but not without me.

'Let's add to your living list and tick places off, one by one,' he'd said, handing me a plane ticket to Rome. Before Dan I'd only dreamed of foreign cities, faraway beaches and foreign suns – my ex Craig was happy with a fortnight in a caravan in Bognor. And so it began. Dan and I started on our quest to tick off my living list and conquer the world. Our trips were short, but always packed with lovely places, magnificent meals and cake. There was always cake.

We'd eaten gateau in a chateau, chocolate torte in a moonlit port, and stöllen kisses in a sparkling Christmas market… and don't get me started on gelato in Milano. And now, here we were enjoying tapas sitting at a table under a palm tree, the sun slicing through the long, structured leaves, the nearby pool as blue as the sky.

'I love this,' I said, lifting my sunglasses onto my head so I could look into his eyes.

'The tapas?'

'No… us.'

He reached his hand across the table and, squeezing mine, he smiled that wicked smile. 'Me too.'

Then he looked intently at my face like he was scrutinising it. 'You okay, babe?'

'Yes… Why?'

'You look… I don't know, surprised?'

'Do I?'

'Yes… You look permanently surprised.'

'That'll be the Botox.'

'Oh yeah, performed by Dr Mandy Frankenstein,' he laughed.

I nodded, and rolled my eyes… which to my relief I was able to do again, despite the two huge spider-like weights attached to my upper eyelids.

'Do you know what one of my fellow students said the other day?' I asked, trying to move my face while biting into a juicy shrimp covered in spicy tomato. Mandy's 'salon doctor' had given me quite a dose of Botox, I wondered if I'd ever be able to express myself facially again.

Dan was concentrating on spiking a huge queen green olive from the earthenware bowl, and missing so that it slid away in its oily garlic bath.

'No, what did she say?'

'She said, "Faye's having a series of one-night stands throughout Europe with a toyboy." When you're nineteen, that's quite the compliment, not a judgement, and the response was a clutch of high fives and murmurings of "You go, girl!"'

Dan laughed. 'When you put it like that, I feel like quite the stud.'

'Yeah, and I feel like quite the cougar.'

'Girl, you got it goin' on,' he laughed, offering me a high five.

'Hell, yeah,' I said, slapping his palm and sipping my wine.

Despite me being 'the older woman' in this relationship, I was like a teenager with Dan. He was the worldly one who'd seen more of life and had a wisdom beyond his years. I would drink him in, listening to his stories of a wasted youth on the beaches of Sydney – a life of girls, surfboards and beer as the sun went down. I longed to chase the waves with him, drink cold beers in his backyard and watch fireworks over Sydney Harbour. When you love someone, you just want to know everything about them, live their lives, and one day I would go with him to Sydney. Until then we'd talk about it and I'd imagine a Christmas filled with sunshine, a place where everything was upside down and inside out and an adventure I was yet to experience. The more he told me about his country, the more I wanted to go. It was now number one on my living list, but the time wasn't right to visit yet. A holiday on the other side of the world would involve longer than a couple of weeks, and I couldn't leave little Rosie.

Too soon our Spanish weekend was over and we were heading for the airport in a beat-up taxi, stealing last-minute kisses on the back seat as the car trundled over the bumpy road.

'Where to next time?' I said, snuggling into his arms as he kissed the top of my head. We always climbed into our little bubble on these weekends away and as much as I wanted to get back to Rosie and Emma and 'real' life, it wasn't easy to leave these wonderful locations. Dan would go back to working his job at the deli and my life would overwhelm me and despite living close to each other, the passion and intensity faded once back. One of the ways we coped with this was by looking forward and planning our next getaway.

'I was thinking...' he started. 'I reckon sometime in April is the anniversary of our first kiss, and I was thinking... it's only fitting to celebrate in the City of Love.'

'Paris?' I asked, excitedly.

'No... Ormskirk,' he teased.

'Oh my God, Paris!' I squealed, sounding like an excited child. We'd been to many capital cities in Europe, but Paris was special, somewhere neither of us had been. We'd always said we'd go there when the time was right, so I was beyond excited. Finally, everything was coming together and life was almost too good to be true. I should have known then that's exactly what it was – too good to be true.

Chapter Two

Skyping Naked with Katy Perry

Two months after our trip to Spain, Dan and I booked into a lovely chateau on the outskirts of Paris. I know this sounds terrible, but I didn't even feel guilty about using the money from the house sale to pay my half. All those hours I'd slaved at work and all those nights I'd sat alone with Craig waiting for something – anything – to happen. If I hadn't had the courage to cut myself free from my marriage, I would still be there, paying the mortgage, worrying about a pension while waiting for life to happen. Instead I was with Dan, two lovers in Paris. This was true independence, and I loved it.

Paris with Dan was magical and we had the most wonderful weekend. It was spring, and blossom covered the parks and pavements like confetti; the weather was warm with a tingle of freshness. On the first night, we ate alfresco at a restaurant by the Seine, watching the early evening sun fill the sky with blood orange and melt into the water, turning it into a million shades of red. We ate salty, garlicky mussels, drank very cold white wine and never took our eyes from each other... except to gaze longingly at the dessert menu.

That evening we clung to each other in the big, ornate double bed, entangled in crisp white sheets, overlooked by a glittering chandelier. Once again, I had to pinch myself: life had changed so dramatically since the end of my marriage. I'd never in a million years imagined myself at forty-five in a Parisian hotel room with my boyfriend. Funny where life can take you, especially if you give things a little push.

Later, I took a shower, and lost myself under hot, steaming needles of water, imagining what it would be like to live here, in Paris, together. I loved the idea of sleeping in the same bed as Dan every night, waking up together each morning; it just felt so free holding hands and heading out into the city for croissants and culture. One day we would live together permanently, side by side, reading to each other in bed, sharing crosswords over breakfast and making love in the afternoons…

I was suddenly shocked out of my daydream at the feel of his strong arms around me, his face in the back of my neck, kissing me under the steaming water. I turned, and within seconds, my legs were wrapped around him, as he gently pushed my back against the tiles. He lifted me higher, his hands on my naked buttocks as he thrust himself inside me, making me cry out in ecstasy, hot water pulsing down, the urgency increasing until we both reached a crescendo. I tried to hold on but almost slipped on the tiles, which made us giggle as I screamed 'Don't drop me,' the water still cascading, my heart still beating.

We finally left the shower, my legs weak, my body exhausted and my heart full. He took the white hotel robes from their hangers and wrapped me in mine, tying the knot around my waist and kissing me again on the lips. He slipped into his robe and we lay on the bed, looking up at the huge ceilinged room, the rosette architrave, the crystal chandelier with its million lights.

'I never imagined I'd stay in a real French chateau,' I whispered into the darkness. 'I didn't even have it on my living list – it hadn't even entered my head to put it on. I feel like I'm in new territory, unbelievable things keep happening to me. I blame you,' I laughed.

'Amazing what life will bring you, if you let it,' he said, and we fell asleep in each other's arms.

I was awoken suddenly the next morning by the alarm on my phone and wondered for a moment where I was. Then I saw Dan and realised my phone was reminding me about something important.

'Rosie!' I said. And he opened his eyes, knowing immediately what I was talking about.

'Wait there,' he said, 'I'll get the laptop. We can't keep her waiting, you know what she's like,' he laughed, as he reached into his bag.

'Hang on, you need to put a T-shirt on; Madam would not approve of you Skyping naked,' I laughed. Rosie would have definitely had something to say and I wasn't sure I wanted to hear it. She was three going on thirty and happy to share her thoughts with everyone and anyone.

Wherever we were and however long the stay was, my grand-daughter insisted we Skype her while we were there. I'd like to say it was because she missed me, but I think it was more about her being a mini control freak – she just liked to check up on me. Regardless, we loved talking to her, and Dan always brought his laptop along, and was a dab hand at Skyping. For a man in his thirties he wasn't perturbed by playing the role of granddad; he did it brilliantly, enjoying time with Rosie as much as I did.

Five minutes later, we were virtually in the living room at Emma's, with Rosie regaling us about her new boyfriend she'd met at nursery. 'It's Josh,' she announced, while nodding agreeably.

'I thought your boyfriend was called Noah?' Dan said, referring to the last conversation we'd had only the day before regarding her busy love life. Today she was wearing a feather boa around her neck and a tiara, her usual headwear of choice for a Sunday.

'No, it's not Noah, you silly boy,' she shook her head so vigorously she made herself dizzy and almost fell off her chair. Emma was smiling in the background ready to catch her, or the laptop if it fell off her knee as she often became extremely animated during these Skype chats.

'Oh sorry, it's just that when we left the day before yesterday I'm sure you told me your boyfriend was Noah?'

'Dam,' she said, reprimanding him for his questioning, her eyes opening wide – she wasn't cursing, she always called him 'Dam'.

'So, Rosie, what's going on?' he asked, seriously. 'You breaking hearts at the nursery again?'

'Dam… you're streshing me out,' she lisped, raising her still-baby hands in the air.

I could see Dan was trying not to laugh, the dimples in his cheeks were straining to appear, but he continued to speak to her like she was in her mid-thirties. Which she thought she was.

'Sorry, Rosie, I just get a bit confused. You're so popular and…'

'Yes, I am,' she nodded, 'it's ridicluss,' she added, folding her arms awkwardly over her tummy. I had no idea where this little diva came from, Emma and I were far quieter than her and I couldn't imagine it was from Craig's side, but her confidence was amazing. I was a very proud grandma and just took her in, aware I had a beaming smile on my face whenever she was around. Then she changed the subject: 'Dam, where are you, where's Nana?'

'We're in Paris, darling,' I said, leaning into the screen.

'Pawis?' she said, like I'd just suggested we were in a running sewer.

We both nodded eagerly at the same time; this three-year-old princess had us in her thrall and she knew it. But then she turned to Emma and asked for her phone, apparently the thrall wasn't mutual.

'You're talking to Nana and Dan, you can't speak to someone on your phone too, that would be rude,' Emma was saying.

This caused a major eye-roll: 'Mum, you're being very silly, I want my phone so I can make a selfie!' She looked back at the webcam and shook her head in despair at her audience.

Emma told her to finish her conversation on Skype first.

'Nana, hugs,' she said, reaching out her chubby little arms and pouting her lips into a kiss. I was being dismissed, which didn't stop my heart from melting over the keyboard, but before I could enjoy this moment she'd moved swiftly on.

'Dam... when are you coming home to play Dowa the Explowa?' she lisped, referring to her Dora the Explorer video game.

'We'll be back tomorrow, get the iPad ready,' he said.

'Can we play for ages and ages and ages, and AGES?' her little arms expanding wider and wider. It seemed Dan was in for a marathon session.

'Yeah... stop swiping swiper!' he said, alluding to the sneaky orange fox in the story.

'Oh *man*,' she giggled, they had their own language.

'Have you been to Millie's party today?' I asked, but she was suddenly distracted by Katy Perry... the cat. 'Katy Pewwy wants her tea now,' she announced, unable to hide her boredom with us.

'What's she having for her tea?' I asked.

'Chips and chocolate,' she answered, 'bye,' and with that, shut down the computer before Emma could stop her or speak to us.

'Rosie, hang on...' I started, but too late, she was gone.

'We have been dismissed,' Dan said, closing the laptop.

'Classic Rosie,' I smiled.

'She cracks me up,' he laughed and we giggled about how Dan had recently decorated the living room at Emma's and Rosie had basically become his boss.

'Every five minutes it was "when's Dam coming to help me with the walls?"' I laughed.

'Yeah, and when she was stood next to me "scraping",' he used his fingers to indicate the speech marks, 'she said, "Thanks, Dam, for helping me with the decowating.'

Age three, my granddaughter had more sass and confidence than I'd ever had and basically ruled the house. She adored Dan – I suppose he was the only father figure in her life as her real dad had dumped Emma when she was pregnant and Craig didn't see much of her. He just carried on with his life after I left – nothing changed, he just stayed in the same routine. It suited him, and didn't affect me anymore, but it meant he saw less of Emma and Rosie – he popped round sometimes when he knew I'd be out, but they weren't close.

I met Dan while I was married to Craig, but I was never actually unfaithful, our relationship started once I'd left. But I think Craig still felt betrayed; I don't blame him, he just never expected me to walk away, he thought we could go on living side by side like grumpy siblings for the rest of our lives. I wasn't prepared to do that. And now, with Dan in this lovely, easy relationship where things happened because we made them happen, I knew I'd done the right thing. I looked over at Dan, who was still laughing about Rosie's commandeering of the wallpapering.

'There was paint and paste everywhere. Katy Perry was licking wallpaper paste off her bum for days,' he said, smiling at the memory.

'I bet that's a sentence you never thought you'd say.'

'That's kids for you,' he laughed. 'You find yourself doing and saying the craziest things... At the park the other day, she made me chase her up the slide as she came down, pretending to be the Hulk. God knows what the other mothers thought, especially as she'd insisted on wearing her tutu and cycle helmet.'

'Darling, it's what they're wearing on the catwalks of Paris this year,' I smiled. 'You're so good with her, you'd be a lovely dad.' I leaned into him, putting my head back on the luxurious pile of pillows. Dan being a dad was something I'd often thought about, and it made me feel sad and a little guilty to think if he stayed with me, it wasn't something I could give him.

'I'm happy with what I've got... I don't need any kids of my own, Rosie's a full-time job for anyone,' he said. 'And I have my nephews back home.'

I noticed a shadow crossing his face.

'Have you heard from your brother?' I asked.

'Yeah, he's great...'

'Really?' I wasn't convinced. His older brother John lived with Huntington's disease, a hereditary condition that Dan had tested negative for. Their mother had died from the illness when Dan was very young and I know he found it difficult to talk about. He'd shared his feelings of guilt on discovering that he'd escaped the gene, but had problems facing his brother's fate.

And now, when I asked about John, he was doing his usual avoidance tactic.

'One day we'll live there, me and you...' he said, skilfully moving the conversation away from his brother. I knew not to push this, and I was aware he found it painful to talk about.

'Yeah, when Rosie's all grown up and Emma's CEO of her firm. So, for now, tell me again about those waves on Bondi Beach...' I said, relaxing into his voice, filled with sunshine and lemon cake.

'Big as skyscrapers...' he started and went on to describe how he and his brother had spent whole days in the sea as kids. I'd heard it before, but never tired of his stories of home. He'd come alive when he spoke and I knew he missed it and the past he'd shared with his brother. 'Wrinkled from the water we'd be... Mum had no bloody idea where we were, she'd send search parties out and they'd find us in the waves.'

I looked over at him, his eyes shielded, but his mouth smiling as he spoke. This was a time before his mother's death, and the later news that his brother also had the gene. I knew this was his happy place. Despite his wisdom, there were childlike aspects to Dan's personality, and I wondered if in some ways he'd stopped growing up. He'd never really put down roots in his adult life, which I suppose for me was part of his charm, but there had to come a point when he settled down. Dan took his fun where he could, with little thought about tomorrow, perhaps because he'd seen the future reflected in the past and couldn't face it?

'What about your nephews?' I said, thinking of the photo of two little blond kids in his wallet. 'Do you miss them?'

'Yeah, but they're grown up now. They don't need me as much, not like Rosie. I'm a sort of honorary uncle to her, aren't I?'

'Or the youngest granddad in the business?' I laughed.

Dan stayed over with me sometimes at Emma's, but it wasn't for the romance. The walls were thin, and the rooms were cramped, and Rosie often got into my bed in the middle of the night. When you're three years old and you're running from the bogeyman it's actually even better when sometimes nanny's fun friend is there too. The first time she'd clambered in between us at three in the morning I wasn't quite sure how Dan would take it, but being Dan, he thought it was hilarious and told her silly stories until she drifted off to sleep with her arms around his neck. I remember lying there in the dark smiling to myself, filled with love for both of them, touched by the way these two people worlds apart communicated so easily and happily. That night we'd carried her back to her room as she slept, only to be awoken an hour later by an indignant three-year-old, standing at the side of the bed, hands on hips, saying, 'Well, *that* wasn't very nice!' before clambering back in, uninvited.

I told Emma the next day and she was mortified – 'Oh, Mum, I'm so sorry, call me next time.'

'Why, do you want to hear Dan's bedtime stories too?' I'd joked. I'd assured her it was all fine, and she could see by the way Dan played hide-and-seek and taught Rosie magic tricks that he was as good for her as she was for him.

'So, you're happy being granddad?' I asked.

'I'm… happy, yeah,' he paused, and for a moment I wondered if he meant it. 'I love Rosie, it's just…'

I suddenly felt a prickle on the back of my neck. 'What?'

'Nothing, I just feel sometimes like I've… given up, you know?'

'Given up what?' I looked at him questioningly. The concern must have shown on my face.

'I love you and I love being with you…' he said, touching my arm to reassure me, but his words had struck me and I wanted to know what he meant, what he felt.

'So when you say you feel you've given up… what do you mean?'

'I mean… sometimes I worry I'm not going anywhere. I'm thirty-six and I don't want to be forty and still living in a little flat above my aunt's business. I like working in the deli, and when I thought I was only there for a few months I was happy, but it's been about four years, on and off, and I just keep seeing more years stretch out before me. It can feel a bit… predictable, you know?'

Unfortunately, I did know, and I could see all the signs; he was feeling just as I had when I was married. I'd done the same thing: found work in a hairdressing salon, planned to stay a few months and twenty years later, realised I was still there. And the fact I'd broken out of the rut by leaving my partner and falling for Dan wasn't exactly inspiring me now. Had karma come to get me? Was

Dan seeing his forty-five-year-old grandma girlfriend as the reason his life was so predictable?

'Do you feel... trapped?' I asked. Wanting to cover my ears in case I didn't like his answer.

'No, no... not really.'

'Not really?' I said, my heart starting to thump in my chest. What was he saying?

'I just sometimes wish we could pack a bag and run away, live on a beach somewhere, open a café.'

The word 'we' calmed me slightly, but I was unnerved by this conversation – even if I wanted to, I couldn't just up sticks like he wanted.

'Perhaps you need to go off and find what you're looking for?' I said, deliberately using the single word 'you' instead of 'me' to see how he responded. If he wanted to run away with me or without me, I couldn't hold him back – he'd already given up so much for me. He'd returned from Australia to be with me, and embraced my family like his own... and being with me meant he'd never have his own.

'I don't know what I'm looking for though,' he was saying. 'I kinda thought I'd be doing something with my life by now.' He turned to me, and still seeing the worried look on my face, touched my cheek. 'Hey, it's all good with us, babe. Everything's great, I promise.'

I gave him a sideways glance – was he really okay? And if everything was all good with us, why did he want to run away?

I smiled, eager to believe he was happy and everything was fine; we were in Paris and we were in love. Me and Dan were bulletproof, nothing bad could ever happen to us... could it?

The next day, we walked hand in hand to the Pont des Arts, where we tied a lovelock to the bridge, along with all the others tied on by lovestruck couples. I wondered what their stories were and I hoped they were as happy as us. Then with a jolt I remembered what he'd said the night before and tried not to think about the possibility that he might not be fulfilled. But then how could he be? He was working and living in a shop in the Midlands that sold fancy cheese, and as much as he loved cheese and everything about it, there was more to life. We both knew he had this dream of having his own café, and making something of his life, but it wasn't going to happen here. His dream was a café in Sydney Harbour, life under a blue sky, near an even bluer sea, a surfboard under his arm, a million recipes in his head… I just hoped this feeling would pass and that he could wait it out with me until we could run away together one day when the time was right. And who knew when that would be? I wasn't leaving Emma as a single mother or walking away from Rosie's childhood. We threw our key into the river and I made a wish.

'It's a sign of eternal love,' Dan said, gazing out onto the water where our key had just sunk. I stared out for a long time, wondering how many keys were lying on the bottom of the riverbed, belonging to couples who'd said goodbye.

We stood for a long time, arm in arm, until dusk fell and the sun began bleeding into the river and I wanted the world to stop here and now by the swirling reds and oranges where we'd laid our hearts to rest. But it didn't – the world moved on, and though I didn't know it then, this had been a very precious weekend, because life as we knew it was about to change.

Chapter Three

Pink Concubines and Frozen Pyjamas

Arriving home late on Sunday evening, I unlocked the front door and crept quietly into the hall so I didn't wake Emma and Rosie. But when I walked into the kitchen, Emma was sitting at the table, which surprised me; she wasn't usually up this late. She looked up from her phone and smiled.

'Had a good time?' she whispered quietly.

'Yes, I'm surprised you're still up.'

'Yeah, you look surprised.'

'It's the Botox... or is it the fake lashes?'

'Mandy really went for it this time, didn't she?' Emma said, scrutinising my face.

'It could have been worse – I'm just glad I only let her at my face,' I whispered, and we giggled quietly, then Emma snorted and that made us giggle even more. Rosie was a scarily light sleeper and we automatically kept our voices low once she was in bed. Having to be quiet in the evening was something Dan could never quite get used to – he'd laugh loudly, shout through to me in another room and be generally noisy at all hours. Then Rosie would appear at the top of the stairs in her *Frozen* pyjamas with a cheeky smile on her face wanting to 'play hide-and-seek with Dam'.

I put the kettle on and showed Emma photos of the chateau, reliving every moment and longing to be back there with him.

'Sounds wonderful,' she smiled.

She sipped her tea, the light from her phone shining on her face – still my little girl. And just like when she was small, I searched her eyes, looking to see if she was happy or sad, and if it was the latter, what I could do to change that? But as they grow older, it gets harder – it's not just about kissing a grazed knee better, it's often more complicated. She'd met someone recently through work, and I know he made her happy, but he lived in Scotland and it wasn't easy for them. Still, I had to leave her be. It was hard enough having her mother live with her, let alone trying to impinge on her love life.

Emma was starting a new job tomorrow, a really great promotion to executive in the PR company she worked for. This meant I'd need to be around more for Rosie, which I was happy to do, but Emma never took me for granted. 'Mum, I don't want you to give up your independence for my childcare,' she'd said, but I assured her I wasn't giving anything up, it was my choice to be there for her. I wouldn't have it any other way and we had enrolled Rosie at the university crèche so Emma could throw herself into her career, I could continue with my degree and Rosie would be with me. Emma would work the long hours necessary in the week and spend weekends with Rosie, while I caught up on essays and worked at my old hairdresser's, Curl Up and Dye.

The salon had always been the craziest place to spend one's days. From staff to customers, all of human life was there, and it wanted its hair done. My old boss Sue had left the salon a couple of years before to live in Spain with the toy boy she'd met on Tinder, who'd rinsed her harder than any shampoo and blow-dry, leaving her in Ibiza in nothing but the clothes she stood up in. Having sold the salon to the beauty therapist Mandy (who'd come into a little money on the death of her granddad), there was nothing left for Sue in the Midlands after the Ibiza debacle, so she'd headed to Devon, where she found work at an ice cream café. She kept in touch mainly by text and postcards, keen to describe her lovely new life, from the amazing ice cream to 'the pink concubines', which apparently grew up her trellis. She still hadn't found love, and if those 'concubines' were anything to go by, it seemed she still hadn't found a cure for those malapropisms either.

I sipped my tea as Emma scrolled on her phone, both happy together in our own little worlds.

'You okay, about tomorrow, first day?' I asked gently.

'Bit nervous,' she smiled, putting down the phone. 'I just hope everyone's nice.'

'I'm sure they are. And they'll love you – how could they not?'

She chuckled. 'You would say that, Mum, you're slightly biased.'

I blew her a kiss across the table and she caught it.

'I'd better go to bed – need to be fresh for the morning,' she sighed.

We caught hands as she left the kitchen, and not for the first time I felt that maternal pang, wishing she didn't have to go through life's tricky bits. It felt like her first day at school and I wished I could be there holding her hand at every turn. I knew I could be a bit of a helicopter mother, but Emma was my only child and I just wanted her to be happy and if I could help that happen, then I was happy too. But all I was feeling now was guilty because I couldn't make Emma confident about starting a new job, I couldn't help Dan feel fulfilled and I couldn't afford to take Rosie to Disney World. Even remembering Sue's advice about putting myself first for a change wasn't helping. She was my best friend who always looked out for me and I missed her now. She'd been the one to encourage me to leave my marriage and it had transformed me, turning me into who I was now: more confident, more happy, more fulfilled and loved. Oh yes, I was to mis-quote Bridget Jones, one of *the 'smug unmarrieds'*.

I just wished I could shake the niggle in the back of my head that had been there since Dan had talked about how he felt like he should be doing something more. I hoped it was just a passing feeling, but it was his free spirit that had drawn me to him in the first place and I couldn't blame him for wanting a change from the daily routine in the deli.

He needed to be stimulated, inspired and the little deli on the little high street wasn't doing it for him – I just hoped I still was. Dan needed something special to take him out of himself, and I thought about us both running away for a few weeks over the summer. I had a long summer off uni but reminded myself that with Emma's new job, Rosie would be totally dependent on me.

It would be fine, wouldn't it? Everything would work out, and Dan had said it was all good, so I had to believe him and stop worrying. Then I suddenly remembered I hadn't finished my essay, 'A Feminist Critique of *The Great Gatsby*', and it was due in the next day. I jumped up, my previous niggles and worries and guilt instantly wiped out by this more immediate concern, and silently chastising myself, I gathered all my notes, my laptop and my copy of the novel (a gift from Dan before I'd started studying) and went upstairs to spend a few hours with F. Scott Fitzgerald.

The following morning I was woken very early by Rosie, who jumped on me from a great height, causing me to scream loudly.

'Nanny... where's Dam?' she said, from her position sitting on my chest.

'He's at his flat, he'll come over later,' I said, rubbing my eyes.

'I want to see Dam.' Her bottom lip was torn between a quiver and a pout.

'Yes, you will see Dan, sweetie,' I said, reaching for my handbag near the bed with one hand and holding my granddaughter upright with the other so she didn't fall. She was watching me like a hawk; I always brought her a little something back from my travels and this time it was a Parisian doll, wrapped in paper covered in outlines of the map of Paris. I could see the excitement in her eyes as she tried, in her three-year-old way, to do as Mummy and Nanny had always taught her and not ask for gifts, but wait to receive them. I had to smile, she was almost sitting on her hands as I gave her the present.

'Look, this is what Paris looks like from the sky,' I said. I should have known better, trying to explain a map to a three-year-old who only wanted what was inside, as all restraint was lost as she tore at the paper I'd lovingly chosen and wrapped, while squealing with excitement.

'LOOK,' she shouted, thrusting the doll at me, once she was released from her paper prison. 'A nice lady,' she waved the doll in her long, green frills and hat in the air, and pronounced her to be 'a dancing Pawis lady…' Eager to tell anyone and everyone of this new acquisition, she leapt off the bed and into Emma's room, shouting, 'MUM, Dam gave me a present, a dancing lady…' She always assumed the gifts I'd brought back from our travels were chosen by Dan, which often they were. She couldn't articulate this, but it was obviously important for her to be ever-present to him, and as she danced and twirled between mine and Emma's bedrooms, I smiled at this.

Rosie had now transformed the elegant doll into an aeroplane. She was making loud, wet, blasting noises as the flying doll crashed into 'the mountains', which were apparently formed by my knees under the bedcovers.

Emma was standing in the doorway of my bedroom, already dressed in her suit and looking every inch the career woman I'd always wanted her to be. It was her first day in the new job and I was so proud. Yes, it would mean longer hours and a huge commitment, but I was delighted to be there so she could take this next step.

'Do you think she's a tomboy?' my daughter smiled, ruffling her little girl's hair as Rosie contorted the doll into an unnatural position I was sure no human could achieve.

'Probably – *you* were, I bought you all kinds of girly toys when you were little, but they usually ended up in a war zone,' I said. I was a little distracted about the role my knees were playing in this plane crashing scenario, as the doll 'crashed' face down on the 'mountain'.

'Do my knees look big in this?' Emma giggled, nodding at the scene around my legs.

I laughed, and Rosie laughed along, always happy to join in, even if she didn't understand a word of what we were saying. It was these moments I loved, just the three of us laughing together over nothing. I knew from experience that these moments were fleeting and precious – and I was glad to be there for my family. I wasn't worrying about what the future held for any of us, just enjoying the here and now, because it isn't here for long.

Chapter Four

Nicole Scherzinger's Bag of Cheese Balls

The following Saturday I was in the salon wrestling with Mrs Johnson's flaky scalp and thinning locks in a vain attempt to grant her wish to 'make me look like that girl from The Pussycat Dolls'. I scrolled down my phone for pictures and we established that Nicole Scherzinger was the 'doll' Mrs Johnson wanted to be. This wasn't an easy ask – she was the wrong side of fifty with a bad case of halitosis and a penchant for cheese balls, which she crunched throughout the process. I doubted this would be the snack of choice for any of The Pussycat Dolls, least of all the glamorous Nicole.

I was thinking how much easier it would be to write my essay, 'A postmodern critique of *Frankenstein* and the nature of the seventeenth-century scientific revolution', than it would be to transform this chunky mother of five into a Pussycat Doll, when my phone pinged. I slipped my hand discreetly into my pocket and saw it was a message from Dan. Seeing his name on my phone never failed to give me a warm glow in my tummy, like someone had just put a string of fairy lights in there. I hadn't seen him much since we'd returned from Paris and usually we didn't get to see each other much in the week. This made our time together all the more special and I couldn't wait to see him, but before I could read his text I had to try and turn Mrs Jackson into a Pussycat Doll. This was quite an ask, and the more I backcombed and curled, all I could see before me in the mirror was John Travolta in *Hairspray*.

I continued with the 'makeover' and twinkled for a while as I put Mrs Johnson under the colour warmer. Sending a prayer that Sarcastic Scarlet would do something miraculous to her elephant grey, I disappeared to take a much-needed break. I sat in the dark little staffroom littered with the detritus of everyone's lunch and opened the text message.

When do you finish tonight?

I texted back that I finished at seven and he asked if we could meet. We hadn't arranged to see each other that evening, so this was an unusual surprise.

Do you have something special planned? I texted.

Sadly not : (I need to talk to you, babe was his response, which was slightly ominous and didn't sound like he had a fun evening in mind. I suggested he come over to ours, but he said he wanted to speak to me privately, which was a little odd. He was usually happy to spend Saturday nights at Emma's with us all. I couldn't think what he might need to talk to me about – the fact he wanted this to be a private conversation suggested something huge. But I didn't have time to call and ask him, so I just texted *Why the cloak and dagger?* I waited a few seconds and his response came back: *Don't want to text. Let's talk later xxx*

I felt vaguely nauseous and agreed to meet him in the nearby pub later. A little tinge of worry marred my day now, but the show must go on and I headed back into the salon, putting a big, bright smile on my face.

Greeting my ten o'clock like she was Beyoncé, I chatted about the weather, *Britain's Got Talent* and Donald Trump's hair, but my mind kept wandering to Dan: what did he want to talk to me about that had to be kept private?

I spent the rest of the day trying to smile, cut, colour, and blow-dry – attempting to work miracles with the strange hair dyes and often even stranger clients. Women of every age, colour and sexual persuasion came through those doors. Today I would welcome Frida – seventy-two, blue rinse, side parting, husband with Alzheimer's and a long-felt desire for Latin men (Frida, not her husband). Later, Thomas would arrive in his work suit and after only a couple of hours would leave with sequinned lashes and his hair teased to within an inch of his life. Mandy's extreme make-up, lashes and tango tanning had made her into a goddess for local drag queens and ballroom dancers. The sights that walked up and down those stairs to the Heavenly Spa were scary and spectacular. I sometimes felt like I was working backstage at the Moulin Rouge, with all the hair and nails and tits and teeth – and that was just the men!

Throughout this madness I trimmed, teased and cajoled hair into all kinds of shapes and styles, while trying not to think too hard about what Dan's text could mean – but I couldn't work it out.

I even shared my concerns with salon-owner Mandy, the twenty-five-year-old slutdropping champion (she had the satin sash) whose proudest boast was that she could drink ten Porn Star Martinis and 'still drop it like it's hot!' Apparently.

'Why didn't he just pop into the salon and talk to me "privately" outside, or in the staffroom?' I said over her usual lunch of choice, a Big Mac with fries and a Diet Coke – which she said 'killed' the calories in the food. I wish! 'And the text was so short and to the point – no heart emoji, no "I love you," just that we *need* to talk,' I added, absently dipping a chip into a pot of tomato sauce.

'Uh-oh,' she said, through a mouthful of burger.

'What?' I stopped dipping and looked at her.

'Bitch, please?' she said, like I knew what she was talking about.

'What?'

'It's obvious, isn't it?'

'Not to me.'

'Bruce has found someone else to play with his bush oysters... Do you think?'

'No, of course not,' I said.

'He could be shagging someone else?' she suggested. 'Just putting it out there,' she added as she chowed down.

I looked at her, 'Mandy, I... you can't just *say* that.'

She shrugged. 'If he has... shagged anyone else... even if he's only grinded on some slapper – then he's a gonner.' She took another huge bite of burger and wiped her whole face with her napkin.

'Mand... I really don't think—'

'Seriously, babes,' she said, emerging from a ketchup-soaked napkin, 'if he has, and you want me to get someone to have a word with him, Jase knows a few blokes in Spain who'd rough him up a bit for you?'

'NO… no… thanks, Mandy,' I said, panicked. I didn't doubt that Jason, the love of Mandy's life, knew men who could 'rough up' other men. But I didn't want Mandy taking this into her own hands and turning a misconstrued text into attempted murder on the Spanish Costas. So I put on a fake smile and feigned hopefulness. 'He might just be meeting up to announce that he's whisking me off to Barbados?' I offered.

'Barbados? Ha, dream on, bitch,' she smiled. She called everyone 'bitch' these days, it was a term of endearment where Mandy was concerned and she patted my arm affectionately. She finished her Big Mac, and when she saw I'd put mine down, offered to finish mine too. I handed her the lot – the talk of bush oysters had suddenly made me lose my appetite.

I went back to the wannabe Pussycat Doll, whose look was more 'Bride of Chucky' after the salon's latest batch of cheap Lithuanian hair dye. As none of us spoke Lithuanian, the names on the tubes had always been a mystery to us, so the former owner, Sue had christened them all in her own tongue and the names had stuck. We still worked with 'Wicked Cinnamon', 'Malevolent Blonde', 'Strident Peach' and my particular favourite, 'Sarcastic Scarlet', which today had done its worst on Mrs Jackson. Being the professional I am, I bravely brushed through and pretended everything was 'fabulous'. While attempting to pile up the vivid monstrosity on the top of Mrs Johnson's head, I told myself I could cope with whatever Dan had to tell me – and it was probably nothing… but I still worried for the rest of the afternoon.

I arrived at the pub just after eight and immediately spotted Dan in the corner, away from the hubbub. He had a half-drunk pint in front of him and a perspiring glass of white next to it on the table, and I softened at the sight of him – and my white wine.

'Hey,' he said, in that lovely lilting way of his, standing up to greet me as I reached the table. We hugged and he made room for me next to him, and as I sat down, I kissed him on the cheek, pushed my arm through his and grabbed my drink.

'So, what's all the drama and intrigue?' I asked, desperate to find out. 'Have you won the lottery or something?'

'I wish! Sorry, babe, I didn't want to worry you, but I didn't want to put it in a text either…' He wasn't smiling, the dimples weren't there and he looked worried.

'What?' My mouth was suddenly dry. 'Put what in a text?'

'I should have phoned you… but you know what I'm like about… difficult conversations. I had to see you.'

'What? What's the matter?' I was going to throw up there and then on the shabby-chic wooden table in front of a pub full of strangers.

'It's my brother, John – his wife Kimmie, she called me this morning, says I need to go home.'

'Oh Dan, I'm so sorry,' I said, shocked at this news even though it wasn't entirely unexpected. His brother had been ill for so long I think it was easier for everyone to just imagine he'd remain in this state forever. 'But hopefully he'll be okay?' I offered, unsure of what to say.

'No… he's really crook,' he said, which I knew was an Australian phrase meaning really sick.

'But it happened before… the deterioration?' I said. 'You went to him then, but he pulled through.' I couldn't begin to imagine how John and his family coped with this terrible spectre over their lives. It had been with them for years and ever since his diagnosis John knew there were no guarantees of a long-term future. I often wondered how he must feel to know he'd probably never see his boys married, never meet his grandchildren; I couldn't begin to imagine how awful that would be. I lived for my daughter and granddaughter.

'Kimmie says this is different,' Dan was saying. 'It's worse than before… Says it feels like time's running out.' He looked sad; he was finding this hard to talk about, he'd never really faced his brother's illness head-on, but it looked like he was now having to.

'But there's still hope, right?' I said, trying hard not to be clichéd, but unable to dampen down my natural optimism.

He shook his head. 'The doctor confirmed things are… bad.'

I could see by his face that he was really shaken – this had been his worst fear for a long time.

'Oh, God,' I said, tears pricking my eyes. I didn't know John, but felt in some ways like I did. I'd heard all the childhood stories about Dan and his 'bro' and it was devastating to think that someone so young – he was only forty – and with a family was looking at the end of his life.

'He's lived with this since he was eighteen – pretty crap, isn't it?' he said, taking a sip of beer. He put down his glass and swallowed, 'He's asked to see me…'

I nodded.

He looked into my face. 'I have to go, Faye.'

'Of course.'

I understood, I really did, and there was no way I would make this any harder for him, but I would miss him. I wanted to know the practicalities; I had to be around... I wanted to know the practicalities. I had to be around for Rosie, but wanted to be able to see Dan off on the flight – but with Emma's new job, it couldn't have happened at a worse time. Not that there was ever a good time for something like this.

'When will you go back?' I asked softly.

'Tomorrow... Monday? Earliest flight I can get, I can't hang about. Apart from anything else, Kimmie needs help and I feel like I have to step up to the plate. I feel so bloody guilty, Faye, you know?'

I nodded. 'Dan, stop beating yourself up.'

'I left him because I couldn't go through another death – not after Mum. I've spent the last twenty years drifting, blaming my itchy feet, but it was my coward's heart that kept me from going back there for good, to face everything.'

'But you did go back, a couple of years ago,' I said.

'I popped in, spent a few months there and left again. Told everyone I had to see the world, but what I was really doing was avoiding the world... *my* world anyway.'

I sat in the silence between us, aware of everyone else starting their Saturday night – friends greeting friends, bursts of laughter, the smell of beer filling my nostrils. I wished I could put my arms around him and tell him it was all going to be okay, but I knew it wasn't.

'So, will you stay… in Australia, until…?' I didn't know how to phrase this delicate question. I was trying so hard not to consider myself in this, but it would have an impact on us and I had to know what he was thinking.

He nodded, but didn't look at me, just kept turning a beer mat over and over in his fingers. 'He's the only family I've got, I should have gone back sooner. I can't keep running around the world trying to pretend it's all okay.'

'I don't know John, but from what you tell me he's a pretty special guy. He wouldn't have wanted you to give up your own life,' I said, my heart beginning to break.

We both sipped our drinks in silence – a silence even I couldn't fill.

Eventually, I said, 'So how long do you think you'll be there?'

He dropped his head and turned to look at me reluctantly. 'That's what I wanted to talk to you about. I won't be buying a return ticket, Faye.'

Chapter Five

A One-Way Ticket and a Magic Carpet

'Oh,' was all I could muster, looking away, trying to hide the tremor in my voice and the tears that sprang to my eyes.

'You're upset.'

'Yes, of course I am. This has come out of the blue – but this isn't about me, and you're doing the right thing. You *have* to do the right thing.'

'I know. And I've been ready for this in my head, he's been getting worse for a while now. I didn't tell you because I didn't want to talk about it, or face it, but now it's happened, there's no other choice. I just feel... lost.'

'I wish I'd known,' I said, a frisson of irrational anger prickling my chest. But this was typical of Dan – he had this attitude that if he didn't talk about a problem, it would go away. It never did. If only he'd mentioned it to me sooner we might have been able to come up with a plan. Mind you, I wasn't sure what plan; it wasn't like I could just pack my suitcase and head off to Sydney for a few weeks.

'I'm sorry, I just couldn't face it... I just don't want to leave you.'

'I hate it too, but you don't have any choice,' I sighed, looking away from him, trying to hide the tears in my eyes, 'it's your brother's life.'

'I know. Don't you think I realise that?'

He was on edge, and he didn't need me to remind him of what he had to do. He was upset but I was also upset. He could have told me sooner that John's condition was deteriorating, instead of smiling and pretending everything was fine. This inability to face reality had made things so much worse because I wasn't prepared – this had hit me from nowhere and I couldn't be the kind, considerate girlfriend I should have been because I had been taken by surprise.

'So that's it, you go tomorrow?' I said.

'Yeah… but it doesn't have to be the end of us,' he replied, still ignoring the huge obstacle and climbing back into his bubble. *Our* bubble.

'Dan, you're going home – we'll be halfway across the world from each other. How can it not be the end of us?'

He put down his drink and leaned into me, putting his arm around me, our foreheads were touching. 'I love you, Faye…' he almost whispered. 'You're everything to me.'

I lifted my head to look at his face and it stung to see how much he was hurting for his brother, and for us.

'I love you too, and I'm trying to be strong. I'm trying not to make this about us… or me, because it's about John and Kimmie, and the kids – they need you. You need to concentrate on them for now, and then when you come back, we can get back to where we were. I'll be keeping busy, don't worry about me.'

'Faye, I'm buying a one-way ticket…'

'I know, but that's because you'll be a while… You don't know how long your brother will… need you,' I said, trying to be sensitive. His brother was dying, of course he couldn't commit to a return date.

'Faye… I've thought about it and when I go, I'm not coming back. Not even after he's gone… I don't have a decent job here, and there's no future… I'm ready to go home.'

I felt like the floor was moving under me.

'And us?' I heard myself croak.

He suddenly sat up, and put both hands on the table, staring ahead. 'Well… I've been thinking… Emma and Rosie are settled, you've got a year left of your degree…'

'Yes?'

'You could come with me and do your final year over there.'

'In Australia?' What the hell was he talking about? I couldn't just up and leave. 'I don't see how that could work, Dan…' I said, trying not to throw his suggestion back at him, to let him down gently. I'd dreamed of going to Sydney with him, but it was a dream for the future, not now.

'Of course it could work. You could carry on with your degree, and I could—'

'You're being unrealistic; you always do this, come up with a ridiculous scenario and expect me to just drop everything and join you,' I said, feeling suddenly irritated that he should put this on me.

'You mean like Santorini? At first you were horrified of running away with me, but you took the leap then and look how much you loved it… so why won't you now?'

'That was three years ago, Dan. Emma was at uni, there was no Rosie, and Craig and I were finished – I had no one else to worry about but myself. But things are different now. I've got my degree course and Emma's just started her new job and I promised I'd be there for Rosie. I can't let her down now – and you know that.'

'But Emma would understand.' He seemed downbeat, like the wind had been taken out of his sails.

'Yes, she'd be lovely about it and say, "You go, Mum," but inside she'd be screaming, "Oh God, what will I do without any childcare?" What kind of mother or grandmother would I be, leaving Emma and Rosie and taking off for the other side of the world with my boyfriend?'

'I have an idea that'll solve everything,' he said. 'I'm trying to build up to it, but you won't let me get a bloody word in…'

'Oh no, wait! I know… don't tell me. Are you thinking about those magic beans we can plant in the garden? No, that would be daft. A flying carpet…?' I said sarcastically, rolling my eyes. There was no answer to this, no compromise; it was an impossible situation, but he couldn't see this.

'No magic beans, no flying carpet… What about a wedding?'

'Whose?'

'Ours… Will you marry me, Faye?'

What? Had he really just dropped that bombshell? I would have been less shocked if it had been magic beans or a flying carpet. But as I looked at him staring back at me questioningly, I realised he meant it. Okay, so he wasn't down on one knee (I didn't blame him, God knows what was on that floor) and he was holding a beer mat instead of a ring, but his face told me everything I needed to know: he wanted us to get married.

A life with Dan was what I'd always wanted; a proposal had been a dream, a secret place I retreated to when life got a bit tough. But this was supposed to happen years down the line, when Emma was safely in her high-powered job and Rosie was an independent teenager. I suppose I'd been naive to think life would pan out exactly as I'd planned it in my head and where Dan was concerned, perhaps I'd been presumptuous and selfish. Who said his life had to be in synch with mine? Just because the time was wrong for me didn't mean he had to wait to live his life, perhaps this was his time? I'd done what I always accused him of doing – I'd put my head in the sand, conveniently forgetting about *his* dreams and *his* family. I knew he had ambitions, that he wanted to go back to Australia, but he'd never given me any warning that he planned to go back for good sooner rather than later – or that he hoped to go back with me as his wife.

He'd just proposed, he'd just garnered all his courage and asked me to marry him. I couldn't ruin the moment, but after a long silence I knew he was agitated, now piling up the beer mats with one hand, shuffling them like a deck of cards. And all I could think as I watched them land was stick or twist?

'Faye, give a guy a break, I'm dying here,' he said, almost under his breath, studying the 'deck' of beer mats like they were Tarot cards holding his destiny.

I sat awkwardly, not looking at him, unsure what to say, not even sure how I felt at that precise moment. This had all come from nowhere. We'd never actually spoken about getting married, we were just happy being together and it felt like for ever – we didn't need a ring. I'd been put off marriage by Craig and as much as I loved Dan, I wasn't going to throw myself into another marriage unless I felt ready, which one day I might – but I'd never seen Dan as the marrying kind. Until a few minutes ago, I'd been happy with my lot: no blot on the horizon, no shadows over me, just Dan and Emma and Rosie and my studies. I was achieving all my dreams in one go, then suddenly, I was being asked to make a choice between a life I was happy in, the family I adored – and the man I loved.

'I… I want to be with you, of course I do, but I can't believe you're making me choose…' was all I could say.

He made a slight groaning noise, like he'd been hit by something sharp. 'Faye, think about it…'

'I am, it's *you* that's not thinking.'

'But this is the only way we can be together and I can be there for John and the kids. You can speak to Emma and Rosie every day, you know how she loves to Skype – and you can carry on studying and… I've got this mate who's opening up a café and he's looking for a partner… I won't be able to get involved straight away, I'll have to see how things are with John, but my mate says there's loads of building work to do first so there's no rush. It means I can go back home and I could even have that café I've always dreamed of….'

'But your time will be taken up with John… and you can't afford to buy half a café…' I started, feeling like a bitch, but thinking perhaps it was time for one of us to live in the real world. This was the first I'd heard of his friend opening a café – what else was he keeping to himself?

'John's my priority,' he said firmly, 'but if everything's okay I can start working there, get involved. My mate's going to lay down the initial deposit, pay the rent on the building and stuff, and when we start making money I'll buy my share off him.'

I was shaking my head, not just because I knew how difficult this would be in reality but because he'd obviously thought it through so carefully without telling me.

'Faye, it's that café in Sydney we've always talked about....'

I was annoyed at his optimism about a new business in the light of his brother's illness. I was also upset that he was chasing a dream that would convince him to stay in Australia whatever happened with John.

'It wasn't real, Dan, the café... it was just us talking, dreaming,' I said.

'It was real for me,' he said, sounding hurt. 'I thought it was what you wanted too?'

'Yes, of course... Oh, I don't know! I'm sorry, Dan. I just feel like there is so much else to consider first before you start to even think about life beyond John's condition. You don't know how long he's going to be... with you.'

'Exactly, but I have to believe there's something after John. If I didn't, I don't know what I'd do... and I can't stay here. I've been feeling like I need something else for a long time now – I want a new challenge, a different way of living.'

He really did believe that everything just fell into place, that all he had to do was click his fingers and everything would be fine.

'After wandering the earth barefoot for twenty years and settling here, you suddenly decide to run away again?' I sighed. I was hurt; he could have gone back to Australia and been with John for as long as he needed to be, but then he could have returned to the UK – to me. I knew I sounded completely unreasonable and selfish, but I just didn't want to lose him.

'I'm not running away, I want you to come with me. I've spent my life just trying to find something good to cling onto…' he said, quietly, and couldn't finish. He didn't need to.

I sighed and reached for his hand. I was merely adding to the pressure, not supporting him in his hour of need as he had so often done for me.

Dan once told me he'd never loved anyone enough to get married, and I knew his proposal must have taken thought and courage at a time when his world was falling apart. As naive and blindly, infuriatingly optimistic as he could be, he had just handed me his heart – something I wanted very much.

'I'd say yes in a heartbeat, Dan. You know I've always wanted to see Australia and… *be* with you,' I said gently. 'Honestly, if I was free, things would be very different, but I'm not, I can't just walk out on Emma and Rosie any more than you can opt out of going to be with John. And besides, I have my course… I'm happy for the first time in forever and…'

'You're happy with me, *we* are happy. Please don't say no. Emma will be fine, she'll do what other mothers do and find childcare. She and Rosie can come and stay all summer, every summer… but she has her own life.'

'That's why I need to be here, so she can be free to pursue a career, make something of her life. She won't make the same mistakes I did and have to rely on a man then give everything up for him only to live to regret it.'

'Is that how you feel – about marriage?' He seemed surprised, hurt even.

'No... Oh I don't know, Dan.' Did I feel this way? I certainly felt like I'd given up everything, including myself while married to Craig. I'd spent much of my adult life hating being married, and my mixed feelings about it might also be influencing my reluctance to say yes to Dan now. 'I love the idea of living in another country,' I sighed. 'It's on my living list... but... leaving here now... marriage?'

'Don't... Don't...' He was shaking his head. 'I don't want to hear you say no.'

'What else can I say?'

'I don't know, but please don't say no yet,' he asked softly, leaning forward in his seat and placing his hand gently on mine. 'Think about it.'

I felt the warmth of his touch, the love in his eyes – this was agony and my head was all over the place. I couldn't bear to say goodbye to him, nor could I bear to say goodbye to Emma and Rosie; it was unbearable.

'Okay,' I sighed, thinking how, under different circumstances, a few years from now this situation would probably have made me very happy. 'I'll think about it...'

He suddenly looked hopeful and squeezed my hand. 'Faye, this could be the start of an amazing new life for us in Sydney.'

'Don't... Don't... I can't promise anything, just let me have some time.'

I hated that Dan was so hopeful and hated myself for even giving him a chink of light. And when he offered to wait to buy his ticket until the following day, after I'd made up my mind, I wanted to cry. But he wouldn't let me say no, and there was a part of me that didn't *want* to say no – that could mean the end for us. How could we come back from that?

Later, when he walked me home, I didn't invite him in or ask if he wanted to stay, even though I knew this would probably be our last night together. The next day was Sunday and we were both free all day. 'Come over to my place as soon as you've decided,' he said urgently. He kissed me on the forehead and put his arms around me protectively, like he wanted to keep me forever.

We stood on the doorstep for a long time, holding onto each other, both wondering what would happen next.

Chapter Six

A Pounding Head and a Psychic Daughter

After wiping my eyes and reapplying mascara in the hall, so Emma wouldn't see I'd been crying and worry, I went into the living room where she was watching TV. She'd just bathed Rosie, and flushed from the heat of the bathroom, she seemed damp but happy, as was her baby, now asleep on the sofa with teddy. My heart melted, but my head pounded.

'You're early,' Emma said quietly, as she looked up. 'Madam's only just had her bath, she's been full-on tonight.'

I laughed, 'I can imagine.' I sat down on the nearby easy chair, 'What's this?' I gestured towards the screen. I wanted to sit and stare at it – I didn't want to talk about what had just happened, I wasn't quite sure myself.

'Oh, some rubbish film. You know they'll end up together in the end – they always do, don't they?'

'Not always,' I sighed, gazing at the two beautiful faces onscreen.

'So… did you finish it?' she asked, turning from the screen to look at me.

Christ, how the hell had she picked up on this? She must be psychic.

'It's not that easy… I need time.'

'What? I thought it was due in yesterday?'

I looked puzzled – all I could think about was Dan getting on that plane and whether or not I'd be with him.

'F. Scott Fitzgerald?' she said, smiling and looking at me like I was mad.

'Oh… you meant the *essay*?'

'Yes, what else would I mean?' Then she sat up on the sofa. 'Why, what *did* you mean? Mum?'

'Oh, love, I'm all over the place, sorry. It's Dan, his brother's ill – he's going back to Australia,' I blurted. It was out there – no point in keeping this to myself, burying it inside and pretending it wasn't happening.

'Oh, Mum, no!'

'It's fine, nothing to worry about,' I smiled. I didn't want to worry Emma, she had enough to cope with as a single mum with a demanding job.

'But you said he was going back to Australia? That sounds like something to worry about.'

'Oh, it's just life – I think a cup of tea will help,' I said, trying to make light of it.

I went into the kitchen and made us both a cup of tea, which I needed, but I also had to compose myself: Emma's concern was likely to make me cry and I couldn't lay that on her. Returning with two steaming mugs, I saw my girls together on the sofa and felt that familiar pull. How lucky I was to be able to spend this time with them. So many kids go off to other cities, get married and move away. Their parents had to make do with a phone call and a visit every other Christmas as they watched their grandchildren grow up from afar, but Emma had accepted the job here, in the town she was born, knowing I'd be there to look after Rosie. Dan's situation had come out of the blue and I needed time and space to think – but my mind fizzed with sadness.

I loved him so much I couldn't help but flirt with the idea of running away with him. What if, against all the odds, there was a way we could be together? What if Emma and Rosie could come with us? They could start a new life there too. The prospect of a new life in a new country with beaches and sunshine, a healthier lifestyle, it wasn't unthinkable, was it? In fact, it was a fantasy for most people. There would be a job out there for Emma, surely, and Rosie would love exploring a new place, making friends, swimming every day and living in sunshine. Perhaps it could work?

I was soon shaken from my reverie at the sound of Rosie waking up on the sofa.

'Time for bed, sweetie,' Emma was saying, but she seemed distracted, trying to do something on her phone. Poor Emma, she worked so hard, sending and receiving emails at all times of the day and night, dealing with problems.

'I'll take her up to bed,' I said, picking Rosie up and holding her little warm body close to mine. She was sleepy, but given any kind of attention she would soon be wide awake and ready for another round of hide-and-seek, which she loved.

'Nan, where's Dam?' she said sleepily as I carried her into her bedroom.

'He's in his house, probably asleep like you're going to be,' I smiled, laying her down and gently covering her up with the pink princess duvet.

'Will his nan read him a bedtime stowy?' she asked, which was Rosie's subtle way of asking for one.

'No… Probably not,' I giggled, 'but I'll read one to you if you like?'

She patted my hand, her eyes barely able to stay open. 'Oh, that's a good girl,' she sighed, and waited for the 'once upon a time'.

Even before the 'happy ever after', Rosie was asleep, and I quietly left her to dream of princesses in pink palaces and padded to my room, my sanctuary, to consider all that had happened. I hadn't told Emma about Dan's proposal – I wanted to think about it all before I talked it through with anyone else. I had twenty-four hours to think about it and I knew I'd be mulling it over for every one of those hours. That night I lay awake in bed considering all the options. Was there a way I could be with my family *and* marry Dan? Ever the optimist, I hoped this was like a crossword clue you think you'll never get, then suddenly the word appears and you wonder why you didn't think of it in the first place. But right now it felt like my whole life was the crossword clue – stuck between a rock and a hard place – and there was no answer.

'Do you fancy Australia then?' I said to Emma the following morning over toast and marmalade. I hadn't slept and waited until I heard her get up to rush downstairs before Rosie and just sound her out. I tried to keep it light-hearted, pretending it was a joke to see her reaction, knowing she'd think I was as mad as I'd thought Dan was by merely suggesting such a move.

'Australia? Oh God, no! All those creepie-crawlies... and the heat. I don't envy Dan having to go back there.'

This wasn't the answer I'd been hoping for.

'Oh, I don't know... There are beaches, year-round sunshine?'

'Nah, wouldn't be my scene,' she said, sipping her tea. 'I'd miss home too much.' She hadn't taken this seriously, but her gut reaction was enough.

'So you'd never consider moving to another country, even in the future?'

She looked at me. 'No way!' she said. 'What about you?'

'I don't know... I'd always liked the idea of living somewhere else, a fresh perspective on life, you know?'

She nodded. 'I think you're more adventurous than me, Mum. I just manage to keep body and soul together here – I wouldn't move it all across an ocean.'

She put down her mug, reached out her hand.

'Are you tempted to go with Dan?'

'No... Well, I don't know, it's such a big thing – I can't leave you and Rosie.'

'But I don't want you to stay here because of us, especially if being apart from Dan makes you unhappy. Has he asked you to go with him?'

'Yes. Actually, he's asked me to marry him.' I was no longer able to keep this in my chest, where it had fluttered all night.

She gasped and clapped her hands together. 'Then what in the hell are we doing sitting here, why aren't we choosing dresses?'

'Because I don't want to leave here and live in Australia,' I said, almost in tears. 'I can't leave you and Rosie and…'

'But it would only be for a while – I can find a childminder for a few months until you're back.'

'No, he's not just going back home for a while, he's staying.'

'For good?' she asked, more uncertainly this time.

'For good.'

'Oh… How would that work?' she said, sitting back, like she'd just been pushed.

'It wouldn't,' I said, and put on my best smile.

'Just because of me and Rosie?' She screwed up her eyes. 'Because we would miss you, of course, but I don't expect you to give him up again, not for us… If you want to go there and be with Dan, you really should.'

I wasn't sure if she meant this or if she was simply trying not to stand in my way, which I suspected was the case.

'I don't… This isn't about you, it's about me,' I heard myself lie.

'Really? You don't want to go and live by the sea in another country with the man you love? You said yourself, there are beaches and sunshine and you've always wanted to see Australia.'

'Yes, but I don't want to *live* there – not yet. And it's not just about you and Rosie, I have my course, a job, I've built my life here,' I said, feeling rather empty, knowing it wouldn't be the same life without Dan in it. 'It just doesn't feel right to walk away from it all now.'

The pull to be with him was as strong as the pull to stay with Emma, and I knew whatever I decided to do, someone would have to be hurt.

Later that morning I called Dan and told him I wanted to come and see him.

'I still haven't bought my ticket,' he said, hope in his voice.

'And I still haven't made my decision,' I replied.

Chapter Seven

A Surfboard in the Kitchen and a Selfie in Venice

'I don't want this to be any more difficult for you than it already is,' Dan said when I arrived at his flat over the deli. He was standing in his little kitchen crammed with pots and pans and clippings of recipes littered the table. A surfboard was propped against a fridge covered with a million photos and magnets – the story of his life scattered over aluminium. Dan had been, and always would be, in Australia in his head. It was part of who he was and I'd been selfish to ever think that life here with me and the deli would be enough for him. My heart lurched, seeing the photos of us together, sipping cocktails in Santorini, a selfie in Venice on the Bridge of Sighs, eating spaghetti in Rome. The narrative of our lives, of our love, for everyone to see – he was proud of me, proud of us and I was lucky to have him. And now the ultimate confirmation of our love, the story of the proposal, was waiting for its ending.

Dan made coffee and we sat facing each other at the kitchen table, both unwilling to say anything, and change everything.

'So,' he said, eventually, 'I'm not always good on picking up cues, but I guess the answer's no?'

I looked at him with a pained expression. It was agony to even think it, but we both knew my answer.

'I can't say it.'

'It's okay, you don't have to. It was a big ask… and looking in your eyes I can see it's a no.' I saw his hurt as he looked at me, moving the hair from my face, stroking my cheek. 'But for what it's worth, I think you're making a mistake. You already said goodbye to me once before to come back here when you left me in Santorini and our lives were put on hold – you can't do this again. To you or me.'

'I don't expect you to put your life on hold, Dan,' I said, frustrated that he thought it was merely my *choice* for things to be this way. Couldn't he see I had no choice?

'I'm sorry, it just feels like I always get the raw end of the deal. We are good together, you and me, and our summer in Santorini was the best time of my life, but Emma was pregnant and you had to leave to be with her… I understood and, as painful as it was, I let you go. I've always gone along with your plans, whatever fits in with *your* life. I've always wanted to go home to Oz, but I stayed here with you. Stupidly, I thought it might be time for you to come with me. When is it *my* turn, Faye?'

I was shocked at this outburst. 'I didn't realise you felt like that.'

He shook his head. 'I'm sorry, most of the time it's okay, I want to be with you and I don't mind that we're here because it makes you happy. But the one time… the *one* time I need you there for me, you won't be.'

'I've always been there for you. Always will be here for you, love you, but my family has to come first… If you had a child you'd understand how hard this is.' I felt hurt at his accusation, and that hurt was fizzing into anger. 'You're the one who wanted to be free, Dan. You're the one who left Australia because you couldn't bear the memories. I never forced you to come here, you could have stayed in Santorini.'

'Without you?'

'Yes, without me. You're going away to live somewhere without me now.'

'But that's because I have to… and because you won't leave your daughter, who's twenty-five!' He almost shouted this; I'd never seen him quite so angry.

'I'm staying here because Emma is relying on me… A year or two down the line, things might be different.' In all honesty I didn't expect anything to be different – Rosie would still only be five and I doubted I'd be any more likely to walk away then – but I just didn't want this to be the end. Even though it was looking that way.

'Well, I can't wait for a year or two… or three… because my brother is dying *now*,' he hissed. 'And I'm sorry if it isn't convenient, if his illness doesn't fit in with your life plan, Faye.'

I must have looked shocked – this wasn't like him. Tears sprang to my eyes and I could see immediately that he felt bad.

'I'm sorry… I just thought that you might be ready to put *us* first. I know it's not an ideal time for you, but Emma's perfectly capable.' He ran his hands through his hair; he seemed exasperated and looked so tired.

'It sounds easy, doesn't it? But it isn't… You've never been a parent, you've no idea what it's like,' I snapped, tired and exasperated by all this.

'I know what it's like to have to go to my dying brother alone, without any support from my partner.'

His words were razor-sharp, but I knew this was his sadness talking, and I didn't want our final memories to be like this, so I touched his arm, 'Let's not fall out, we don't have long left together.'

I understood his hurt and resentment, but it wasn't just about me and Dan, it was about the way our lives entwined with other lives, like branches in an oak tree. And how could we extricate ourselves from all of that?

He turned on his phone. 'I have to book my ticket,' he said. 'I guess it's just one. Single?' He looked at me, but I didn't answer and waited for him to go back to his phone and he clicked away, booking a return to his old life, and all that sunshine and pain.

'I can get one first thing in the morning. I'd need to leave here about six, but it's cheaper than a later one – quicker too,' he said, scrolling through his phone.

'Okay, go for it,' I said softly, knowing it would all be settled within minutes, that this would be goodbye.

I waited for him to say something, but he didn't, he just sat scrolling on his phone, and I felt like he'd already gone.

When he finished, he looked up at me and I could see my own despair reflected back at me. But if this was the end of our story I had to remember him in a good way, and see him smile one last time.

'I don't want our final few hours together to be sad – we're a happy couple, let's be happy until we can't do it anymore?' I asked. 'Please?'

'I'm sorry, I kinda thought you might just change your mind.'

I shook my head.

'Faye, at some point, you're going to have to let Emma go and live her life so you can live yours.'

I didn't respond, but it struck a chord and, rationally, I knew he was probably right. But I kept thinking of Rosie's little face when we baked together, her excitement at simply watching TV with me, going to the park, playing with her teddies – and my heart just couldn't say yes, because it would also mean saying goodbye to my granddaughter.

'You're right, let's not be sad,' he said suddenly, standing up from the table and walking into the bedroom. I could see him through the open door as he picked up his rucksack and threw it off the bed into the doorway. 'Let's not talk about it anymore,' he said, 'let's just have fun until the plane leaves.' He walked back into the kitchen towards me, his arms outstretched and I stumbled into them, trying not to hear his words replay over in my mind 'until the plane leaves'. Tomorrow, he would be gone and I knew my heart would break into a million pieces, but right now I needed to make one last memory to hold onto.

'Sounds good to me,' I mumbled between our kisses, now more intense than ever.

He carried me into the bedroom, like a groom carrying his bride over the threshold, and I was aware of his physical strength as he held me. It made me wonder what being married to Dan would be like, to have that first night, the rest of our lives together stretching before us.

He was so sure of what he wanted, and I lay back as he kissed my breasts, moving down my body slowly, sensuously. This would be the last time between us, and knowing this somehow made the pleasure more intense even as I fought back the tears. I wanted him inside me as he moved back up my body and I let him in. We were soon damp with sweat as we rolled around on the sheets, my legs wrapped around his back, holding him inside as he thrust into me. I never wanted this to end and as we gazed into each other's eyes, fireworks were exploding around us and I gasped, clutching him even closer. I would take this moment and hold it to my heart forever.

Afterwards, the air was charged with pain as we lay side by side. There was now a physical separation, neither of us touching the other for fear of hurting or being hurt. As if we weren't already broken.

'What shall we do then?' his voice sliced into the silence, the lovely Aussie sunshine now dimmed. 'I mean, should we stay in touch, will you come out to see me?'

I shook my head, tears filling my eyes. Oh God, how I wished that might be possible, that I could hear his voice every now and then, go out and visit him, but it was no good.

'I don't think that would work. We'd see each other a couple of times a year at best, and that's not a relationship.' I smiled, and touched his cheek and he took my hand, holding it to him as he closed his eyes.

As dusk shrouded the bedroom, I watched him sleeping, taking in every centimetre of his face. I needed a close-up to keep in my head for the rest of my life. It would be all I had left of him, of this time, of us, and I hoped remembering what we'd had would be enough. What Dan and I had was special – some people live a lifetime and never have that connection and if this was all I'd ever have, then I was lucky. I'd let him go to live his life, while I stayed here with mine. And it occurred to me as I lay in the dimming light, fresh tears cool on my cheeks, that I'd probably never love like this again.

Twelve months later
Chapter Eight

Love, Lemon Cake and Ladies' Night

On the morning Dan left for the airport, I'd returned home to begin my life as a single woman. I put all my mementoes of him in an old hatbox of my mother's and hid it in the back of the wardrobe. I packed away the photographs of our weekends in Italy and Spain, pressed the blossom confetti we'd collected in the Parisian park and locked our last weekend in Paris in my heart. Then I deleted his number from my phone and pressed restart.

He'd been gone a year and I was now absorbed in studying for my finals and taking care of Rosie. I tried to look forward and not back. I told myself and everyone else that I was fine, but even now my heart hadn't caught up with my head. I often cried myself to sleep – I missed him so much. He'd texted a few times at first, and despite deleting his number from my phone, when a message from him popped up I realised I knew it by heart anyway. So much for deleting him from my life.

He'd only been in Australia for three weeks when he called me to tell me his brother had died. I almost offered to fly out there and comfort him, but I resisted. Nothing had changed: Emma was still fully committed to her career, I was knee-deep in my course and there was Rosie. If I'm honest, the selfish part of me wondered if his brother's death might change things, that he might decide to leave Australia and come back to me – but he didn't. He told me he was glad he'd been there at the end, that his decision to go back was the right one, even though he missed me every day.

Not long after, he texted to tell me he was opening the café in Sydney Harbour with his friend. Apparently, his brother had left him some money, and things were looking up for him. It was only then I finally began to face it that he wasn't coming back, he'd put down roots in Australia now and he wouldn't just be able to walk away. The next call came a few months on and he left a voicemail to say the café was doing well and he wished I could see it. 'There's an open invitation for you here at Lemon Myrtle,' he said. Just hearing his voice gave me a pang.

I googled the café and the homepage showed a lovely plate of pale coral salmon, pink shrimp, fronds of seaweed garnished with lemon myrtle. Then I clicked onto the café itself and it was just as I'd imagined: a small, but fashionable eatery in Sydney, with exposed brickwork and hanging copper ceiling lights. My heart did a little dance. I was genuinely happy for him. He'd achieved his dream – something he would never have done if he'd stayed here with me.

I recalled the lemon cake he'd once made for me, his mother's recipe with the secret ingredients: love and lemon myrtle. He couldn't find lemon myrtle in the UK so just used love and lemon juice instead, and it was always delicious. I began to text him to ask if he'd thought of me when he named the café, and then realised that way madness lay. I couldn't ask such a loaded question, so deleted the message without sending it, and when he called again I didn't pick up. I put his number on silent, hoping that in time my heart might also be silenced, and after a few months he stopped texting and calling completely. I knew it was for the best, but it felt like I was losing him all over again.

I threw myself into everything so I could try and forget him. Writing essays on romantic novels, I tried not to think of my own romantic story and the blossom paths in Paris. Sitting in the park with Rosie on a sunny afternoon I'd try to forget how the evening sun had melted over us as we'd sat in a bar by the Mediterranean. I'd pass the deli and wave to his aunt, but I couldn't bear to go inside and talk to her because then I'd think of him. I had to erase him, or I'd weaken and who knows what fresh heartache I'd be inviting in?

I had lots of friends and family giving me support and advice throughout this time. 'Mum, for Christ's sake, just call him, you're unhappy without him,' from Emma. 'Nana, for Christs *you* need to get a new boyfriend because Dam isn't bruddy here,' I was told by my now four-year-old granddaughter. I knew she missed him almost as much as I did, but she couldn't yet vocalise her own loss. And then there was Mandy's advice, which was to, 'Go to the Funkin' Fusion in a low-cut top on Ladies' Night, get on the mic and shout "Hello, boys!"' Apparently, they would 'come flocking'. Whoever 'they' were, I doubted they'd hold a torch to Dan, and I definitely didn't want them to come 'flocking' down the Funkin' Fusion. Sue, of course, was full of advice, mostly regarding the world being mad because Mercury was 'in reprimand', by which I guess she meant retrograde. Her final words on the subject were to move on, find a nice toy boy on Tinder and 'illiterate' him from my memory.

Eventually I stopped listening and decided to take my own advice: work hard for my finals, take care of my granddaughter and her potty mouth and do my job without yearning for unavailable horizons. Emma seemed happier – she told me she'd met someone at work and this 'someone' turned out to be Richard, an accountant who worked in the Edinburgh office. As the weeks went by, I noticed she laughed more, had a lovely glow and I was pleased she'd found someone to spend time with who made her happy. It was just what she needed. Even though he was based in Scotland, he came to stay a few times and Rosie liked him, as did I. He was divorced, intelligent, caring and great with Rosie. What was not to love?

Emma was doing really well, but worked long hours. Fortunately, my granddaughter was there to take care of me – even though it was supposed to be the other way round. Yes, she bossed me about on a daily basis. 'Come on, Nana, we have to go to uniwersity today,' she'd shout, bouncing on my bed and doing a great impression of a too-vigorous alarm clock at 5.30 a.m. most mornings (even when 'we' didn't have 'uniwersity'). I'd pretend to refuse to get out of bed, which gave me a few precious minutes under the covers while Rosie yelled and tried to tickle me. I'd leap up and tickle her back, which made her scream with shock and delight – the mornings were raucous and hilarious. Emma said Rosie was the more sensible grown-up of the two of us and I had to agree. She was the one who told me not to eat too much sugar as I bit into a doughnut, and at the supermarket would remind me that we had to have 'five a day, Nana'. I wasn't sure if she actually knew what it was we needed in this particular quantity, but she'd announce this in a rather earnest voice. It was, I suspected, the same voice the nursery teacher had used when informing her class about the magic number of fruit and veg.

I was discussing Rosie and me and the whole role-reversal thing with some of my student friends after a seminar later that week. One of the girls (Kate – seven facial piercings, a back full of tattoos, midnight hair and black lipstick) was saying how she felt like she was the sensible one with her mother these days. Looking at her outward appearance, I wasn't convinced.

'My mum's gone bloody mad,' she said. 'She's having actual sex... I mean, like literally, with a man,' she said, pulling a face that indicated sheer revulsion.

'What's wrong with your mum having sex?' I asked.

'Oh my God! It's disgusting...' She threw her hands in the air, almost knocking over her peppermint tea. She curled her lip as the others sitting around the canteen table curled theirs in unison. 'I mean, she's forty... so fucking OLD.'

I covered my smile. *And you're so fucking young*, I thought, recalling myself at her age when I believed women over forty should be seen and not heard.

'Your mum's probably enjoying herself,' I said. 'She's earning her own money, living her life, and there's nothing wrong with sex in your forties,' I added, aware these kids saw me and my kind as sexual freaks. 'And I'm not just talking about sex in bed with your nightie rolled up,' I laughed, warming to the theme as their faces grew pale with horror. 'You aren't the ones who invented blow jobs and sex toys and...'

The girls were mesmerised (or scandalised?), gazing at me as I went on to list various acts in ludicrous positions. Their faces were a picture, and I hoped I was making them realise how alike we all were, that being forty-something was just like being twenty-something – without the flexibility. God, these kids were naive – I really was amazed at the way they reacted, like bloody Victorian ladies.

Continuing with my masterclass on 'Sex for Ageing Mothers', I went back in for a final thrust, as it were: 'Hey, and let me tell you, blow jobs aren't just for the young, neither is the back of a car – and even these forty-something thighs can still take a knee-trembler!' I laughed, slapping my own legs for endorsement, but the girls looked even more horrified, if that was possible. In fact, Kate was doing something strange with her eyebrows, and then I heard a faint cough behind me, and to my horror turned around to see Dave Bronson, my tutor.

'I'm glad to know that, Faye,' he said, seriously. 'About the knee-tremblers. Bravo!' He was standing by my side – he'd heard everything.

Everyone was open-mouthed, clearly trying not to laugh, but losing the fight.

'But the question on my lips,' he continued with a wry smile, 'is this. Tell me, Faye, can those forty-something thighs climb out of the back of that car and make their way to my room, where we can begin the tutorial which was due to start twenty minutes ago?'

I died. On the spot.

'Oh, Dave,' I started, blushing furiously. 'Oh... you must have thought I meant... me,' I said, putting my hand on my chest in a way that hopefully indicated surprise at the mere suggestion I was talking about my own sexual adventures. 'No, I wasn't talking about me. When I said, I have sex in *cars*, I don't… *Sex*? Me? *No*.'

This caused a ripple of stifled laughter and even Dave now had a twinkle in his eye. Throughout this encounter I'd been struggling to pick up my rucksack, which I hadn't realised was caught under the chair, and in my embarrassment was saying far too much, as always.

He smiled. 'You may want to stay here and talk about sex while fighting a chair for the remaining forty minutes we have left of the tutorial, but if you're aiming for a First, might I suggest we go and discuss the works of Shakespeare instead?'

I nodded, and the girls snickered as I heaved up my rucksack with brute force, knocking several drinks over.

'Yes, I'm coming now,' I said, rushing to catch up with him after turning to pull a silent screaming face at the girls, who were now hysterical.

'Dave, can I just clarify…? When I say forty-something, I wasn't referring to my *own* thighs, I was trying to explain that young people – well, they didn't invent sex, did they, Dave?' I kept on going, when I knew I should have stopped and moved on. 'The knee-trembling thighs was theoretical, Dave… in *theory*.' I'd finally caught him up as he reached his office, but rather than go in, he stopped and turned towards me. Despite being a mature student, I still reacted to teachers like a child in kindergarten and felt quite intimidated by this brilliant man. I wanted him to like me, to respect my work – I didn't want him to think I was a nymphomaniac grandma with a penchant for sex in cars. But Dave was oblivious and keen to get on.

'Shall we?' he said.

'Shall we what?' I asked, wondering why he was now facing me.

He looked at me like I was mad and gestured towards his door. Oh, of course! I moved and let him open it, following him into the room. Now I was hot, very hot and sweating, which was partly my age and partly the situation I'd got myself into.

Dave's office was very small, and we had to sit quite close – I just hoped I could stop sweating for the next forty minutes. I also hoped that I could stay calm enough to discuss my essay like an adult and prevent the phrases 'knee-trembler', 'blow jobs' or any kind of 'juice' from leaving my lips for the duration of my tutorial.

'So, are we doing a feminist perspective of *The Great Gatsby*, or that other profound literary work, *Fifty Shades of Grey*?' he asked.

I laughed uncomfortably and told him (again, unnecessarily) that sadomasochism wasn't 'my thing'. Then spent the rest of the tutorial in agony, wondering why I'd felt the need to point this out. To my tutor.

An agonising forty minutes later, when the words 'juices' and 'knee-trembler' had inexplicably escaped my lips while discussing aspects of the great American novel, I looked at my watch and said I had to go. Apart from the obvious, it had been an enjoyable tutorial, especially after I'd calmed down and Dave seemed to be warming to the theme. He was leaning back, spouting on about Shakespearean anti-heroes with quite some passion, but I had to cut him short. I hated having to rush off, but I was due to pick up Rosie from the crèche, so I made my apologies and left, running along the corridors, scared to be late. Rosie was not pleased if she was the last child left at nursery and had been known to reprimand me severely with hands on hips, much to the amusement of the nursery staff.

I loved studying, but this was my favourite time of the day, when I opened the door of the little nursery building, taking in the scent of warmth and sawdust, talc and paint laced with overcooked cabbage. It sounds revolting, but if you could bottle it, every mother everywhere would want a bottle to sniff at when her kids were grown.

Rosie and I had all kinds of adventures together, from jumping in puddles all the way home to dancing with umbrellas, chasing our shadows down the lane and singing our favourite songs. That particular evening we put fish fingers in the oven then produced a live version of *The X Factor* with a furry camel as 'Simon Cow'. He proved to be quite a hit with Rosie, especially when I made him dance from his judging chair.

'Nan, he's not dancing… he wants to wee,' Rosie squealed with delight as I crossed his legs, which made her scream with laughter. I smiled to myself, thinking how mad and wonderful my day was. I'd gone from chatting about sex with a group of students to being overheard by my tutor, to having an hour's conversation about anti-heroes in Elizabethan literature. And now I was cooking fish fingers and making a celebrity cow pretend to go to the cow toilet. You couldn't make it up.

I remembered playing crazy games with Emma when she was Rosie's age and when she grew up so quickly (as they do), I'd missed our time together, never realising that I would be given a second chance so soon. Rosie was my bonus, another opportunity to weave precious childhood memories. Emma's work was taking her all over the country, but that wasn't a problem because I was there. And when she started seeing more of Richard, I was happy to step in at the weekends and be with Rosie. I felt like the luckiest woman in the world.

Chapter Nine

We Need to Talk About Gatsby

Sometimes at night when I couldn't sleep I googled Dan's café and it seemed to be going from strength to strength, with great reviews and an extended eating area. So Dan was becoming the man I knew he could be and following his own path, alone. But as I curled Mrs Bennett's hair for the Social Club Barn Dance, and twisted and plaited the chignons of the prom queen wannabes who I'd known since they were babies, I was sometimes filled with overwhelming sadness. Nothing was the same here without him.

There were moments when I wondered if I should just call him to say hi, but I had to be strong for both of us. I'd told him we needed a clean break, and he'd respected that. I hadn't heard from him in months – so when, at work one day, I saw a text from him, I panicked. I was colouring Judy Mack's hair and she was looking a little pale under all the 'Violent Violet'. I didn't want to put my glasses on and read Dan's message while I was applying her colour – she was clearly worried enough about the resulting shade without me scrolling on my phone while she turned purple (damn those Lithuanian hair products!). So I threw my phone to Mandy, who happened to be passing through on her way to the laughingly named 'Heavenly Spa'. There was nothing heavenly about the way Mandy attacked a person's eyebrows, or attempted a 'heavenly treatment', like a wrestler on steroids, kneading and pummelling at her clients while discussing her latest sexual exploits with 'Jase'.

'What the f——' she started, looking from me to the phone. Then she seemed to remember that she was the owner and she wasn't allowed to say the f-word in the salon.

'It's from Dan,' I hissed. 'He's texted me, but I can't answer it. It's like I've got some extra-sensory perception, I just know when he's texting.'

'That's because you've put him on vibrate, you daft cow,' she laughed. 'Hey Jude, every time Bruce texts her, she starts vibrating!' She slapped Judy on the back, which quite frankly, was the last thing Judy needed. Not only was she acclimatising to the apocalyptic purple of her hair, the woman was a slave to her bowels and had just been to hospital for an exploratory. God only knew what one of Mandy's harsh slaps could have unleashed below the waist.

'So,' I grimaced, looking into the mirror at Judy. One could only pray she was going to leave the salon with a human shade of hair and bowels firmly closed.

'So what?' Mandy said, leaning on the mirror, looking at the same head of purple and curling her lip.

'What does the text say?'

'Oh…' She started scrolling. 'He says… he wants to have you every way he can until your legs… One word… operation! He says you will need an *operation* after he's finished with his…'

'Stop it, Mandy, just *tell* me,' I said, knowing she was winding me up – Dan would never be texting me with stuff like that. But I was desperate to know and irritated now: why would he suddenly text after months of silence? Was he going to sell up and move back here to live with me after all? Stupid, I know, but this was one of my daydreams. Despite splitting up, I hadn't even begun to move on. 'TELL ME!' I said a little too loudly. And okay, aggressively. Poor Judy flinched and went scarlet – who knew the strain this was causing on those flawed and fragile bowels?

'Okay, calm down. He says, "Call me. It would be good to meet, don't want to discuss over a text – need to talk about Gatsby."'

I felt my heart thump slightly in my chest. It was a signal, this message was his way of getting me to go out there. Suddenly, I didn't care about Judy's hair, I had to ask Dan to stop doing this. My heart couldn't stand another goodbye.

'Oh, this is too much,' I said.

'What you talking about...? He said he wants to talk about Gatsby, not stick his—'

'NO,' I shouted, in an attempt to stop the vile filth that neither I nor Judy needed to hear – the woman was traumatised enough and I was in bits. 'You don't understand,' I said, more calmly now. 'He bought me a copy of *The Great Gatsby* before I started my course; it was our favourite book, he used to read it to me... It's symbolic...'

'Oh!' She was either unimpressed or hadn't a clue what I was talking about – probably the latter.

'We both had our favourite passages,' I sighed.

'I'm sure you did, but we don't need to know about that, do we, Jude?' Another slap across Judy's back. The woman was a wreck and at this point I could only imagine the state of her intestines.

'Anyway, I haven't got time to discuss Bruce's passage or your symbolics,' she winked. 'I've got an eyebrow tattoo at four, so do you want me to text him back for you or not?'

'Yes... Yes, please...' I nodded gratefully. I had to finish Judy's hair and without my glasses it would be easier to dictate a message than fumble blindly around myself and leave what I wanted to say at the mercy of autocorrect. I'd been there so many times. Only the day before I'd texted for a client who was having her hair washed. 'Can you ask my daughter to bring my epi pen – I have allergies and am not meant to leave the house without it,' she asked. 'No problem,' I said, quickly sending the message without my glasses on. But within seconds her daughter called up, horrified, asking to speak to her mother. Apparently epi pen autocorrected and I had in fact asked if she could bring her mother an 'epic penis' because she couldn't be without it!

No, I wasn't going there again, and though dictating in the salon wasn't very private, it was better than anything autocorrecting to 'penis' and giving Dan the wrong idea – he'd think I'd got text Tourette's. I glanced at Judy, who was about to hear everything I said to Dan, but she'd seen and heard enough in her years coming to the salon. She'd witnessed the breakdown of Sue's marriage, Mandy's slutdropping and was only too familiar with Gayle, the head stylist's, ovulation cycle (don't ask). My text to 'Bruce' would be a day in the park for Judy after all that. 'Okay, Mandy, please don't mess about. This is important, okay? So say this... "Sorry, but you can't just text me like this. What we had was magical... Erm... You are the love of my life, but this can't happen, full stop... WE can't happen. I think about you all the time, but you have to stop texting me, it's too painful. Goodbye." Full stop. Have you got that, Mandy?' I asked.

'Yes.'

'You haven't put "penis" in there, have you?'

'No, but I can if you want me to,' she said in all seriousness. I shook my head vigorously, 'No, please don't.'

'Suit yourself,' she said, screwing her face up and still punching out the last few letters. 'Don't send it yet,' I cried. 'Read it back to me, so I know you've written it down right, and please do NOT add anything disgusting – I'll never forgive you.' I had to trust her not to add her own colourful asides.

When I'd first met Dan in the deli where he worked, Mandy had told me to ask him for 'a bush oyster sandwich' for her – which I stupidly did. Imagine how red I went when I discovered this is in fact Australian slang for kangaroo testicles.

'And don't mention...'

'I know, I know... bush oysters,' she said slowly, in a bored voice, then read out the text, which was surprisingly accurate.

'Would you send it now, please,' I said.

'Okay, my queen. I'm pressing send,' she sang.

'Thanks, Mandy,' I sighed, sad that I'd had to say this to Dan and at the same time relieved I'd been strong and made my feelings clear.

She stood at my side for a few seconds, watching me 'transform' Judy. Call me psychic, but I had a strong feeling she was about to say something tasteless about someone in the vicinity – possibly me.

'Are you okay?' I asked, waiting for a tsunami of vileness.

'Yeah. I thought Bruce's name was Dan?'

'It is... You know, it's not bloody Bruce. Not all Australians are called Bruce,' I added, returning to Judy's violet hair.

'I know. So why is he calling himself Dave now?'

'He's not.'

'Is Dave a new one then?'

'New one? I haven't got *a new one*, as you so delicately put it.' I rolled my eyes at Judy in the mirror, but she didn't look up – I think she might have been pretending to be in a trance so she could pretend none of this was happening. I'd definitely seen her flinch at 'bush oysters'. Her hair was purple and Mandy's language was blue – God alone knows how the woman had survived this long.

'You are one crazy bitch,' Mandy was laughing as she skipped off to rugby-tackle a client into her heavenly spa and I thought little of it until later that day, when I received another text. This time I put my glasses on to read it.

I had no idea you felt this way. I only wanted to discuss your dissertation on Gatsby.

And when I looked at the sender it was Dave Bronson… my lecturer from college.

My mouth went dry and I scrolled up, willing for it not to be – but yes, the previous text that I'd thought was from Dan had been from Dave. I died on the spot. I couldn't face this now, but I wondered what on earth my college lecturer must think of me. He'd merely asked to arrange a chat about my work and I'd told him what we had was 'magical', that he was 'the love of my life', but that 'WE can't happen' and he had to stop texting me because it was 'too painful'… Shit! Looked like I'd have to brace myself for one very awkward chat at some point in the near future. Even more awkward than the last one regarding my forty-something thighs and sex in a car…

Chapter Ten

Three Arrests and a Bruddy Rabbit

One evening in May, I noted Emma seemed quite agitated. She was unable to sit still, constantly texting and smiling. She'd been away to Richard's that weekend and I understood how she felt — it was sometimes hard to come back to real life. I was cooking dinner, and Rosie was drawing on the kitchen table, while Emma continued to be completely lost in her online world. I guessed she was looking at the photos of the two of them on their weekend, savouring every moment in retrospect. I used to spend hours doing this when I was with Dan.

'Mummy, do you like my picture?' Rosie suddenly said, having finished her masterpiece and waving it in Emma's face. 'Mummy… Mummy!' She was yelling now.

I turned to see why Emma hadn't responded, surprised to watch her gently waft Rosie away and continue texting, which wasn't like her.

'What a lovely cat drawing,' I said, stepping in, so Rosie would feel satisfied and Emma wouldn't be disturbed.

'It's NOT a cat, Nana,' she yelled, 'it' a bruddy rabbit!'

I found this quite funny, but I didn't let Rosie know that and glanced over at Emma, fully expecting her to pick up on this and chastise her daughter for saying a naughty swear word. I waited for rolling eyes and gentle admonishment, but Emma was completely oblivious.

Later, when we'd had supper, Rosie was in bed and Emma and I were settling down to watch some old reruns of *Prime Suspect*. But just as Helen Mirren began to instruct the 'coppers' about the latest killing, Emma's phone rang. She immediately answered – after all, it had been glued to her hand all evening and I could tell by the way she said 'Hey' in a sweet sing-song voice that it was Richard and that me and Helen, aka DCI Tennison, would have to solve this case without my daughter's help. She smiled over at me and took the call upstairs, while I continued to work out who did it.

She was gone for ages. Me and Helen Mirren had made three arrests and discovered a 'bent copper' before she was back in the room. At the risk of sounding a bit nosy, I asked Emma if all was okay.

'Mum, he's asked me to marry him!'

I picked up the remote control and paused the investigation. 'Richard has?'

'No… Ryan Gosling. Yes, Richard!'

This was a surprise – they'd been together a while, but they lived in different cities and I knew more than most how impossible that was. But Emma was flushed with happiness and I had to join in. 'Oh darling, I'm delighted for you.'

'He says he doesn't want to hang around. We want to get married soon.'

'Oh… great… okay. How soon?' This was all so sudden. I was happy for her, but couldn't help but feel she was rushing into this.

'In a couple of months… July?'

'You want to organise a wedding in two months?'

'Yeah, we'll work it out. Thing is, he's stuck up there in Scotland and we're finding the distance a big problem.'

I knew about that, only too well.

'You're not pregnant, are you?' I said, torn between panic and elation, immediately trying to work out the childcare arrangements for a potential second child in my head.

'No, we just don't want to waste time being apart – like you're always telling me, life's short and we want to get on with it.'

'But can he just leave Scotland so quickly – his job, his kids?' I asked. 'I know his kids are a bit older… in their teens, aren't they?' I knew Richard had been divorced five years, his wife had had an affair but he seemed to get the rough end of things, handing her the house and the kids. He adored his kids and saw them regularly at weekends. I knew this was going to be difficult, there was no way he was going to come and live here permanently.

'Yeah, his kids are thirteen and fifteen,' Emma said.

'Well, I suppose they could come down here, stay with us some weekends…' Then I suddenly realised Richard and Emma might not want to stay living in this little rented house. 'Of course, you might want to move somewhere together. There's a house down the road that's for sale – that would be handy for me to collect Rosie and…' I started.

'Thing is, Mum, we've been talking about it for a while, but I don't think that would be right for us, not with work and Rosie.'

I tried not to look too relieved. 'I can see what you mean, you wouldn't want Rosie to be moved around too much. Having a new daddy will be a big change, probably best to stay here until everyone's settled... I mean, you're introducing another man into her life.'

'*Another man*? Richard's the first man I've introduced into her life, Mum – I'm not the bloody village bike!' she snapped, and I heard Rosie's 'bruddy rabbit' echo and realised where she'd heard the word.

'Emma, I wasn't saying that – I just meant there's a lot to think about from Rosie's perspective. You're dealing with long hours at work and now she's going to have a different family dynamic...'

'In a different place.'

'Different? I thought you said you didn't want to move Rosie around.'

'No, Mum, I didn't say that, you did. And actually, I've talked to my boss and I can move to the Edinburgh office, where Richard is. In fact, it'll be a slightly bigger role, a bit more money... and more responsibility.'

Now it was my turn to bristle, and it dawned on me that I wasn't part of this plan.

I stared at the TV screen, like Helen Mirren might be able to give me some advice, but she had enough on her plate with three murders and a stroppy deputy. My foundations suddenly felt very wobbly. Given my huge capacity for worrying about situations that were never going to happen, I'd managed to miss this one which was staring me in the face completely. I was trying hard to be pleased about Emma's wedding, and trying even harder not to think of myself and where I fitted into this strange new world my daughter was now producing from nowhere.

Emma and Rosie were leaving. I felt like I'd been punched in the stomach; this wasn't supposed to happen.

'Talk to Richard...' Emma was now excitedly dialling his number and handing me her phone.

'What do you want me to say?' I asked, still in shock, not ready for this conversation with my soon-to-be son-in-law and holding the phone like it was infectious. What do you say to the virtual stranger who's about to marry your daughter and become dad to your granddaughter – and turn your own life upside down? But I didn't have time to dwell on it as he'd already answered...

'Congratulations, Richard – it's lovely for Emma to have finally found someone. When I say, finally... I mean, it's not like she's been frantically searching... she's had lots of boyfriends. Ha, when I say *lots*, I don't mean she's slept around... It's not like she's the village bike or anything... although, of course, she's not a nun – she's had her fair share of...'

At this point a rather horrified Emma whisked the phone from me: 'Mum, for God's sake, he doesn't need my sexual history! Sorry, Richard,' she said, putting the phone to her ear, 'Mum's a bit surprised and she tends to go on a bit when she doesn't know what to say. I'm sure over the next few years you'll get to know this and be as embarrassed as the rest of us by the stuff she comes up with,' she giggled.

I put my head in my hands and watched her through my fingers. Emma was right: when I was nervous I attempted to fill awkward silences and didn't know when to stop.

Eventually Emma put down the phone (not before some girlish giggles and secret whisperings) and we laughed about my incoherent ramblings. She was excited and wanted to talk cakes and dresses and venues, but it was all a bit much for me: my ship had hit the rocks. Everyone else was making plans and I suddenly felt like a gooseberry in my own life, not that I knew what that looked like any more. So much of my life had been about being there for Emma and Rosie and now that was ending. Naively, I'd imagined us all living together for years, with me there to help Emma guide Rosie through school and the awkward teen years and all the madness that came with it. But now I wouldn't even see her start school.

'I am just so tired,' I said, 'and I have lots to think about if we're going to plan a wedding – so I'm off to bed, let's talk tomorrow.'

Emma nodded, but she wasn't really paying any attention to me – she was already back on her phone. If I'd done a mega slut drop right there in front of her, she wouldn't have batted an eyelid, she was just so involved in the moment – and Richard. Having only just spoken to him, she was probably now texting him and I realised with a jolt that my little girl didn't need me any more. I heard Dan's words in my head, 'Let Emma go and live her life so you can live yours'. How wise he was and how much I missed him now. Dan knew what I didn't – that Emma hadn't needed me for some time, I'd just been too 'bruddy' stubborn to admit it, even to myself.

Chapter Eleven

The Crazy Bitch in the BIG Pants!

'So, do you have an actual date yet?' I asked tentatively the following morning over coffee and toast.

Perhaps now wasn't the time to suggest it was all too much too soon and they just wait a couple of years or longer, until Rosie was eighteen. I'd come up with this idea at 3.47 that morning, while unable to sleep, but in the cold light of day, I realised it wasn't going to work as a suggestion.

'You're okay with this wedding and moving and everything, aren't you, Mum?' Emma said, sitting at the kitchen table. 'I mean, it will have an impact on you too, I suppose?'

'I suppose it will,' I said, trying to hide the sarcasm in my voice and faking a smile, but feeling bereft. I'd slowly travelled from shock to worry throughout my sleepless night, but just before dawn had come to the conclusion that Emma and Rosie would be fine without me. Now I was at the stage of wondering how I would be without them… and for that matter *where* I would be. I was a couple of weeks away from my finals, had no life partner, was about to lose my daughter and granddaughter and my home. *Yes, I suppose it might just have an impact on me, Emma.*

I didn't want to rain on her parade, so girded my loins, patted her hand and put on a brave face.

'It's wonderful,' I continued, then repeated, 'wonderful,' before hiding my face in a sip of coffee. 'Wonderful' wasn't a word I would use to describe this whirlwind of madness that had the potential to unsettle Rosie and leave me homeless, but I had to at least appear to be positive.

As much as I tried to be 'delighted' though, I couldn't help but feel a little resentful. I knew she'd said I should go with Dan if that's what I wanted, she also said they'd cope without me, but I didn't hear it. Consequently, I'd pretty much given up my own life little more than twelve months earlier so I could be there for her. I didn't exist as an independent being, I was an extension of my daughter's needs and wants – and it was all my fault.

'I'm taking Rosie to Scotland with me next weekend, and we're going to spend it together with his kids – as a family. The children have only met a few times, be nice to have the whole weekend,' Emma was saying now.

'Great, I hope they all get on,' I said, ashamed of my mixed feelings, but aware that it wouldn't be hard to win over our feisty four-year-old in a weekend.

'Oh, you know Rosie – buy her an ice cream and she'll love them to bits,' Emma laughed.

'A relationship with a child isn't built on ice cream, it's built on love and trust and years of nappy changing and playing games and singing songs,' I heard myself say. Aware I was sounding like a disgruntled nanny from the Victorian era, I stopped short of listing the up-all-night nursing a fever and not being able to attend lectures because the little one is poorly and Mum has her career. But Emma had seemed to conveniently forget the bond I'd shared with Rosie wrought from tears and sweat and love and endless hours of hide-and-seek – and let's not forget *Frozen* on an endless loop! Okay, I'd just thought of a vague silver lining to this – I might never have to hear or sing another chorus of 'Let It Go', but that didn't work because I loved duetting with Rosie – even if she did always have to be Elsa, the beautiful blonde one.

'Dan seemed to win her over with ice cream and funny faces, so I'm sure we'll be fine.'

That hurt. Dan may not have actually fathered a child, but that didn't mean he couldn't look after one. I was probably being over-sensitive, but the way she said it, it felt like she was implying that's all he could do – and if *he* could win Rosie over, anyone could. But Dan wasn't just about ice cream and funny faces: we'd spent a lot of time together, the three of us, when Emma was working. He would sit patiently with her while she drew pictures, watched TV with her and was always there to wipe away her tears if she fell over. Rosie thought the world of him and they'd had a lovely friendship. I knew I was being childish, but I suddenly felt like everything me and Dan had been to Rosie was being dismissed now Richard had come on the scene.

I didn't want to fall out with Emma though – she was so happy, perhaps for the first time in a long while. I wasn't going to rain on her parade, so I kept my thoughts to myself. I understood Emma didn't want to stay single all her life and it would be good for Rosie to have a father figure. Now Dan had gone, the only male in Rosie's life was Craig, her granddad, with his monosyllabic conversation and unhealthy obsession with ballcocks.

Rosie had now come into the kitchen for more toast and asked for 'an espwesssssso', which made us smile, and I made her some warm milk with chocolate sprinkles.

'There you are, Madam. I hope it's to your liking,' I said, placing a small cup and saucer in front of her and sitting down.

'Is that weaaaally espwessso, Nana?' she lisped, looking at me like I was in court and she was cross-examining me.

'Yes, that's what they drink in all the fine coffee houses of Europe.'

'You cwazy bitch!' She rolled her eyes and Emma and I looked at each other over our coffee steam. We both knew where she'd heard that expression.

'Don't worry, she won't be going into the hairdresser's much longer,' I said pointedly, before Emma could say anything.

'Oh, Mum, don't be like that.'

'Like what?' I feigned surprise. 'I was just saying, you two won't be around here for much longer, so there won't be any bad influences.'

'I never said anything about bad influences.' She sipped her coffee, then carefully placed the mug back on the table. 'Mum, are you okay with all this? I know it can't be easy for you. I was saying to Richard on the phone last night that I didn't want to upset you with all the changes.'

I was hurt and angry to think Emma had been discussing me with Richard. I knew I was being unreasonable, it was inevitable that she would talk to him, but it changed the dynamic of our relationship, which was painful for me.

'I'm not some infirm ninety-five-year-old granny who has to be "discussed", I'm not "the family problem",' I snapped.

'Mum... I never said you were, you're overreacting...'

'I'm sorry,' I huffed. 'Yes, there are a lot of changes, but I can cope. I'm perfectly capable of accepting and adapting to new situations, whatever you or Richard might think.'

I picked up my mug and plate of toast crumbs and stacked them in the dishwasher, realising she was absolutely right – I wasn't remotely ready to accept this.

'Don't be so defensive, I just mentioned to Richard that I feel bad leaving you here on your own.'

'I'm fine, I'm not some arthritic old lady with three cats and a heart condition,' I said, almost slamming the dishwasher shut. 'I'm a forty-six-year-old student, not some pensioner. Jesus, Emma!'

'Mummy, Nana just used a swear called Jesus,' Rosie politely informed her mother, as she delicately picked up her 'espresso' cup and sipped daintily. I usually loved Rosie's commentary and I'd have laughed if I wasn't on the verge of tears.

'Sorry, Rosie, Nana shouldn't say things like that,' I patted her arm. 'But, Emma, I have to be honest – I feel like you're doing this without considering anyone else...'

She put down her mug with an eye roll, the implication being that my overreaction was just what she'd warned Richard about.

'And yes, I'm overreacting,' I said. 'Damn right I am!' I added, hoping to God the swear police was too busy with her fancy coffee to remark on this. Emma needed to know exactly how I felt for once. 'This is a big life event for you, but it's also a big family event with huge implications for Rosie... and for me – yet if I say anything, I get the feeling you think I'm just being obstructive or annoying, and now I'm being defensive, *apparently*,' I said. Defensively.

A rather heated exchange followed, throughout which we both smiled through gritted teeth and did what we always did when we said anything mildly controversial in Rosie's hearing: we changed the names to protect the innocent. Rosie had quite the gob on her for such a little one and, apart from reprimanding me and her mother if we argued or swore, had been known to share all kinds of intimate and embarrassing information later with whoever cared to listen. Aged just three, she'd once informed a stranger in Tesco that 'Nanny and Granddad don't love each other anymore because Nanny goes to sleep in Dam's bed', as well as passing on the news that 'Mummy has a moustache' to her crèche teacher. My personal favourite, 'Nana wears very BIG pants', was announced to a group of my fellow students at uni and accompanied by a visual demonstration with her little arms spread as wide as physically possible to give some indication as to the enormity of what one might laughingly call lingerie.

'So, can you please tell the Wicked Stepmother exactly what's going to happen and when?' I asked Emma now, with gritted teeth. 'Is Snow White definitely going to live in the Highlands with her Prince? Has a decision been made, and can we all be told yet when the happy day will be?'

Emma shook her head. 'I don't know, and I, er, Snow White is sorry she upset the Wicked Stepmother.' Then she lifted her palm off the table in a 'not now' gesture, glancing over at Rosie. 'Rosie, as you've finished, you can go and watch some TV while Nana and I finish our coffee,' she said, stretching her mouth into a smile, panic in her eyes.

'No, thanks, Mummy. I'd like to stay here and talk about Snow White's wedding.' With that, she rested her little chin on both hands and waited for the next comment, looking from one to the other like she was at a tennis match. If the situation hadn't been so horrific and I hadn't felt that life as I knew it was hanging in the balance, I would have been hysterical. 'So, Nana, what are you going as?'

'I'm sorry, darling?'

'Jesus, I mean the bruddy wedding!' She threw her hands up in frustration.

'That's enough, Rosie – that's very rude,' Emma frowned. 'You mustn't say swear words.'

'But Nana said a swear called...' Her little chubby index finger was pointing directly at me.

'That's *enough*,' Emma repeated, with a warning look, and Rosie looked at me with an 'Oh God, she's at it again' face, and I tried not to catch her eye.

We all sipped in the silence. I didn't know what to say, but Rosie did.

'Mummy's going to the wedding as Snow White and I'm having a unicorn costume, aren't I, Mummy?' she said, turning to Emma.

'Not for the wedding, sweetie,' Emma replied, no doubt relieved her four-year-old had stopped swearing like a trucker.

'I AM, I'm going to the wedding in a unicorn!'

Rosie was now threatening tears and as this subject really wasn't the top of anyone's agenda (except Rosie's, of course), there was no room on the current agenda to explore this. Given that I wasn't even aware the wedding had been discussed at 'costume' level, I just sat and looked at Emma and waited for the relevant information.

'I'm having a unicorn bedroom,' Rosie continued. 'Richard told me I can. Hey, Nana, don't be sad! You can come for sleepovers in my unicorn bedroom… yes, you can,' she nodded vigorously as she reached for my arm and gazed into my face.

'Lovely, darling, I shall look forward to that,' I said, unable to imagine her waking up in that bedroom without me there to make her breakfast, help her choose her outfit for the day. I swallowed back tears, thinking how the two of us had been quite the team.

After a reasonable interval, I continued my conversation with Emma, still smiling through gritted teeth.

'So, have you and… the *Prince* named the day?'

At this, Rosie leaned into her mother and whispered conspiratorially, but loudly, 'Nana means Richard…' This was accompanied by more vigorous nodding, like she was imparting something quite revelatory. She then turned to me, 'July… Mummy's getting married in July, Nana – but don't be sad – you're invited too. Of course you are!'

It was now my turn to roll my eyes, torn between bursting into laughter, panic or tears; I opted for all three.

'It's okay, Nana. You can go as a mermaid if you like?'

Emma passed me a box of tissues and assured a slightly alarmed Rosie that, 'Nana's okay. They're happy tears, darling.'

'The twenty-first,' Emma blurted. 'That's the day.'

I nodded and attempted a smile for Rosie's sake, but felt like shouting, *so that's something else no one has bothered to tell me. And, no, they bloody aren't happy tears! These are tears of hurt and abandonment and panic at the prospect of you both leaving for another country – after planning a wedding in a ridiculous time frame.*

But I didn't. I wiped my eyes, dampened down my own feelings and, slipping into my mum safety net, asked: 'So, what kind of wedding cake would you like?'

Chapter Twelve

Golf Pros and Tennis Hoes

So, that was it. The wedding was a matter of weeks away and my family was leaving me for a new life and a unicorn bedroom in Scotland. Meanwhile, I'd let the man I love leave and all I was left with was an endless guest list and a huge bill for Emma's wedding. I'm not complaining, I insisted on making a large contribution from my house money.

I was in the middle of my finals, and as tutorials had now ended and we were well into revision mode, I'd managed to avoid Dave, thankfully. After my last text he hadn't responded, but his radio silence spoke volumes – he clearly thought I was deluded and believed we were having an affair. I knew I should deal with this, but I also knew that I'd end up saying too much, behaving weirdly and making things worse. So, I decided it was best to leave well alone – I wasn't going to let anything cloud my last few weeks of living with Emma and Rosie. Emma and I both knew things were about to change, so we made the most of our time together. I spent the days revising and finishing my dissertation, then taking my exams, while Rosie enjoyed her last few weeks at the uni crèche. The rest of the time was spent wandering in awe through white tulle, floral bouquets and cake tastings. Despite my initial apprehension I couldn't escape the feelings of love and joy I had in sharing in this moment with my daughter – it's what every mother dreams of. The wedding was to be in Scotland at a big old castle, which I was invited to inspect, along with the groom, who looked at Emma with such love, and treated her and Rosie – and me – with such kindness, I began to accept what was happening.

I did contemplate how the people I loved always moved far away from me but tried not to take this personally. This pre-wedding time was happy. We shopped for Rosie and Emma's dresses – white fishtail lace for Emma and a ballerina pink flower girl dress for Rosie, who was furious because she'd planned to go as a unicorn. It was an unusually warm summer, and some early evenings, Emma and I would sit in the garden with a chilled white while Rosie played with her toys on the grass. Other times, we'd order pizzas and watch Rosie-chosen DVDs (which turned out to be *Frozen*, *Frozen* and *Frozen*). We also went to the zoo, theatre, cinema and out for tea far more than we should – I just wanted to enjoy these last few weeks because I knew once family life and school kicked in up in Edinburgh, I wouldn't see much of Rosie. She'd promised to Skype, but as she'd pointed out, 'Don't be surprised if I don't because I can get very busy.' I was slowly coming to terms with everything, and though I'd had a few tearful moments in private, I wanted to throw myself entirely into making Emma and Rosie's farewell a memory we could all hold onto.

A week before the wedding, Mandy offered to give us all beauty treatments, including Rosie, which worried Emma slightly. I promised that the treatments Mandy gave her drag queen clientele would not be used on a four-year-old, but I crossed my fingers behind my back as I said it, and off we went.

'She hasn't had a bloody hen night!' Mandy screeched accusingly in my face as she painted Rosie's nails pearly pink.

I held my breath and cringed at what might come next, but I reckoned Mandy was already ordering the fake penises, if she didn't have a stockpile in her garage.

I couldn't whisk Rosie away with her nails half-done – divas always complete their grooming – so I just had to hope Mandy didn't swear too much or say anything too sexual – which was like asking her not to speak, really.

'I don't think Emma wanted a hen night,' I said, aware that Rosie was looking at Mandy like she was a goddess and was likely to repeat *everything* she said.

'Your Emma should have a party at least. I know, a fancy dress? I know... I know,' she could barely speak with excitement and I was too slow to get in there before she finished, 'tarts and bloody vicars?'

'Tarts and bruddy knickers?' giggled Rosie innocently, shaking her head like Mandy was a crazy bitch, which could easily have been the next words out of her little rosebud mouth, had I not intervened.

'I don't think... tar— *that*... would be appropriate,' I said to Mandy, nodding in Rosie's direction, hoping if it stopped now, Rosie might forget she'd ever heard it.

'Nah, you're right – your Emma's a bit classy for tarts and vicars,' Mandy said, repeating the bloody sentence, stopping the nail painting and gazing into the ceiling for hen night inspiration as Rosie looked on in awe. 'I know, what about something a bit more posh… Golf Pros and Tennis Hoes?'

'Not sure…' I said, though I was very sure – adamant, in fact – but it was clear Rosie was intrigued by the idea, even though she didn't understand what the hell was going on.

I was now at the stage of defeat, almost abandoning any kind of censorship. It was like holding back a tsunami as Mandy went on to list the various possibilities of my daughter's hen night themes and accompanying props. 'Naughty nurses… Erm… Playboy bunnies?'

'Hardly.'

'You crazy bitch!' she laughed, like I was the mad one. 'I know, I know, what about S&M? Whips and chains and…'

'I always think the simplest ideas are better,' I cut in, trying to stop this tsunami of filth being washed over my granddaughter's innocent ears.

'Okay, it's looking like really big blow-up penises,' she said before I could do anything to stop her.

Which is why, when Richard arrived the following day in a big van to move their stuff to Scotland, Rosie greeted him by telling him, 'Nana's going to the wedding as a *really* big penis!'

The day of the wedding dawned and I woke to mixed emotions. My head knew this was right for Emma and Rosie, but my heart ached to think I wouldn't see them every day, or even every week. It would be tough on all of us, but Emma had Richard, and Rosie had them both, so hopefully they'd be okay. It was just me who would struggle, and I felt truly alone – especially without Dan to hold my hand and tell me it would all be fine.

I tried to push thoughts of him aside and think 'happy thoughts' because if I didn't get a grip, I might well end up sobbing throughout this wedding. I stepped into my new powder blue dress and shoes, applied my make-up carefully and added a blue feathery fascinator, which looked good on my blonde hair. I wanted Emma to be proud of her mum; I knew the wedding pictures would be pored over long after they'd left for Scotland and I wanted to look good.

Leaving my hotel room, I closed the door, knowing our lives would be quite different when I returned later that day. I knew the occasion was supposed to be happy, but I was sad to say another goodbye and tried to keep my composure as I entered the reception area where drinks were being served before the wedding. I greeted friends and family, was introduced to some of Richard's side and, checking the table planner, managed to hide my sheer horror at the prospect of spending the wedding breakfast seated next to Craig. I'd seen my ex-husband as little as possible since I'd left him, and he'd avoided me too – not because we were broken-hearted and couldn't bear to see the one that got away, but because we couldn't bear to see each other full stop.

For years we'd lived with a deep, mutual, burning dislike of each other. This sometimes slipped into pure, unadulterated hatred, and in my case sometimes trod the very fine line between letting him live and murdering him as he slept. On the sofa. Mouth open. Snoring. In the middle of *Silent Witness*. Thankfully, those days were behind me and I only had to get through the next hour or so – how hard could that be?

Unfortunately, I saw him as soon as he entered the castle chapel where the ceremony was taking place, and to my dismay he joined me, pushing me up the pew with his ill-judged plonk down. Although he visited Rosie and Emma occasionally, I'd always made myself scarce, so it was all a bit awkward as he gave me a nod and a monosyllabic grunt. Emma didn't want Craig to give her away; she said it was 'perpetuating the patriarchy' and he'd said that was fine by him because he had a dropped flange to fix first thing and might be a bit late anyway. Sadly, it seemed the flange hadn't proved too problematic and he'd made it with time to spare, which meant I now had to make non-plumbing small talk with him until the ceremony got underway. I glanced over at him, waiting for some acknowledgement of the occasion, but he was staring ahead, probably dreaming of hard setting sealant and brass flange nipples.

'Looks beautiful, doesn't she?' I whispered, trying to open up the lines of communication, if only for the day. But he just nodded and checked his phone and I felt the years of frustration, resentment and anger come back up between us like a brick wall. Having Craig around made me miss Dan even more, because he was everything my ex-husband wasn't. I thought about Dan every morning when I woke up, every night before I fell asleep and a million times in between, and here in the church, on this special day, I'd have loved him by my side.

He would have obsessed over the wedding breakfast and insisted on baking the cake, which was white chocolate and raspberry, sweet and delicious. Dan was a fantastic cook and a brilliant baker, and though self-taught, he had the knowledge and passion of a great chef. And later, as we ate canapés made from goats' cheese, figs and drizzled basil oil, I imagined Dan savouring every mouthful, discussing the flavours and ingredients intensely. He'd have pondered the exact origin of the Scottish beef for the main course, and I'd have teased him, saying it was the cow called Daisy who lived on the third hill from the left. He'd have loved the crisp, bubbly Prosecco, and the rich, fruity Merlot, allowing it to roll around his tongue, while he considered the grape.

This was in complete contrast to darling Craig, who, while shovelling in two canapés at once, was heard to remark, 'This is rubbish! Don't know why they don't just give us a sandwich until dinner comes.' His only comment to me throughout the elegant wedding breakfast was, 'This wine tastes like battery acid, I'm going to suffer with my guts later,' causing my fascinator to droop. Wherever Dan might be, things could be worse – I could still be with Craig, I thought as he belched loudly into his napkin.

As for Emma, she was magnificent, and as Mother of the Bride, I tried to ignore the Father of the Bride and just enjoy the day. I was so proud and happy for her. I wept loudly as she walked down the aisle, causing Craig to tut beside me and shift uncomfortably. But this was merely a prelude to my uncontrolled blubbing at the sight of my little granddaughter in baby pink with a basket of roses. To everyone's amusement, her sudden sprint up the aisle caused my restrained sobs to erupt, reaching levels of what can only be described as climactic hysteria. Even the registrar waited until I'd composed myself before she started the ceremony. But Rosie reacted to my blubbing with her usual candour and, standing with the bride and groom at the altar, one hand on her hip, she rolled her eyes and shouted, 'Nana, you *crazy* bitch!'

Chapter Thirteen

Filthy Foreign Words and Nice Men on Timber

While Emma and Richard honeymooned in Ireland, Rosie and I spent the week in her old home. I was staying on for another couple of weeks – the rent was paid for a month and I was considering my options. But for now it was a treat for both me and Rosie to spend time together before she moved and, despite being forced to watch *Frozen* for the 538th time, I valued that week together. I wanted it to be special, and filled with everything about her life here, because once she was in Scotland, I doubted she'd remember our favourite pastimes. So we did lots of lovely things, from play dates with her friends from the crèche to walks in the park, to afternoon tea in our favourite local café. I also planned a visit later in the week for 'beauty treatments' with Mandy, but I'd have to ensure this was after Mandy's vajazzle 'promotion', which left little to the imagination. The staff were wearing T-shirts with 'Life's short – get a vajazzle' emblazoned in rhinestones, which I just knew Rosie would find fascinating. *Too* fascinating. I could only imagine Emma's face when Rosie asked for one of her very own. I could also only imagine Emma's face if I'd been working on 'Vajazzle Week' and had been forced to wear a T-shirt with a rhinestone vagina emblazoned across the front.

'Come into the salon and I can demonstrate on you,' Mandy suggested when I'd popped in earlier that week to ask about bringing Rosie in to have her nails done. 'Go on… I'd put shedloads of crystals on it this time, we could have big posters of your lady garden all over the shop.'

I couldn't hide my horror at the prospect of close-ups of my jewelled vagina all over the walls. 'Tempting as that is, I'll give it a miss, Mand,' I said, knowing the sarcasm would be lost on her.

I wanted to provide memories for my granddaughter when we visited the salon, not post-traumatic stress.

I was aware Rosie's new life would be quite different, full of new and exciting things, but at the same time it might be a little overwhelming. So I photographed everything we did and all that was familiar and planned to put the pictures in an album so she could go back there sometimes.

Of course, I'd visit them in Scotland and they would come and see me, but I'd been doing some thinking and I wasn't sure how long I'd be here. I was still in 'analysis' mode from my degree course, studying every text, every film – looking for the meaning, the subplot, the message. And it kind of hit me one evening, while watching *Frozen* (for the 539th time), if you try to hide your emotions and isolate yourself in a frozen ice castle, everything you've been holding inside will eventually blow up and cause a lot more harm than if you just – as the song says – 'Let It Go'. So the answer had been in front of me all the time – Disney knew it, Rosie knew it – it had just taken me a little longer to see what was right in front of my face.

I'd done this with my feelings for Dan – since he left, my life had been taken up with studying, my family and the hairdresser's. I'd avoided communicating with him, I'd avoided anything to do with love – and if I didn't do something about it soon, I'd be… frozen! Okay, I really needed to stop watching that film.

That night, I lay awake and thought about his proposal in a way I hadn't before. As painful as it was for me that Emma and Rosie would be living so far away, it also meant that I was now really free, with no ties, no responsibilities, and I could go anywhere I wanted to. Could I live in another country now? Could I marry again? And what about my career? Could I be a teacher? How difficult would it be to get work somewhere like… Australia? How would Dan feel about me now saying I'd changed my mind? What if his feelings had changed in the fifteen months since we'd parted? Then I thought of those eyes, and the way he loved me, and I just knew in my heart he'd still be waiting, because that's what I'd been doing: waiting. Waiting for him, waiting for an opportunity, waiting for a time when, like now, I was finally ready.

I woke early the next morning and called Sue, my old boss from the hairdresser's, for some advice. As I heard the ringing on the other end, I wondered why on earth she was the person I'd turned to in my hour of need – her love life had been a car crash for years. It started when her beloved husband Ken ran off with the next-door neighbour (Sue put it down to the slut having O-level French and apparently using 'filthy foreign words' in his hearing, which had inflamed him). Relying mainly on looks and star signs, Sue had since been used, abused and dumped by men throughout the United Kingdom and various Spanish holiday resorts. But before

I had chance to renege, she picked up the phone and I apologised for calling at such an ungodly hour.

'I'm sorry for calling so early, but I need to speak to you before I ring him,' I said quietly, trying to keep my voice down so I didn't wake Rosie, who'd seen and heard enough this week. Fortunately, she was unable to pronounce 'vajazzle' after hearing it in the salon – but she'd certainly given it a good go.

'Oh love, you can call me any time, day or night – it's no bother,' Sue replied, through her yawns.

'I just don't know what to do, Sue,' I said, after explaining my dilemma.

'I say go for it. I mean, look at me – I took a risk, abandoned everything, ran away to Devon and it's the best thing I ever did. And I've met some very nice men on Timber.'

I think she meant 'Tinder', but with Sue there was no telling – her love life had known such tragedy it could indeed have been a dating app for rampant lumberjacks.

'I'm glad you've found happiness, Sue, you deserve it. Thing is, I wanted to ask you… Do you think I should call Dan and try and give our relationship another chance?'

'Of course you should, love.'

'But I wonder if he can ever forgive me. I rejected his proposal and let him go off to Australia alone and…'

'He'll forgive you, love. Look at me, when my Ken left for that hussy next door, I thought I'd never forgive him, but ten years down the line I'm over it.' She *so* wasn't – I could hear the venom in her voice down the line all the way from bloody Devon! 'My only regret, Faye, is never having kids, but I reckon he was impudent anyway.

Mind you, he was a cheating, womanising Virgo, who I should never have married in the first place, but that's another story.'

So much for forgiveness, I thought as Sue went on to cheerlead me to Australia, insisting I call Dan immediately and pointing out that with the sun currently in Venus, I should strike while the iron was hot.

'But be careful,' she warned, 'Sagittarians aren't called the bachelor sign of the zodiac for nothing – they like to sow their wild oats.'

'Oh, he'd been there and done that before he met me,' I laughed.

I listened on to Sue's astrological, malapropism-punctuated nonsense, knowing it was just what I needed after all. She was my friend, always would be, and despite being quite bonkers, she'd tell me what I wanted to hear. And as we said our goodbyes, her final words rang in my ear: 'Go for it, love! Death is not the greatest loss in life, the greatest loss is what dies inside us while we live.'

I was impressed, but this was *too* meaningful and malaprop-free for Sue. 'Wow, Sue, that's profound... Is that Proust?'

'No... Pinterest,' she said. 'Bloody fabulous, isn't it?'

I laughed, said goodbye and put down the phone. I thought about what she'd said (well, what Pinterest had said) and started to type his number, then sat and stared at my phone for at least ten minutes. I hadn't even told Emma about what I was contemplating, but I assumed she'd be okay with it. 'Mum, I hope you meet someone... or that Dan comes back,' she'd said at her wedding. We were both a little tipsy at the end of a long, but beautiful (apart from Craig) day and feeling happy but sad, the way weddings make you feel. 'I don't need to meet someone,' I'd replied. 'I don't need a man in my life, it's full enough without having to cook someone else's dinner. I'm going to concentrate on me and my career now – I've worked hard for this.'

'Just don't throw yourself into work and neglect the real stuff,' she'd sighed, her veil a little askew, but her heart in the right place. 'I just wish you'd fall madly in love so I don't have to feel guilty about leaving and living so far away.'

'Emma, guilt is a wasted emotion. I know this because it has ruled my bloody life and I won't allow it to rule yours! I'm perfectly happy on my own,' I said, 'so no more of it.'

Yes, I thought, holding my phone in both hands, staring at the screen – this is exactly what Emma would want me to do. So I held my breath and I dialled his number (the one written on my heart) and I heard it ring. Strange to think it was ringing somewhere on the other side of the world. God only knew how much this call would cost, but I didn't care.

It rang and rang, and eventually went to voicemail: 'Hi, it's Dan at Lemon Myrtle – leave a message.' My legs felt weak, my stomach was doing somersaults just hearing his sing-song sunshiney voice. He sounded slightly different – older perhaps? I suppose a lot had happened with his brother, and now he was a grown-up and a fully-fledged business owner, he'd probably been through plenty of ups and downs, which had taken their toll on that carefree voice, those eyes that were about to laugh any minute. No surprise if his light had dimmed a little. Perhaps me being there would bring the light back for him, because we were both at our happiest together.

I gave it a few minutes, then called again. The second time I was even more nervous and as the voicemail picked up once more, I clicked off. I sat there tapping my feet. My whole life was hanging in the balance here – this could be the phone call that would change everything. I made a mental note that if I didn't get through the third time then perhaps fate had other things in store for me and I would give up (knowing I had no intention of doing so. I'd made up my mind, and as Sue had said, 'Leos are very detrimental' – I think she felt it was a posh way of saying determined, but who knew with Sue?).

Eventually, after trying for about an hour, Dan answered, and I heard that lovely voice. He only said, 'Hi, it's Dan,' but my heart was immediately flooded with warm chocolate.

'G'day, Dan, it's me!' I said in a fake Australian accent. I don't know why, I just felt like being silly – being me again.

'Faye…? Oh jeez, I never expected… I saw the number but thought it was my aunt.'

'Oh – didn't my name come up on your phone?' I felt slightly deflated at this.

'You told me to delete it, remember?' *Yeah, but I didn't mean it.*

Okay, I suppose asking him never to contact me again was pretty much the same. And clearly he hadn't remembered my number. But I remembered his, along with all of the quotations for my finals and the lyrics to 'Let It Go'.

'How is everything… your sister-in-law, your nephews?'

'They're good. Talking about moving back to be near Kimmie's parents, which is a shame – I'll miss them. Thing is, their memories aren't so good here – John had a rough few years…' he tailed off. 'Anyway, how are you? How's Rosie? I bet she's really grown up!' he said.

'Yeah, she has. Still in charge, still spends her days in royal costumes, though she's starting school in September. And I got my degree.'

'Oh, that's just fantastic, Faye! Really, really great.' He was genuinely pleased, but I got the feeling he was distracted. Then again, we hadn't spoken for a year and we were thousands of miles apart.

'And Dan, you won't believe this – Emma got married.'

'Wow, what a turn-up!' he said, and he asked about the wedding breakfast and the groom (in that order). I gave him all the details, from the canapés to the cake, and he was as engrossed as I knew he'd be – food was his language.

'So... you said you never wanted to talk again, but you've called?' he asked, once he'd heard all about the wedding.

I'd been hoping for more small talk, more catch-up, some mild flirting even, so him asking me why I'd called made me feel slightly uncomfortable. I couldn't blame him – I was lucky he didn't tell me to sod off, and say I had a cheek, calling him up out of the blue over a year after I'd broken his heart. Luckily, he was still lovely Dan and despite wanting to get down to why I'd called him, he seemed pleased to hear from me.

'I wanted to talk to you because... I miss you,' I suddenly said, aware my voice was catching. I knew in saying something like this, I was opening the floodgates and I waited for his response. It wasn't easy to get back to where we had been but just hearing his voice the magic had begun again for me. 'Are you there?' I said, into the silence, wondering if we'd lost the line.

'Yeah... yeah... I'm here.'

'I'm sorry to just call you up out of the blue like this,' I said. I could tell from his voice that he was upset – the emotional impact was huge for both of us and I'd taken him by surprise.

'No worries… Faye… It's good, all good.' But I wasn't convinced – I reckoned he was still hurting after losing his brother, grief can change you.

'It's just that, well, things have changed around here… You know I said Emma was married now?'

'Yeah?'

'Well, they've moved to Scotland. That's where Richard's from, and I was upset when they moved, of course. It took a bit of getting used to but now it's happened, I've been thinking…'

'Oh?'

'About us.'

'Oh.'

'You needn't sound so excited,' I giggled, unsure of what to make of his one-word reaction.

'No, it's not that, it's just… Faye, you said it was over. You said there couldn't be an *us* ever again.'

'I know, I know, but that was then, this is now. I'm free… Dan, I'm finally free… No baby-minding, no daughter-minding, I can concentrate on us… We can do a road trip through Australia, you can show me…'

'I have the café, Faye…' He sounded surprised, not to say slightly underwhelmed, but I understood it was all so sudden for him – I hadn't given him a chance to take it in.

'Oh, I know you have the café and I wouldn't *make* you go on a road trip…'

'That's good to know.'

Christ, he was making this tough for me.

'… But I was thinking, if you still want me…?'

Silence. I felt a little uneasy at this, especially as it was followed by more silence. Which I of course had to fill.

'Then I could come to Oz. I don't want to wait another minute… I don't mean… I'm not saying we have to get married. Though I would marry you – gosh, of course I would… But you might not want to get married anymore, right? Then again, you might? I just want to make it clear I'm not just calling you up and saying let's get married, unless of course you…'

'Oh… I don't… That would be…'

'Forget that last sentence,' I said, feeling like an idiot. Why did I always say what I was thinking instead of being more thoughtful, more sensitive to his feelings? 'Not just the last sentence, forget everything I just said for the last three minutes… at least.'

He laughed and I felt a little easier.

'I'm just thinking, I could come over there, get a job, stick around and see what happens? I want to teach English and I'd love to live somewhere like Sydney… with you. I stayed behind for all the right reasons, but now I'm free… Dan, just think about it. We can drink cocktails all night, stay in bed all day, lie on the beach – when you're not working, I mean.' I didn't know what else I could say; I hadn't thought this far, to be honest – I'd just assumed after 'Dan, it's me,' his response would be 'When will you be here?' But we'd been apart over a year now. Our lives had obviously changed, how could I possibly expect him to be in synch with me?

'I was all mixed up about ending things with you and being there for Emma and Rosie, but now I know this is the right thing to do,' I started up again, tired of my own voice. 'I just keep thinking of the fun we used to have and how we can do it all again, only this time with no responsibilities… just you and me.'

The silence, *his* silence, was unnerving. So I kept talking.

'I know I'll need a job, there's only so much irresponsibility a girl can have…' I laughed, aware I was waffling and in my nervous state now in danger of saying too much and behaving weirdly. 'But I could work anywhere… A school, a university? I don't know if I'd have to be married to an Australian citizen, that would be you,' I giggled nervously, wondering when I would stop behaving like some wannabe wife desperate to bag her man. 'I'm forcing myself on you, aren't I… am I? I'm not… am I, Dan? Please say something so I stop.'

'No, no. You're not forcing yourself…' He hesitated. 'But I just… This has all happened so suddenly, you have to understand I thought I'd never see you again, Faye.'

'I know, and I'm sorry. I've messed you about, I've been an idiot.'

'Yeah. Well, I wouldn't put it like that, but you did piss everything away… I mean, I was ready to get married, make it forever and you just said no.'

'Mmm, I did,' I said, slightly irritated at his retelling – it made me seem selfish, like I'd only considered myself – but then again perhaps I had?

'I'm sorry if I made you feel bad, Dan. I knew you had to go, I just couldn't go with you – but now everything's different. I've got enough money from the house sale to afford to fly over to you, spend the summer there and…'

Silence. Horrible. Silence.

'Look, Faye, there's nothing I'd love more than to spend the summer with you... here. But, babe, I just can't do it.'

'Oh, okay.' I couldn't quite get my head round this. He was the guy, the only guy, who'd do anything for me, who'd walk through hot coals to be with me – so what had changed?

'It's... I'm working. I'm working really hard, it's great – the café – it's what I always wanted. I feel like I'm finally doing what I wanted. Wonderful ingredients, locally sourced... It's more like a restaurant since we started opening in the evenings.'

'Hang on,' I said, stopping him mid-speech. 'I don't expect you to abandon your life just because I've decided to come over.'

'No, but it's just so busy, I wouldn't be able to see you...'

'I understand... but hey, I just had a brilliant idea,' I said, not listening to him, excited at my plans, 'why don't I come and work for you? There won't be any teaching work until September anyway, so it would be perfect! Oh Dan, imagine, you and me working in the restaurant together... It's what we always talked about.' I could see it now, side by side in the kitchen, planning menus, Dan wiping flour from my cheek and kissing it gently.

'I don't know, Faye, you don't have any experience...'

I felt crushed. He didn't have to say that – I wanted to be his girlfriend, not an employee. Since when did he care about experience? He'd taught himself to cook, and had always encouraged me to do new things, take risks, scare myself. He believed in me before I believed in me – he showed me I could dive into deep waters, literally and metaphorically. I glanced at my upper arm and remembered how he'd convinced me to have the little lemon cupcake tattoo. It was still there – but he wasn't.

'Okay, so I don't have experience,' I said, still smarting from this put-down, 'but I could work with you, learn from you. Dan, I'm so proud of you. Going home was so good for you…'

'Yeah, yeah, it was...'

'And I could be with you in a couple of weeks! I need to sort out flights, give my keys back to the landlord for this house, but Emma's back from her honeymoon in Ireland tomorrow night…' I laughed, but it was hollow. He'd usually have picked me up on this and said something about *our* prospective honeymoon. But he didn't.

'Faye, I should have said… I'm at work, it's a bit difficult to talk,' he said, like he hadn't even been listening to me.

'Oh, I'm sorry. I had no idea you were still at work, you should have said… But it's after midnight…'

'No worries. I'm just getting tomorrow's menus done.'

'Okay,' I said, slightly relieved now. It explained why there were so many silences; his awkwardness wasn't about me, there were other people around and he didn't want to say too much. 'So, shall we talk in a couple of days? Or…?'

'Hey… yeah, let's do that.'

'Okay,' I said, thinking that perhaps he might also still be pissed off at the way I'd rejected him last time we saw each other.

I was about to put the phone down when he said, 'Faye?'

'Yes?' I said, uncertainly.

'It's… good to hear your voice.'

I smiled a secret smile to myself, and clicking off the phone, sat in bed, watching the curtains drift in the summer breeze, but instead of feeling excited, certain of my future, I was left wondering what had just happened. Had the early morning

sunshine gone behind a cloud, or was I just being stupid? Of
course he was pleased to hear from me, but he was at work, he
was busy... Or was it more than that? How bloody conceited
I'd been to think I could just call him up after all this time and
expect him to drop everything. He had a lot on his plate and I
might not be top of his list of priorities at the moment. I had to
accept that I might have to work my way back to being the love
of his life – I had to earn it and not just expect that I'd be able to
step in and carry on as we were. But I was prepared to do that,
because he was worth it.

'Who were you talking to, Nana?' a little voice asked from the
doorway.

I opened my arms to Rosie and she ran to me, clambering onto
the bed. I swept her up, burying my face in her shampoo-scented
hair. Children are a great antidote to any kind of pain and just
hugging her soothed me, and at the same time reminded me she
wouldn't be here much longer. I had to make the most of these
Nana and Rosie days before Emma came back and whisked her
away to Scotland.

'I was talking to Dan,' I said. 'You remember Dan, don't you?'

She smiled a cheeky little smile and said shyly, 'You mean Dam...
He's your boyfriend.'

I nodded. 'Yes, he is... Well, he was.'

'Do you love him, Nana?'

'Yes, I do.'

'Are you going to marry him, like Mummy married Richard?'
She was cross-legged now, arms folded across her tummy. 'Can I be
a unicorn... and have a hens party night with the vicars?'

'Mmm, something like that. One day... perhaps. Now, come on, Little Miss Busybody,' I said tickling her, 'let's make pancakes for breakfast.'

'Yay! Let's bake pancakes,' she yelled and we put on our dressing gowns and raced downstairs.

'Is Mandy coming to your wedding? I like Mandy,' Rosie said a little later as I stood her on a chair to reach the kitchen worktop to help with the pancakes.

'Probably.'

'Can I have a T-shirt like Mandy's?'

I was slightly distracted as she broke an egg outside the bowl in her efforts to 'bake'.

'A T-shirt, sweetie?'

'Yes, like Mandy's, with jewels and a front bottom on.'

'Probably not,' I said gently, horrified that she'd been able to decipher the picture on Mandy's 'Vajazzle Week' T-shirts.

'I think we'll stick to the unicorn, darling. Now, shall we weigh out the flour?'

She lifted the bag of flour with a great deal of effort and I managed to catch it before it landed on the floor. I watched the concentration on her little face as she put the flour on the scales – painfully slow spoons, half-full, wobbly, flour dust everywhere. It seemed to last forever but I didn't mind, I just took her in, aching with love and missing her already.

Along with my theory that children are a cure-all, I find stacks of pancakes smothered in sugar and spiked with fresh lemon are also a great soother. I was confused and inexplicably stung by my conversation with Dan, and dreading Rosie's departure, therefore several pancakes would be required. Large ones.

Mandy had offered to do Rosie's nails before she left for Scotland, and as the salon was one of the places Rosie had grown up visiting, I wanted to take her for a farewell outing. So that afternoon we popped along and were soon swept up into the gentle camaraderie of women together. To my relief there wasn't a vajazzle T-shirt in sight, and no sign of blow-up willies or whips and chains, which was always a possibility when Mandy was in the vicinity. Everyone called hello, smiling at Rosie, waving from under hairdryers, all of us recognising a fellow soldier of life – all fighting the fight, hoping one day to win the lottery, meet the man, retire to Benidorm. For most of us it would never happen, but while we waited there were worse things to do than kill time with other women and have our hair done. Stories, secrets, laughs and lies were all shared under the dryers and as the water sprayed in the backwashes, women of all ages and stages shared tales of scandalous affairs, wicked husbands, and long-lost children. I loved it here, among the curlers and hair dyes, where no subject was barred – even Mandy's colourful sex life, which, frankly, should have been. Rosie loved it here too, in the whirring of hairdryers and the kindness of old ladies in rollers, with sweets in their pockets and time on their hands.

Everyone in the salon knew my own life story, and when I'd left Craig for a summer in Santorini with Dan, my customers and colleagues had been my cheerleaders. Mandy even gave me a goodbye fake tan (which was so orange, it might have jeopardised my relationship with a lesser man). I was back in that lovely summer of rebirth and new experiences when I was rudely awakened.

'Hello GORGEOUS!' came a loud voice from the Heavenly Spa at the top of the stairs. Mandy was in the building. She appeared wearing half a head of heated rollers, full lashes with sparkly bits and apparently she'd just had Botox, which explained the screams coming from the spa and the surprised look on her face.

On hearing Mandy's voice, Rosie turned, abandoning some old lady's Werther's Originals, her face lit up. Mandy was all noise and colour to a four-year-old and often insisted on slapping creams/eyelashes/lip gloss on Rosie, which she loved, but Emma found a little disconcerting. 'Mum, she looks like one of those pageant queens they have in America,' Emma had gasped in mock horror the last time Rosie had paid a visit to Mandy's dreaded spa. I'd laughed it off, which was easier than wiping off the tan and the fake lashes later, which I'd insisted to Emma were only temporary. 'God, Mum, promise me you'll never let Mandy near her with that tattoo gun,' she'd half-joked.

Yes, Mandy had recently been fully trained at the *Tattoo You* school of cosmetic tattooing, had a licence to mark people for life – and the certificate to prove it. When she concentrated, Mandy created some beautiful nails, and eyes, her tattooed lips and brows could also be lovely. But the problem was that she sometimes took her eye off the ball – or the face, or whatever body part she was tattooing – she was so busy gossiping, suffering a hangover, or demonstrating her slutdropping prowess. Consequently, the visions that sometimes appeared from the spa after a long session were like something from Madame Tussaud's Chamber of Horrors.

'How's my gorgeous little Rosie posy?' Mandy was now addressing Rosie as she descended the stairs like a queen entering her court. The staff didn't even bat an eyelid. Gayle, who billed herself as 'head stylist to the stars'. was enjoying 'a celebratory Prosecco' (though I wasn't sure what she was actually celebrating) and laughing at a video on her phone. Meanwhile, Camilla (still the junior after five years) was meditating on a large cushion on the floor. Mandy had always seen Camilla as great sport – she'd once sent her to Ann Summers, telling her it was a bookshop and told her to ask for *The Karma Sutra*, and would shout across the salon that 'Mr P Ness' was on the phone for her, to which of course Camilla would innocently call back, 'P Ness?' This alarmed some of the older clientele, but provided Mandy with deep, unbridled joy. Somehow against the odds, these two had become firm friends, Mandy giving the very straight Camilla some life and daring, while Camilla in turn provided the calm antidote to Mandy's madness.

Mandy had now handed Rosie a bright pink lollipop from a bowl on the reception counter and was asking if she'd like her eyebrows 'on fleek'. I immediately declined on my granddaughter's behalf, just imagining Emma's face when she came home from honeymoon to a tattooed child.

'Oh, she just needs a bit of definition,' Mandy was saying, weighing up the four-year-old's eyebrows. 'I can't wait until she's a bit bigger – we'll knock a few highlights in that hair, a set of lashes and a sparkly mani and pedi and she'll knock 'em dead down the Funkin' Fusion.'

'Yeah, lovely,' I said non-committally, while pretending to share her vision. 'We'll just have a manicure for now, eh, Rosie?' I said.

Rosie took her seat and Mandy painted her nails and asked her about her boyfriends, which delighted Rosie, who told all. And when she was finished, Mandy hugged her and we said our goodbyes as she downed a Prosecco and began wiggling her hips. I rushed Rosie to the door, fearing a sudden revival of the great salon slutdropping competition of 2014 when in an attempt at the world record, seventy-two-year-old Joyce inadvertently landed in the splits. Paramedics were called and Joyce was whisked to the Royal, where she was in traction for six months. She said her sex life had never been the same since that day, and she'd only come in for a root touch-up.

'Do you want me to come in to work on Saturday, Mandy?' I asked, from the doorway as we were leaving.

'Ooh, yes please, love! Me and Jase are having a date night Friday, and you know what that means, don't you?'

I certainly did, but really hoped she wasn't going to share it in front of my little granddaughter, so I got in there first. 'Yeah, it means you'll be late in on Saturday,' I smiled, opening the door and gently pushing Rosie towards it before Mandy spilled.

'I'll be pissed on all fours…'

Too late.

'We'll get off then… See you Saturday…' I didn't want a repeat of our previous week's visit when Mandy had been to a glitter party and couldn't remove the glitter from her body. This in itself was perfectly acceptable before the watershed, but when she announced that her crotch looked 'like a bloody glitterball', I saw Rosie's eyes widen and knew the word 'crotch' had just been included in the Rosie Dobson Dictionary. Emma would kill me.

'Two words…' Mandy was now shouting after me as I attempted to remove my innocent granddaughter from the scene. 'Carpet burns,' she roared, laughing, and slapped a nearby stylist on the back, which caused her to take a large slice out of a customer's hair. 'We were doing it on the kitchen floor the other night – and it's linoleum! LOL, I was sliding all *over* the show,' she yelled at me across the salon. 'Then Jase got a bit too excited and I was doing hundred miles an hour up the kitchen.' She shook her head, in peals of laughter now. 'Faye, take my advice, love, never lube up on lino.'

'I won't,' I muttered, like this was sage advice I might need to take. I was now trying to bundle a protesting Rosie out of the door with my hands over her ears before Mandy could offer any more sage advice on sexual matters.

Eventually I rescued the poor child and when, over supper with Emma later that evening, Rosie chatted animatedly about, 'Mandy and loob and dino,' I laughed it off, saying how it was funny what children picked up at nursery. And sent up a little thank you that she still couldn't pronounce 'vajazzle'.

Chapter Fourteen

Kung Pao Chicken and a Burning Oesophagus

After a lovely week with Rosie, Emma returned from honeymoon to collect her and the last of their stuff and head back to Scotland to start married life. Richard had taken a flight directly to Edinburgh to be in work the next morning, and Emma planned on driving her and Rosie up the following day.

I was looking forward to a final evening at home with Emma, but just as she'd arrived, I received a text from Dan. I quickly checked it while Emma greeted Rosie.

Hi, sorry couldn't talk yesterday. It's 4am here, I'm tired and I can't sleep. I hope you're okay. I miss you. X

It literally took my breath away. All the doubts that had plagued me since our phone call dissipated, and I wanted to sing loudly and dance like Beyoncé round the kitchen. Everything was fine between us and he missed me. He. Missed. Me.

After I'd chatted with Emma and heard all about her honeymoon and bathed Rosie, I locked myself in the toilet (four-year-olds think it's okay to sit and chat everywhere) and tried to call Dan back. It was 6 a.m. in Australia by then, but I didn't care – I just wanted to let him know I missed him too. The line rang and rang, and Rosie was soon knocking on the toilet door, shouting, 'I'm coming, ready or not!' and Emma was suggesting a Chinese takeaway and there's only so much multitasking a woman can do. So I decided to concentrate on them for now – I could talk to Dan later, or tomorrow when they'd gone and I was alone again. I had all the time in the world now, and he and I could plan another magical summer – only this time I wouldn't be coming home.

I abandoned my bathroom sanctuary to deal with the important matter of Rosie's game and the question of sweet and sour chicken or pork. We were just going through the takeaway menu when there was a knock on the door. Suddenly my heart was in my mouth. Having received that lovely text, my mind could think only of Dan and I know it was stupid because mathematically, it wasn't possible because he'd texted only a couple of hours before from Australia, but I wasn't thinking straight. As I got up and went into the hall to answer the door, I hoped against hope it wasn't him. As delighted as I would be to see him, I was tired and hungry, my roots had grown and I looked like an old dog with day-old make-up and tied-back hair. The joy of my Dan weekends away was that I could be glamorous and carefree and didn't have to be Mum or Grandma. I could be blonde, funny Faye, who made Dan go weak at the knees, and I wanted to be that again for him. But right now all I could do was hold in my stomach, push my hair back and wish for the best. As I opened the door, I felt breathless – my heart doing a little dance…

Then I saw Craig and I stopped holding my stomach in, my heartbeat now pounding out a dance of death.

'Oh hi,' I said, unable to hide the disappointment on my face.

'What's up with you?' was his opening gambit.

In that first sentence he'd managed to conjure up all the years of our marriage. What I wanted to say was 'What's up with *me*? You cheeky bastard, *you* are what's up with me! You stole my youth, took the joy away from everything and turned me into a bored, bitter, empty woman who hated you. But more than that, Craig, you taught me how to hate myself.'

Of course I didn't say any of that because it was pointless; he would look at me like I'd lost it and then I would want to kill him. I was also in the presence of my daughter and granddaughter and whatever I might think of Craig, he was still their family.

'Nothing's wrong with me,' I said, standing back for him to enter, like a teenager letting a hated stepfather in. Honestly, I *tried*, but he was so infuriating. And he'd only just arrived.

'Thought you were in Greece?' he muttered as he walked down the hall.

'Yes, I was… four years ago,' I answered, wondering if it would be rude to order the Chinese now so he'd be obliged to go when it arrived. Then I remembered how thick-skinned he could be. In fact, I decided I'd hold off with the sweet and sour chicken because he might see it as an excuse to stay. I didn't share my Chinese with anyone, least of all Craig.

I wandered after him into the living room. Emma greeted him – she'd told him it was her and Rosie's last night before they went to Scotland for good, and apparently he'd felt obliged to pop round.

We all sat down on respective chairs and the sofa and looked at each other. It felt awkward, like my past and my present had collided. I sometimes felt a bit mean about how I felt towards Craig, but he only had to say hello and it annoyed me. And I know the feeling was mutual; I irritated him just as much.

He'd never been able to understand why I'd left him and couldn't see why I'd wanted to travel or do a degree. A mutual friend once told me that he'd said he hated the fact I was now 'one of those students'. Apparently he'd said I should grow up and get a job and stop dreaming – which sounded just like him. Funny, when I think back to the blushing (pregnant) teenage bride I'd been, believing it was forever, that this was the man I would grow old with. At forty-six, with a failed marriage behind me, I was less naive now and knew nothing was forever – and looking over at Craig, now picking his teeth, I decided that was probably a good thing.

Rosie seemed quite happy that Granddad had arrived. Kids always like someone different appearing on the horizon – to them it's someone new to play with, fresh blood for hide-and-seek. But Craig was socially awkward and had little imagination. *Good luck with that, love*, I thought, as Rosie attempted to adorn him in a pink feather boa from her dressing-up box.

I was finding the whole scenario intense and irritating, the three of us all looking at each other and poor Emma trying to make small talk. She tried to include me, desperately hoping I'd catch her rope, but for once I had no inclination to fill the silence. I removed myself by offering to make a cup of tea. I was angry at his intrusion. I knew it was selfish and immature of me – he was Emma's parent too – but this was our last proper evening together at the house. It was supposed to be a girls' night, with Chinese and *Frozen* and a nice bottle of Pinot – and monosyllabic Craig dressed in a pissing pink feather boa wasn't part of that, he never had been. I went into the kitchen and boiled the kettle, hoping he'd feel he'd done his duty and would leave after a cup of tea.

I took the opportunity to sneak a look at Dan's text again and felt a warm fizz in my chest. After a while, when I'd made the cups of tea as slowly as I could so I didn't have to go back into the room, Emma wandered into the kitchen (it seemed even the small talk had dried up now).

'Everything okay, Mum? Did you want to order the food now? I don't think Dad will be staying much longer.'

'I don't mind if you'd like Dad to stay and eat with us,' I said, trying to smile while holding my breath and hiding my horror at the prospect. I wasn't going to be unreasonable – this was her dad, and Rosie's granddad, so I made an attempt at being mature and behaving like a grown-up. I never once gave any hint that if he were to stay for Chinese, he was likely to be wearing a chopstick up each nostril, kindly inserted by me.

'No, Mum, it's fine,' she said. 'Dad doesn't like Chinese anyway, remember? It gives him terrible heartburn.'

'Oh, of course,' I said, nodding vigorously in faux sympathy. Somehow I'd forgotten that particular joy – the romantic Chinese dinner where Craig retched over a kung pao chicken in front of the whole restaurant. No, the only thing he wanted in his mouth was of English origin – accompanied by chips and peas. 'Foreign muck' was Craig's generic term for anything that wasn't chips. Now I knew why I loved Chinese food so much; anything that made my irritating ex-husband's oesophagus burn hotly was a friend to me.

I went back into the living room with Emma, handed Craig his cup of tea and sat down on the edge of the same sofa he was sitting on. I had no choice, Rosie had covered every seating area with toys – it was a hospital and apparently the patients were sleeping and couldn't be moved. I was holding my tea by the handle, one arm folded around myself, clear in my body language that I was ready for fight or flight, whichever came first.

'Granddad, do you love Nana?' Rosie suddenly said into the silence, while checking a zebra's 'blood pressing'.

Craig almost choked on his tea, the spluttering made Rosie laugh and I looked away, unable to watch. Or listen.

'Rosie,' Emma said, stepping into the breach, 'that isn't a question we ask grown-ups, is it?'

Rosie began to protest, but Emma picked up her iPad and held it out to her. She wasn't usually allowed the iPad 'after hours' so this was a rare treat and an indication of how much Emma didn't want this discussion to be pursued. Neither did I!

'Nana?' Rosie turned to me and I held my breath. 'Don't you love Granddad any more?' she asked, taking the proffered iPad and pushing it to the side for later, along with the zebra's 'blood pressing'. Rosie wasn't bothered about the hospital or the iPad now, there was more sport to be had from torturing the adults. She clearly had more pressing matters to deal with before operating on teddies or enjoying any *Dora the Explorer* interaction.

'Don't keep asking questions, Rosie,' Emma snapped, returning the iPad to her daughter's hands. But Rosie apparently felt the need to have a frank and open discussion about the breakdown of her grandparents' marriage.

'Nana loves Dam now, Granddad,' she said gently, bending her head to one side and touching his knee like she was the first one to break this to him.

I didn't know where to put myself. I adored my granddaughter, but she had a tendency to keep going when other four-year-olds might have given up and moved on to the virtual world by now.

I grimaced at Emma, she mirrored back with a slight raising of the eyebrows, and I realised it would be easier for everyone if I made myself scarce. Rosie clearly had ambitions of the marriage guidance kind, and was keen to probe the relationship, deal with the tensions and bring them right out into the open. She was a mini Jeremy Kyle and it was only a matter of time before she was demanding lie detectors and paternity tests. And before this happened, one of us had to leave.

'I'm just popping upstairs,' I said brightly, placing my cup on the coffee table, and running up the stairs two at a time, like a teenager escaping questioning parents.

As soon as I was inside my bedroom, I leaned back on the door for a few seconds in case the mini marriage guidance counsellor chased after me, keen on an intervention.

I had this urge to climb out of the window and flee from Craig, the man who'd spent a lifetime making me feel worthless, stupid and insignificant. I'd even have foregone the Chinese and the Pinot – I just wanted Dan. And like a teenage girl, I unpacked my old rucksack, taking out the pressed Paris blossom, the postcards we'd sent each other, and the photos of the two of us in sunshine, somewhere in Europe.

Seeing Craig was always a good reminder of why I'd walked away from my marriage, my life. If I ever doubted myself, I would think about him and the life we had and remember why I left.

Dan's text may only have been four sentences, saying he missed me, but it was so much more. I realised his apparent lack of enthusiasm or engagement when I called was probably more about hurt and pride and fear of being rejected all over again on his part. So, as I was now free as a bird for the summer, I was going to fly. Straight back to him.

Chapter Fifteen

Katy Perry and a Rabbit Called Keith

I said a tearful goodbye to Rosie and Emma the following day, and it was one of the hardest goodbyes I'd ever had to go through. I didn't tell Emma of my summer plans – I didn't want to overload her with too much at a time when she already had enough on her plate. So for the next few weeks I worked at the salon and waited for my degree results to come through, and talked to 'my girls' most days. It would start as just a quick call from Emma but then Rosie would grab the phone and before we knew it, we'd been talking for an hour. There were Skype calls too.

I was able to chat to Rosie about everything that was familiar. I told her about bumping into her friend Elsie from the crèche who said hi, news from customers and staff at the hairdresser's, with cleaned-up messages from Mandy (without the punctuating 'yaas, bitch'). Meanwhile, Rosie shared snippets of her new life with me, usually from her laptop in her bedroom, supervised by Emma.

'I love your room,' I said, admiring the pink princess bed, the princess wallpaper, the princess cushions, princess lamp and every tomboy princess's must – a Darth Vader. I longed to sit in there with her, playing princesses with the teddies, both in our tiaras. 'So, is that a new princess dress too?' I asked.

She nodded vigorously, so vigorously in fact that she lost her balance and disappeared from view. I leapt up, wanting to pick her up and help her. Thank goodness Emma was there to rub her forehead and plonk her back on her seat. Of course she was – they didn't need me to look after them anymore, which caused a little pang in my heart.

'Well, Nana – *that* wasn't supposed to happen!' she said, looking at the camera, rolling her eyes and straightening her crown.

I laughed softly. I didn't want her to think I was laughing at her, but she was just so funny. How I missed her camp little mannerisms and pseudo-grown-up remarks about how she was finding her new boyfriend 'difficult', her friend Megan 'tricky', which she didn't expand on, just rolled her eyes and folded her arms. I knew where she was coming from – I'd had a few 'tricky' friends in my time, they didn't need expanding on. I'd been so involved in her big little life when she lived here, I sometimes felt an emptiness where she'd been. I also found it hard to accept that Rosie had new friends, new interests beyond what we'd shared – and would soon be starting school. I'd miss the watersheds, the special moments, the impromptu dancing, the swirling, twirling madness that made up a four-year-old.

'Nana…' she was saying now.

'Yes, darling.'

'I'm not a *real* princess, you know.'

'Oh really, I thought you were?'

She shook her head again and laughed loudly. 'Nana, you're silly – I'm a bruddy unicorn really!'

I could hear Emma in the background muttering a reprimand, as Rosie pulled a face reminiscent of Emma's when she was fourteen and I said she couldn't stay out late. Here was a little girl who was ten steps ahead of everyone; her confidence, her humour and her character were testament to the fact that she was happy and secure. It was everything I wanted for her, and though I wasn't there, I was strong enough to see this move had been good for both Rosie and Emma.

Katy Perry (our cat) had stayed behind with me because Richard suffered allergies. Obviously, Rosie was sad to leave her, so I promised she'd Skype and Rosie insisted on this at the most difficult times, like when Katy Perry went missing for three days – 'She's gone on holiday,' I'd said.

'She has to talk to me. Nana, get her back from her holidays now, there's a good girl.'

I knew Rosie would be devastated if she thought she was missing, so I made the lies more elaborate. 'She's gone off in a hot-air balloon today,' I offered, then she was out on a date with her boyfriend, gone to a birthday party, a cat fashion show. None of these were questioned; in fact, I was expected to tell Rosie all about Katy Perry's adventures until she eventually turned up late one night, meowing for food. Today she joined us at the screen and wandered along the keyboards of my laptop, looking for somewhere to settle. 'She's writing a book,' I told Rosie, who roared with laughter.

'Read it to me, Nana,' she said, and I realised I'd just signed myself up for the next six months to 'reading' a non-existent literary work supposedly written by a cat.

'The End,' I said one afternoon after regaling her on Skype with a particularly hilarious adventure involving Katy Perry, Keith the rabbit from next door and an empty cardboard box. In the days since Emma and Rosie had been gone, I'd been thinking a lot about my own life, and the phone calls and Skype sessions had convinced me even more that there was no reason now why I couldn't follow my own path and head out to Australia. But I still had to break the news to Rosie – and Katy Perry was going to be my way in.

'So, Rosie, Nana's going away for a little while. What do you think Katy Perry would say about perhaps doing a long sleepover with Mandy?'

'Oh, that would be *fuuuun*,' she said, big, long nods almost causing the tiara to wobble off. 'Will Katy Perry have her nails done?' Probably, I thought, knowing Mandy, who had been delighted when I'd asked if she'd have Katy Perry. I reckoned it would be a match made in heaven because Lady Gaga (Mandy's hamster) had died some years before and she said she'd never really got over it. According to Mandy, Lady Gaga had committed suicide because she was depressed. Despite us explaining that hamsters only had a lifespan of about two years and she'd probably died of old age, Mandy couldn't get over it and for some time had pondered the reasons for her hamster depression. 'It was that bloody wheel, round and round and round… You'd top yourself if you had to do that all day and night, Faye,' she'd sobbed. Yes, Katy Perry would be as good for Mandy as she would be for her, and she'd clapped her hands like a child when I'd asked if she'd mind having her for the foreseeable.

So, telling Rosie and finding accommodation for Katy Perry had been the easy bit. Later, I called Emma to break my news to her.

'Wow!' she said, 'Australia's a long way, Mum.'

'You're okay with me going, aren't you?' I asked.

'Absolutely I am. Mum, it's exactly what you should do – and we can still talk to each other whenever we want. Rosie knows Nana is only a few clicks of the computer away and I think that's really helping her settle here.'

'Good,' I said, pleased I was still part of Rosie's life. Being able to chat whenever we felt like it had helped me adjust to them being away too.

So that was that. I had the blessing of my daughter, granddaughter and cat – I was on my way to Sydney and a new exciting adventure. I couldn't wait to see Dan. We'd texted a few times, but I'd kept things cool – no declarations of undying love yet. I realised a rekindling would take some effort on my part. I had a lot of making up to do, but once I'd booked my flight and made my intentions clear, it would all come together. I just missed him so much. I wanted to be with him, sharing his new exciting life, tasting his recipes, feeling that sun on my face and his kisses on my lips – we had so much to look forward to. I was finally free to run away to Australia and a brand new life and finally say yes to the only man I've ever loved.

Having made up my mind, it took a matter of weeks to pack up the rest of the house (leaving my stuff in storage at Mandy's) and book my flight. One-way. I wasn't messing about, this time I had to show Dan that I was prepared to commit. I'd taken his heart and I'd basically turned it into mincemeat, but it was now my turn to hand my heart to him, and knowing he might still be feeling wounded from my previous rejection, I'd be upfront and clear about my feelings. So, once I'd booked my flight, I called him, eager to hear his voice, and excited to tell him I was a matter of days away.

'Dan, I'm jumping on a plane… to Sydney.'

'Oh.' Silence, then, 'You're kidding, right?'

I was sure he wanted me there, but was probably just scared that he was letting himself in for more heartache. 'Hey, Dan, I'm not going to back out this time – this is it, me and you for good.'

'Oh.'

'Is that all you have to say?'

'Yeah, well, it's just… There's a lot to think about.'

I couldn't believe his response. Jumping on a plane at a moment's notice so we could be together was the kind of thing Dan did without a second thought. He was the one who always told me to 'dive in', 'say yes to everything because life's short', so why wasn't he on board with it now?

'Unexpected? But I thought it was what you wanted?'

'It was… It is, I just…'

'What?'

'I'm just surprised at this sudden… change of heart.'

'It isn't a change of heart, Dan,' I said, a little hurt at this – he knew my feelings were genuine. 'You know why I stayed here, it wasn't about us.'

'But it was though, and I kind of feel like you put me through it and now I'm starting to get over it, you want to fly over, like nothing happened. Do you have any idea of what you put me through, Faye?'

I took a breath. 'Don't be like that… I feel bad, I didn't want to hurt you. Let's just… I'm so sorry… Can we talk this through when I'm there?'

'Yeah, but… I don't know how I'll *feel*,' he said, suddenly.

'About me?'

'No, I know how I feel about you. Unfortunately, there's nothing I can do about that, though for a while I wished I could. I just wonder how I'll feel if I see you… I'm not sure I can go through it all again – I think it's only in the last couple of months that I've been able to wake up without feeling like shit because you're not there.'

The words made my heart beat quicker, but his delivery was a little harsh, and made me feel guilty and sad. We'd both been through it, I understood how he'd felt, and I knew it was all my fault.

'Of course, I want you to come over…' he said into the silence.

My heart lifted in relief, but I tried not to let the excitement show in my voice; we needed to work through this. I needed to show him how much I meant it this time and take it gently. 'I understand you'll be busy. You don't even have to meet me at the airport, I could just come directly to your place?'

'No… no, don't do that. I'll come and meet you…' he answered.

I was finding it hard to read him without facial expressions and body language. One minute he seemed to be up and his usual happy, carefree self, but then other times he'd seem down, like he was choosing his words carefully, which wasn't the Dan I knew. I wasn't quite sure what was going on; I wanted to get back to *us*, to who we were. It all felt so distant, but that might be because we were talking over the phone, thousands of miles away from each other.

'I don't have your address anyway, but I could *find* it,' I said, trying to lighten things by teasing him, but coming over like a pupil from the bunny-boiling school for girls. With a GCSE in Stalking.

'Faye, I just think we need to organise it properly, no surprises.'

'I never thought I'd hear you use the word "organise",' I laughed.

Dan never 'organised' anything 'properly'. In fact, he never 'organised' anything full stop. The word wasn't even in his vocabulary; he was the man who loved life and lived it to the full, rode mile-high waves, climbed mountains, was excited about the very existence of fig jam. He loved surprises, he was a free spirit who threw stuff into a rucksack and just went wherever the mood might take him – and now he was suggesting we 'organise' my arrival. Really? This was feeling slightly weird, but I told myself perhaps this new and improved Dan was a good thing. I loved his spontaneity, but perhaps his brother's death had made him take on some responsibility and he was more in charge of his life these days?

'Well, things are *different*…' he was saying.

'Different?'

'Yeah, a lot's happened, Faye.'

Chapter Sixteen

A Taste of Wedding Cake and a Tingle of Dread

What was he talking about? I felt really uneasy now; I wanted to ask him what had changed, but was almost too scared to know the answer.

'I understand that things might have changed, and you and I won't be able to just fall back into the life – the relationship – we had,' I said, unwilling to push him for any details. 'I know what I put you through and don't want to force myself on you, but now I can give you what you wanted… what I wanted. Can you forgive me?'

'I… It's just… I feel like we've probably both changed and…'

'Yes, I'm sure we have,' I said. 'We've probably both grown a little, Dan, and that's a good thing. I'm not messing about, I want to be with you and I want to prove to you that this time it's for keeps. We don't have to make any decisions, any commitments, we just need to spend some time together, do some talking. I'm free to come to Sydney, where we can regroup and… If you still want me to?' I felt slightly unsure of him, and I'd never really felt unsure of Dan before.

He didn't answer, and I really couldn't get used to this rather cool Dan, who didn't seem to be all that excited about me travelling thousands of miles to run into his arms. The silence down the phone line was agony and though it may only have lasted seconds, it felt like hours.

'We can watch those fireworks over Sydney Opera House…' I tried, convinced I just needed to find the right words, the magic key to unlock him again. 'You *have* to show me that beach with the skyscraper waves.'

'Yeah. Yeah, of course… But I meant what I said, don't just turn up. I'm busy at work and… I'm not in the market for surprises,' he said, quite seriously.

'God, as if I'd just turn up without letting you know. I was only joking,' I snapped, humiliated by his reaction. I wasn't joking – I'd had every intention of landing on his doorstep looking pretty damn fabulous, with freshly highlighted hair in my new mid-calf blue dress and denim jacket, shouting, 'Surprise!' Perhaps not. Thing is, I'd always assumed Dan would be ready, excited, waiting for me – I had it all planned, right down to the underwear. And in the film of my life that I'd run in my head, he'd open his front door looking gorgeous, slightly dishevelled, a little subdued, only for his face to light up when he saw me. Then he would lift me in his arms, carry me into his home and close the door with one foot as the credits rolled on our happy ending.

This call had gone from me phoning excitedly about us finally being together to feeling like I was being put off. He'd talked so fondly of his country, what we'd do, where we'd go – yet now I had this feeling that he wasn't sure about me being there. I'd been hoping for so much more than this, even contemplating a second proposal, but I understood how he was still carrying the hurt. Emma's wedding had made me believe that Dan and I could be forever; I'd daydreamed about flowers and the taste of wedding cake ever since. If he still wanted forever when I got to Sydney, I'd have to prove to him that my heart was for keeps and I would get down on one knee and ask him myself this time. If the unthinkable happened and he couldn't get over my past rejection, then I'd have to rethink my stay. I just kept my fingers firmly crossed that we could work this out when I got there, but talking to him, I realised it wasn't going to be as easy as I'd thought.

'Faye, I'll book you a room somewhere,' he was now saying, which didn't exactly sound like the romantic encounter I'd envisaged after being apart for so long. 'My apartment's small and cramped.'

His flat over the deli had been tiny and I'd stayed over many times, so why couldn't I stay with him now? He knew I wasn't bothered about bloody dimensions, I just wanted to be with him.

'I'm not some diva who demands specifications for my sleepovers, *give me your room proportions and I'll tell you if I'm available*,' I laughed. 'You know I'm not bothered about stuff like that, Dan.'

He didn't answer me.

'I just want to see you,' I said earnestly.

'Yeah, me too. I do.'

We couldn't work this out over the phone, we had to see each other to understand what was happening between us. Perhaps it wasn't all about me? Perhaps he was disappointed with how things had worked out in Sydney for him? He seemed pleased about the café, but he probably hadn't had a chance to concentrate on his living quarters yet. Dan had always said if he moved back to Sydney he'd live in a stylish place with a pool. He probably thought I'd be disappointed with a cramped little apartment, but I didn't care, he could live in a box and I'd still want to be with him.

'Okay, book me a room near where you live. That will be fine,' I said. This didn't feel right, but I didn't want to put him under any pressure so would go along with what made him comfortable.

'Okay. I'll meet you at the airport,' he added. 'Just let me know when you'll be here, it's easier on text.' Was he asking me not to call him?

I didn't feel the time was right to question him on something so small when there were already so many unanswered questions between us.

'Okay,' I said, trying to hide the catch in my voice, my throat swollen from holding back tears of disappointment. I put down the phone, looking around at the few boxes and bin bags that were now my life. I just hoped I hadn't messed everything up, and I'd have to spend the rest of my life without him. But I wasn't letting him go without a fight. I was going to get on that plane and head off for Dan and a new and exciting future under a different sky. Nothing was going to stop me. So why did I feel a tingle of dread in the pit of my stomach?

Later that night as I lay in bed, I went back over everything we'd said on the phone. I thought about all our times together, the wonderful places we'd been, the kisses we'd shared. I recalled the way he'd smile whenever he saw me, his eyes never far from mine in a room full of other people. Dan had always been there for me, but speaking to him over the phone it seemed things had changed between us. And I finally let the thought in that had been buzzing around my brain since that first call… Was there something in Australia that Dan didn't want me to know about?

Chapter Seventeen

Brexit,
The Spice Girls and Beyoncé's Beautiful Twins

I woke the next morning feeling dreadful after worrying all night. I was getting a slight case of cold feet, but I told myself not to think about 'The Dan situation' because until we met, there was nothing I could do about it. I thought instead of the waves on Bondi Beach and Sydney Opera House in the sunshine and all the places in between that Dan had talked lovingly of. Ideally, I'd discover those places with him by my side, I just hoped everything would be okay.

So, three days later, with my too many bags, floppy hat, blue linen dress and lashings of factor 30, I landed in Australia. I'd texted Dan (as requested) to let him know my arrival time. It felt rather polite and formal, but after that strange phone call, I wasn't taking anything for granted. This was the love of my life, the man I'd shared my deepest secrets with, but we weren't back there yet. He texted back, equally polite, saying he'd booked a room at a hotel for me.

'I've taken two days off so I can get you to your hotel and then show you around,' he added.

Two days? I'd travelled thousands of miles to see him, we hadn't been together for over twelve months – I'd expected more than two days! This was the man who'd talked for hours about the waves on sun-drenched Bondi Beach, where he'd grown up and learned to surf as a tiny kid, and the glittering Sydney skyscape by night. He'd been desperate to show me these places, take me through his childhood, eat in every café he'd ever eaten, taste every brand of 'amber nectar' and consume Vegemite and Anzac biscuits like a native. He was passionate about his homeland, wanted to open it out to me like a gift. His very soul danced in the waves, made sandcastles, and climbed the Blue Mountains that framed his amazing city. And he wanted to share this with me. Didn't he?

What the hell was going on with him? I just kept going over and over our conversation and texts and went from 'he loves me' to 'he loves me not'. Going through passport control, it occurred to me I might just be making the biggest mistake of my life. Me and Dan had been wonderful together, but perhaps we weren't meant to be? Perhaps we were just a holiday romance that had gone on too long, his proposal a moment of madness, and now I was turning up at his home trying to make something of nothing? Why was I having these thoughts now? It was too late, I was here! And just a little bit tipsy from all the gin I'd drunk on the plane. Medicinal, to calm my nerves – besides, it was free, so it would have been rude not to.

Standing alone in the middle of this huge airport, all I could see were strangers' faces looking back at me as I walked through arrivals. I'd imagined this moment for so long: us seeing each other across acres of shiny flooring, me dropping my bags to the floor and both of us running towards one another, him lifting me off the ground and twirling me round. People would look enviously on, wishing for a moment that they could have a little taste of what we had. We'd be the accompanying gif to #RelationshipGoals on everyone's social media.

I tried to hold in my stomach, lift my face slightly so I'd look younger – I could only imagine the extra lines and chins I'd developed since I'd last seen him. Mandy's dubious Botox could only do so much, and this would be Dan's first glimpse of me. I wanted him to fall in love all over again and any doubts to dissipate at the sight of me.

But first I had to find him and the more I looked, the less I saw. So many expectant faces, so many fair-haired men dressed in T-shirts and jeans making my heart jerk in my chest until they turned or got closer and I saw it wasn't him. And then, I saw him. It was him. Definitely. A glimpse of fair, tousled hair, a movement of both hands through that hair, a nervous gesture I knew so well. I'd seen it the first time we'd kissed, the first time he turned up at the salon and was accosted by Mandy – and the time he'd asked me to marry him.

The sight of him standing in the near distance had a physical impact, like something had slammed into my chest. He was wearing sunglasses, his face was tanned and a little stubbly, his hair beach blond; he looked a little older, in a good way. And if I'd ever had any doubts about venturing this far, about putting myself on the line, about whether or not we had a future together, just seeing him standing there looking gorgeous erased all doubts. This was no holiday romance – on my part, at least – this was true love. It was heart-in-your-mouth roller-coaster, thirst-quenching, nothing-else-matters love and though it had never really gone away, it now hurtled into me, throwing me off balance. I felt giddy and dizzy, my limbs like liquid; one of those dreams where you're walking but not going anywhere, each step pointless, like being underwater. And trust me, it wasn't the gin.

I walked in the direction of where he was standing and felt a little rush as he pushed his sunglasses onto his head and gave me that familiar, twinkly smile, a moment of relief – yes, he *was* pleased to see me. Everything would be okay.

He began walking towards me (he wasn't running as I'd hoped). The distance between us felt so short, and at the same time endless. As we grew closer, I tried to search his face for clues, but he was giving nothing away. Suddenly we were together, and we automatically moved into a hug. I tried to let myself go, to relax into his arms. I let my head drop onto his shoulder and immersed myself in his smell – seaside, sunshine and lemons. I wanted to kiss him, but as I looked up into his face, his expression told me this wasn't something I could do. There was resistance in his eyes, a hardness in his limbs that caused me instinctively to pull back, and a word kept going through my head as I gently stood back and surveyed him – cautious. Dan was being *cautious* around me. This was not a word I would ever have associated with him before. He was here on home turf, and I wondered if this was the real Dan. And for the first time I had to ask myself how well I really knew him.

'Hey,' he said. 'I can't believe it, you're actually here.' A genuine smile, but his stance was still awkward as he gestured for me to hand him my bags.

'Thanks for meeting me,' I said, my hopes of hurling myself into his arms and kissing away the past year in the first ten seconds now gone. This wasn't how it was going to be.

'Come on then,' he said, picking up my bags with one hand, and I noted, not taking my hand with his other. I didn't feel I could take his hand – I didn't know why, but I felt like he might not want me to. This was so unlike the 'us' we used to be. I could grab him and kiss him in the middle of the street, burrow under his arm and into his chest. But now, without words, he was somehow keeping me at arm's length, and it hurt like hell.

We headed towards the exit, me running alongside him, trying to keep up.

'So, where are we staying?' I asked brightly. I kept things light, no difficult conversations yet about feelings, telling myself he just needed time to get used to me being here.

'I booked a little hotel near The Rocks. The area's a bit touristy but the hotel's good, clean – there's a place nearby that does good breakfasts,' he added, a glimmer of the old smile at the thought of breakfast.

I smiled back. Our mutual love of food always brought us together.

'Is that okay with you?' he asked, turning to look at me properly for the first time.

'Yeah, it sounds good.'

'It's just that you look a bit surprised.'

'Oh… no, it's Mandy and…'

'The Botox?' he laughed. 'I don't know why you put yourself through it, you don't need Dr Frankenstein, Faye,' he smiled, and for a moment our eyes met. But it was fleeting and he quickly put his sunglasses over his eyes and turned away. 'Come on, we've got a train to catch,' he said, picking up speed as I ran along beside him.

'So, breakfast?' I said, returning to food, trying to engage him so I could get a feel for what was going on. 'It sounds great, haven't eaten since yesterday.' I looked up at him, still searching for a clue, hoping for a return of that glimmer when he'd looked at me, but he seemed to have closed off again. 'I was a bit… nervous, coming here… seeing you,' I said.

'Nervous?' He was still walking fast, still looking ahead.

'Yes, I wasn't sure whether I was doing the right thing… coming here.' Again I tried to see a reaction, but nothing.

'It might be a bit late for breakfast,' he was looking at his watch, without acknowledging my last sentence. 'But fortunately this café I know does an all-day brunch,' he smiled.

He must mean Lemon Myrtle. I longed to see it, but I was torn between feeling excited and scared about this whole trip. For the first time ever I didn't feel completely sure of Dan.

Boarding the train at the airport, he nodded for me to climb on first. He caught my eye but there was no recognition of the shared love between us, and I wondered if the problem was simpler than I'd imagined. Perhaps he just didn't love me anymore.

I tried to focus on what was happening. I was going to his café for breakfast, and perhaps once he started showing me round and talking food, the old Dan would return. His exuberance around baked goods was always something I enjoyed and surely he hadn't lost that? I had to stay positive for now and have patience; we both needed to reacclimatise to each other. The very prospect that he didn't love me or want me there was too impossible to consider, so I pushed it away like a meal I couldn't eat. I wasn't ready to give up on him yet.

Our train was busy, and sadly, we couldn't sit together. Dan stood with my bags, while I found a seat, unhappy that my first glimpses of Sydney were blue skies and sunshine without him. But even the stunning panorama of sun-blazed beaches opening up into the Pacific couldn't drag my eyes away from him.

'So, you have two days to show me around?' I asked, when we finally got off the train and started walking. Again, me almost skipping by his side as he forged on through the crowds of people.

'Yeah, most of today and I can take tomorrow off,' he said. I'd hoped he'd changed his mind now I was here and would try to get a few more days, but it seemed he was sticking to two – it was all I was worth, even in my new blue dress with my new fake tan done by Mandy. She'd offered me a free vajazzle: 'Sydney Harbour in rhinestones?' she'd said. 'Life's short – get a vajazzle,' she'd added, like that would sway me to have an iconic building in jewels glued to my vagina. I'd declined with some force, and she didn't make me have the treatment against my will, which was a blessing as she often did.

The way things were, I didn't think a glittering Sydney Harbour on my lower regions was the icebreaker Dan and I needed just now. I'd hoped that when we met it would all become clear: I'd see the old Dan, we'd fall into each other's arms and within minutes we'd have planned our future. If I'm honest, I even stupidly hoped he'd realise from my obvious 'hinting' that I was ready to take him up on his proposal. I honestly thought there might be a chance of him greeting me on one knee in airport arrivals while everyone cheered around us and took photos on their phones. But, of course, he hadn't. In fact, he'd whisked me out of that bloody airport in indecent haste, without even asking if I needed a drink or a rest.

As someone who valued her independence I made up my mind as I ran alongside him that I wasn't going to make a fool of myself or stick around where I wasn't wanted, but for now I'd keep going.

'There's so much I want to see! I feel really lucky to have a native showing me around,' I said, wanting to fill the air with my voice instead of this emptiness.

He was being pleasant, pointing out things as we walked by and of course he was carrying all my bags. Anyone who didn't know us might imagine we were new lovers, or old friends, but we still weren't being *us*. Where was the Dan who'd be giving me the bloody history of every single place, along with the kind of sandwich that originated there?

Arriving at the café, it looked nice, better on the website – but the view was good. The deck looked out over the water, at the white sails of the Sydney Opera House, its soaring, sculptured roof skimming the clouds, framed by the brilliance of a Sydney morning sky. We wandered in and found some seats and I started to feel a little better. Dan was smiling and seemed more relaxed.

'Dan, it's lovely,' I said, gazing at someone's waffles as they were delivered to the next table.

'Yeah, it's good food too,' he said, as the waiter approached and we ordered. Dan went for huevos rancheros and I couldn't resist the waffles with fresh berries, honey and whipped cream.

'Does he know who you are?' I asked as the waiter walked away from the table. I was surprised he didn't seem to know Dan.

'No... Why should he?'

'Because you're the owner.'

'Oh no, this isn't The Lemon Myrtle, that's the other side of Sydney.'

I was shocked. 'So why are we here? I thought you'd be keen to show me your café?'

'Well, that's work and this,' he said, lifting his glass of orange juice and clinking it with mine, 'is pleasure.'

'Oh, okay,' I smiled, not quite convinced. I took a gulp of orange juice and watched him over the glass. This made a kind of sense, this way we could be alone, me and Dan in our bubble again without colleagues and customers interrupting us. 'So, the hotel is near here and also miles away from your café?' I asked, this thought colliding with my temporary acceptance of his explanation.

He nodded. 'Yeah. Like I said, I think we need to spend some time together, away from everything else. We need to talk and... I don't want anyone else distracting us and... being there.'

'That's fine,' I smiled, wondering who 'anyone' might be. 'I agree, we've got a lot to catch up on.' I continued to sip my juice.

We sat in silence until our food arrived. I tried to swallow any lingering doubts along with the spiky berries and clouds of whipped cream that topped the lightest waffles I'd ever had. I told Dan he must get the recipe, and offered him a forkful, which he took in an unguarded moment. Our eyes met over the delicious morsel, and my heart began beating as I piled cream on the berries and chewed in brunch bliss.

About an hour later, we arrived at the hotel and the minute we closed the bedroom door, we were in each other's arms. Well, to be accurate, I fell into his arms, fully expecting to land on something soft, but again there was resistance. His chest felt like concrete and as he gently took my wrists in each hand and moved me away, I almost died.

'What's the matter?' was all I could manage, in little more than a whisper.

He pointedly moved to sit on a chair, not the bed.

'It's okay, Dan. If I repulse you, just say.' I was trying to be light-hearted even though inside I felt crushed.

'It's not that... You know it isn't.'

'Well, don't sit over there. You're quite safe sitting on the bed – we don't have to touch, I won't come near you,' I said, anger and fear now lacing my words. I was hurt, and I wasn't sure what was going on, but I was waiting for the next part of our story, which I was sure would leave me in no doubt at all. 'What is it?' I asked softly. I didn't know how to handle this slightly vague man who didn't seem to want me near him.

He didn't look at me, just ran his hands through his hair and stared at the ceiling. 'I feel so bad. And I don't know what to do... I don't know where to start, and...'

'Dan, tell me!' I was feeling panicked now.

'I was so hurt when we split... angry with you, which wasn't perhaps fair, but I couldn't help how I felt.'

'I understand – and now you're worried I'll change my mind again, aren't you?' I said, almost willing this to be the issue. 'I'm not here to see the Opera House or the waves, I'm here to be with you, for as long as I can. But only if that's what you want too.' I was facing him, sitting on the edge of the bed as he sat on the upright chair – the distance between us seemed ludicrous. 'I know you think I'm suddenly going to feel guilty about Emma or Rosie and just when things are looking good, I'll run away again, but I won't. Not this time,' I said, putting my head to one side to look into his eyes, trying to engage him. 'I know they're fine, they're both happy – it's me that isn't. And that's because we're apart.' But I didn't feel like he was listening, and Dan always listened. 'Dan?' I said, longing for him to get up off the ridiculous chair and come and sit by me. 'Hey, I feel like I'm being psyched out in a bloody job interview,' I added.

He looked up and smiled and it broke a little of the ice.

'Come on, sit by me. I promise I will be able to resist you,' I smiled.

He stood up, walked towards the bed and, with some reluctance, sat down next to me.

'I understand if you don't want to rush things,' I continued.

He looked at me, 'I'm not sure you do understand.'

What was he trying to say, that I was coming on too strong? I flushed and started to speak without any filter. 'I'm not chasing you, Dan. For God's sake, it's not like I was going to propose or anything! Jesus... It's not like I'm looking to get married.'

'Married?' His face flushed slightly.

'Exactly, who wants to get married? Weddings? No one mentioned any wedding... What the hell? I mean, it's not like anyone's getting married, is it? I wouldn't, oh no, not me... I mean, if I were asked, I don't mean you...'

'Stop,' he said, and almost smiled as he looked down at me. 'You still haven't found any meds for that then?'

I smiled, shook my head and then lowering my bottom lip, pulled an 'awkward' face. 'You know me, Dan, I just blurt it all out and then try to take it back by repeating it and adding layers. And then another layer, until…'

'You're doing it again.' I saw the twinkle in his eye; he was coming back to me, bit by bit.

'Okay, so we might need to take it slowly, just talk, not kiss each other, or have sex or… I'm not saying I wouldn't, it's just that… Sex isn't… I'm not obsessed or anything…'

'Oh Faye,' he sighed, turning to me and kissing me full on the lips, his arms slowly coming around me, his tongue pushing into my mouth. It was warm and loving. The promise of passion tingled through me and it felt like the first kiss of my life. Until he pulled away. Suddenly. As if I'd given him an electric shock.

'You're being all weird, Dan. Yes, it's been over a year… A lot of water's gone under the bridge, but *we* haven't changed, even if other stuff has.'

'That's the trouble, everything else has,' he sighed, and I suddenly got the feeling we weren't talking about the same thing. When I said stuff had changed, I was thinking US presidents, Brexit, The Spice Girls reunion and Beyoncé's twins, but he was definitely thinking about something else.

I looked at him, waiting for an explanation, but he seemed to be having trouble finding the words.

'So, what is it? What "other things" have changed that could affect us? I've had this weird feeling since I first got in touch with you again that you might not feel the same about me but I thought when we actually got together we'd be okay, like we always were. But you're different.'

He seemed almost tense, which was the opposite of the Dan I knew – or the Dan I thought I knew.

'Faye, you turn up out of the blue like nothing happened, despite having told me you'd never be able to live here. You said you'd never marry me and we were wasting our lives even trying.'

'You understood the reasons why, they had nothing to do with you and me.'

'They had everything to do with you and me, and for a while I was crushed. Then you just contacted me to say you've changed your mind.' He still wasn't looking at me.

'I can see how it looks, but I'm not just here on a whim. I can't live without you – I can't sleep, I can't concentrate, I can't get on with my life. Hell, Dan, even cake tastes horrible without you! Nothing's the same when you're not there, Dan.'

He didn't react, just lay back, staring at the celling now, unable to look at me. What the hell was going on? I'd always been surprised at the level of commitment from this free spirit who'd turned up in my life at a time when I needed him. Throughout our relationship he'd had plenty of opportunities to dump me, forget me, pretend I'd never existed – but all the time he said he couldn't live without me. When we'd said our final goodbyes, it was Dan who'd continued to text me, who said he'd wait forever. So why, when I turned up in his home city, did he suddenly seem to have changed his mind?

I'd always had this vision of him standing by an altar waiting for me in a cheap suit. A rushed wedding, me in a short dress, a budget bouquet walking towards him; the wedding meant nothing, but the marriage meant everything. But right now, weddings and marriage seemed like the most impossible things imaginable.

Becoming the sixth Spice Girl seemed more feasible, and that wasn't going to happen.

'Is there someone else?' I asked into the silence, fully expecting him to reject this vigorously, but looking for something to say.

He closed his eyes, and I felt my skin begin to slowly peel away. No… Oh, not this… I hadn't imagined this in my worst nightmares, but the longer he stayed silent, the more my mind lurched. His distance, his reluctance for me to be here, no public displays of affection, bringing me to one side of the city when his life was on the other, his inability to meet my eyes. I hadn't imagined any of it. This wasn't about Dan protecting himself, it was about Dan hiding someone from me – and hiding me from someone else.

Chapter Eighteen

The Icing on the Bloody Lemon Cake

'So there is someone else?' I heard myself say once more.

He stood up, putting his hand in his pocket and taking out his wallet. I watched, wondering if perhaps this was some kind of joke, that he was teasing me.

'If that's anything other than a new puppy, I don't want to see it,' I snapped.

'It isn't a pet, it's… Well, take a look… Meet Clover.'

'Is she furry, because if not…?'

He shook his head, so I brushed his hand away.

'I can't, Dan,' I said, unwilling to engage with whatever/whoever was in the photograph, the beginning of tears stinging my eyes. 'All these years we've been seeing each other, I thought we'd been honest and now you've lied… you've lied to me.'

'Faye, listen… Yes, I met someone. I didn't want to tell you.' He reached out both his hands and tried to hold me gently by the shoulders, make me listen to what he had to say, but I shook him off. I couldn't hear this, and within seconds, I started to cry – lurching sobs I couldn't keep down, a horrible out-of-control hysterical cry like I hadn't experienced since I was a child. Who knew as adults we could still cry like this?

I grabbed my bag and blindly headed for the door.

'I don't want to know about your wife or girlfriend or whatever she is.'

'Faye, don't be stupid.'

'I am being stupid because I AM stupid,' I said, through mucous and nose entrails. 'I finished it. I can't blame you for moving on with your life. It's what I wanted you to do, but I can't believe you let me come all this way without telling me…' I headed for the door, slamming it behind me – so hard my arm was still ringing when I'd got down the stairs. I just had to get out of that room, that bloody photograph he obviously kept safe in his wallet. I was almost knocking people out of the way, like I'd committed a murder in my bedroom and was running from the police.

I ran outside and the blazing sunshine whacked me in the face, almost knocking me over with its dazzle. But I kept running; I couldn't stop. I ran along past the shops and cafés. I was, I think, in shock – real medical 'let's get her onto a stretcher' shock. Along with heat, jet lag and heavily-laden waffles that was quite a cocktail, but still I kept running.

Eventually, after about twenty minutes, I was zigzagging along the road, exhausted and dehydrated, so I stopped to sit on the steps of a waterside building. Even the stone steps were hot under my lovely blue linen dress, bought for this reunion, now damp with sweat. This wasn't the romantic event I'd planned – and Dan wasn't who I thought he was. He hadn't waited for me after all. I should have taken the safe option – I should have stayed at home, taken a teaching job and settled into a quiet existence with Katy Perry. Instead I'd set off on a journey of thousands of miles only to end up with the love of my life having met a new love of his own life. This was the icing on the bloody lemon cake! He let me travel here without a mention of his new love, just to hand me a photo from his wallet when I arrived. What did he want me to do, say, 'Oh good on yer, she's a looker! You're punching way above there, mate.'

At the thought of this, my already overheated body fainted in a heap on the hot concrete. I blacked out for a matter of seconds, but every interfering do-gooder in Sydney was stood round me when I came to. Given my previous zigzagging walk and my collapse, everyone wanted to help, or at least watch what the crazy lady would do next. I couldn't believe the commotion – I was being fanned by an elderly woman while a teenager threw a paper cup of cold water at me and some tramp shouted, 'She's dead!' at the top of his voice. Even in this state all I could say was 'My hair, my bloody hair!' and 'NO, I'M NOT DEAD!' I sat up, pushing everyone away. I stood up on wobbly legs, assuring at least twenty nosy buggers that I was fine, I didn't need a doctor, ambulance or psychiatrist. What I needed was a man who'd tell me the truth and the services of a good hairdresser.

I eventually dismissed my unwanted entourage and headed to a van selling ice-cold lemonade, bought two cartons and was so thirsty, I knocked them both back too quickly. It was while puking up the second carton into a waste paper bin on the picturesque harbour overlooking the Opera House that Dan appeared.

'You okay?' he asked.

'Never been better,' I said sarcastically, still with my head in the bin, a pool of vomit at my feet, where I hadn't managed to get there in time.

'Faye, you're overtired, and overreacting.'

'Overtired? Overreacting? Oh yeah! That'll be it, nothing to do with the fact that you just handed me a photo of your wife and said "Deal with it".'

'I didn't say that, and she isn't my wife...'

'Oh whatever, girlfriend, partner, lap dancer...' I was now frantically rummaging in my bag for some kind of tissue to mop up the remains of what I'd just puked... Silently lamenting the fact I'd never eat waffles or drink lemonade ever again.

Dan ran his hands through his hair and wandered over to one of the food vans, returning with a handful of napkins and giving them to me.

Hating the fact I had no tissues of my own, I was forced to snatch them from his outstretched hand. I swiftly wiped the tissue round my mouth, hoping I'd got it all and trying to retain what little dignity I had left. Even then, at the pinnacle of my hurt and hate, I didn't want his last memory of me to be one in which I was covered in vomit.

'I called and texted and said things about still caring for you, and you never said a thing. I couldn't understand why you were so weird with me... Now, I know,' I said, emerging from a wad of napkins.

'Yeah, because I was in a relationship with someone else and I don't cheat.'

'So why didn't you tell me you were with someone else and stop me from making a total dick of myself?'

'Because I love you and you're not a dick. *I'm* the dick... I tried to tell you, but every time I got cold feet.'

'So who is she?' I said, still standing by the filthy bin like an old bag lady, my hair now sticking to my head with the heat, my dress damp with sweat and sick. Might as well face whatever he had to throw at me and get this over with, because I couldn't possibly have felt any worse than I did.

'She's a lovely woman I met after my bro died... The night of his funeral, actually.' I searched his face as he spoke, but could see nothing, just my own horrified face mirrored in his sunglasses.

'Oh God,' I said, flopping down on the hot steps again.

Dan sat down next to me and we both looked out on to Sydney Harbour. The water was blue, the sun high in the sky – ironically, a perfect day. How many times I'd imagined us doing exactly this, but in none of my fantasies was I covered in sick while Dan was declaring his love for another woman.

'I'm sorry I'm being dramatic. Of course you met someone else, you're a good-looking, lovely guy. Why wouldn't you?' I suddenly felt a bit wobbly and started to sway slightly.

'Let's get you out of this heat – go and get a coffee. We need to straighten this out...'

'Okay,' I said, feeling completely lost. 'But I can't go anywhere, look at me.'

Dan agreed, and suggested we go back to the room, have a proper conversation and then I could decide what to do.

Arriving back at the hotel, we went straight to the room and sat together on the bed.

'So,' he started, after getting me a towel, a waste bin and a big glass of water from the bathroom. Under normal circumstances I wouldn't have hesitated to take off my dress and wrap the towel around me, but not now. I felt like Dan was a stranger, and what's more, he was someone else's stranger. I don't know which was worse, the hurt or the humiliation.

I sat on the bed as the silence fell between us.

'So?' I said, then before he could open his mouth added, 'I want to know, but I don't. So please don't tell me the love story, I just want to know where things are now… with *her.*'

I was feeling slightly more composed now (well, I suppose anything would be more composed than vomiting in the middle of tourist central), but that didn't mean I didn't hate this woman instantly.

'First of all, we're not together now. We ended things a few weeks ago.'

I have to admit to feeling a sense of deep joy and relief at this and a little chink of light started to appear, but was still a little uneasy. If they weren't together, then why did he have a photo of her in his wallet?

'I'm sorry I got myself into quite a state,' I said, shaking off my questions – they would have to wait.

'Yeah, I know.'

'I just feel so stupid. I'm annoyed with myself more than anything. I missed all the signs. The texts suggesting it wasn't time, the way you never answered my calls, avoided talking about us whenever we did speak,' I looked at him and realised he was right, I was being unreasonable. 'Then there were the "Faye, please whatever you do, don't come to Sydney" postcards you sent,' I joked.

He smiled at this, then put his head in his hands. 'Faye, you and I were over,' he said calmly. 'I met someone *after* you'd told me we had no future… "Go and find someone else," you said.'

'Not quite…'

'That's exactly what you said.'

'Okay, I did. But I didn't mean go back to Sydney, stop in the first bar and find a woman.' I softened this with a smile; I wasn't angry at him, I was angry with myself for letting him go in the first place.

'It wasn't quite like that,' he said, giving me a chastising look. 'We didn't even date, we just "hooked up" every now and then.'

I'd heard Mandy use this expression, but she'd also said 'shagged', 'bonked' and 'banged' – 'hooked up' somehow always felt a little more restrained. But however I wanted it packaged, there was no escaping the fact that Dan was telling me he'd had a sexual relationship with someone else when we were apart.

'She was single, I was single… We talked, had a few drinks, swapped numbers, then the night of my brother's funeral, I called her and we met up and…'

'Oh Dan, I'm so sorry. I should have been there for you.' I blamed myself for everything that had happened. I pushed him away, and now I was paying the price. I wasn't sure how I felt. I know it sounds arrogant and stupid, but this hadn't been on my radar. How naive was I to expect this wonderful man to put a hold on his life just because I wasn't in it?

He gently reached out and touched my knee, then he reached into his wallet for the bloody photo again and I put my hand up like a stop sign.

'No! Dan, I can handle that you had a hook-up thing with a woman last year, but I don't need photographic evidence. I'm not possessive, but I can be a little insecure and I really, really don't want to see a photo of her standing around in tiny cut-offs or a string thong thing on a beach. If I don't see her, then I can pretend she never existed. As long as she isn't in your life now.'

He looked me straight in the eye, shifted in the bedroom chair and said, 'Clover will always be in my life.' He was looking down at the photo like she was a bloody goddess. This didn't augur well for our happy ever after and I was ready to call the airport and get a plane out of there.

'Saffron and I… We tried to live together, tried to make a go of it, for Clover's sake.'

'Clover? Saffron? Who are these women? Do you have some kind of harem?' I asked, confused and wondering if we were now in a polygamy scenario.

'Look at the bloody picture! Clover is a *baby*,' he said, thrusting the photo in my face. 'She's my daughter.'

I was in shock. *Dan was a father? My* Dan, the carefree spirit who chased waves and rainbows was now somebody's dad? This wasn't happening, it was all too weird.

'You are kidding me?' I said, unable to take my eyes from his, searching for the flicker of humour.

He shook his head. 'No, this is real… Clover's real.' He lifted the photo in evidence.

'You really have a daughter? A baby? What the hell! Why didn't you tell me this?' I said softly, taking the photo he was now holding under my nose. Looking at the picture of this gorgeous baby with big brown eyes and a mop of dark hair, I almost melted. 'She's beautiful. I'm not sure it's appropriate coming from me, but congratulations,' I said, wondering again how he could keep something so big from me.

'I didn't know how to tell you. She was born two months ago. Saffron didn't tell me until she was almost seven months gone and we kind of shared a place for a while, but it hasn't worked out.' He was looking at the photo, unable to hide the flicker of a smile as he gazed at his child.

'She's nothing like you,' I said. 'She's dark haired, dark-skinned, and beautiful,' I sighed.

'She's like her mum... I mean, the dark hair and skin...'

'It's okay, I'm sure her mother is beautiful too,' I sighed. 'You can say that to me without me crumpling into a heap.' I said this with fake certainty, I was quite devastated by all this and just trying not to overreact – again.

'So, now you know,' he said.

'Yep.'

'What do you want to do?' he asked, like he'd just shown me a menu and was wondering what I fancied for dinner that evening.

'I have no idea what I want to do,' I sighed. 'I don't think it's really up to me... There's a large cast list,' I added sarcastically.

'I'm so sorry, this must be hard. I was going to tell you so many times,' he said, now searching my face for a reaction. He looked sad and guilty and I didn't know what to say or how to feel. 'But when you got back in touch you seemed so excited about having your freedom and no responsibilities,' he continued, 'I didn't think you'd want me, with a child. And I didn't seriously think you'd ever come here.'

'I know, I know. So where's everything at? Is the baby here, in Sydney? Do you see her?'

'Oh yeah. Saff and I are muddling through, trying to make it work. She's an artist and often away working so we have to rota the childcare.'

'Wow, a childcare rota! You really have changed,' I said, still taking all this in.

'Saff's worried about Clover growing up with no dad, and we need to be more organised... At the moment it's just a mess, me trying to work at the café, Saff all over the country doing exhibitions. She stays over at the apartment on days she has Clover – and I stay over on my days, that way Clover doesn't have to move. As you know, babies come with lots of equipment, so we keep it all at the apartment.'

'So that's why you didn't want me turning up unannounced: I'd discover your secret,' I said. This explained why he wasn't exactly jumping for joy at the prospect of my arrival, and why he'd been so insistent I called him. Instead of falling onto his bed in a passionate heap, we'd have been falling over pushchairs and baby clothes.

'Yeah, well, I was always going to tell you, but when you said you were coming over to Sydney, I panicked. Then I thought about it and Saff and I ended things... and I wanted to see you. I felt it was only fair to tell you face-to-face.'

'I... I'm still finding it really hard to grasp. You have a baby, Dan,' I sighed. Things would never be the same now. Even if we did get back together, it would never be just about us, there would always be Dan's daughter to think of. Life always had an unexpected card to play and just as I'd become free, Dan had life-changing responsibilities. I couldn't help but wonder as I watched him gazing at the photo of his daughter and seeing the light in his eyes when he said her name that perhaps this was what he'd wanted – or needed all along. When he'd told me he was happy with just me, and being a surrogate granddad to Rosie, perhaps deep down he'd wanted more, something I couldn't give him.

'She wasn't planned, this wasn't how things were supposed to be, but she's here and she's wonderful. The only thing is, Saff's away such a lot, it tends to be me and Clover most of the time, which is great – but I also have the café to think of. It's not easy.'

'I can imagine.' I felt genuine empathy for him, I knew too well how tough it was to balance children, work and family.

'I thought I was doing the right thing moving in with Saffron once she found out she was pregnant. Then Clover was born and I just loved her so much, everything fell into place, but as a couple we couldn't make it work. It was after yet another row you called me once just to say hello.'

I smiled. 'God, yes... I was having doubts about coming to Sydney and wanted you to tell me I had to come... You didn't.'

'I'm so sorry, but just talking to you that night had such an impact on me. I remembered in those few seconds what love sounded like – and it wasn't me and Saff.' He now had his head in his hands and I heard him say, 'What was I supposed to do, Faye? I had a baby and the woman I love was telling me she's finally free to stay up all night drinking cocktails, spend whole days at the beach. But now I have a daughter who needs me.'

'The irony,' I said, still trying to get my head round all this.

'And every time I tried to tell you, you'd talk over me,' he continued with a smile and a slight roll of the eyes. 'You'd be telling me how wonderful it was that now you had no one to worry about. I didn't want to piss on your bonfire…'

'No, you waited until I got here to do that,' I sighed, wondering where I stood in all this and if we even had a future together.

'Do you still have feelings for Saffron?' I had to ask. I needed him to be open and honest, and I would take that truth, painful as it might be. It was the only way we could move forward, to wherever that might be.

'No… I don't love her, if that's what you mean. We were kind of thrown together, we both needed someone and the other was there. She's the mother of my child, so there'll always be something between us, but it's not romantic love.' I nodded, relieved, but still unsure where this left me. Where it left *us*. 'Saff knows you're coming here and she's okay about it.'

'I'm not sure I'd be okay if my partner's ex suddenly turned up,' I said, suddenly feeling like the third wheel.

'It's not like that. She gets it and we both want to move on, in different directions… One of us has to move out and…'

'So you're still living at the same apartment… Together?' My heart sank like a stone.

'Not like that. Saff and Clover stay at the apartment when she's around and I stay there with Clover when she isn't. The rest of the time I stay in a room over the café. It's got a bed and that's all I need, but it isn't a home. I don't have a life apart from Clover and work.'

'Oh Dan, we're both in limbo, aren't we? I can see how tough it's been for you, but I feel really weird about this.'

'Why?'

'Because as much as it hurts me to think of you being with someone else, me being here isn't giving you a chance. You're parents and you might rekindle things if you were alone with your child.'

'No. We weren't working, you know how I feel about you. Saff does too, and now you're here and she's totally cool with this...'

I looked at him doubtfully: it felt awkward, uncomfortable, that he had this whole life that I wasn't part of.

'I feel like an intruder in your lives,' I said.

'Well, you're not. We're not this little family unit, we're two people with our own lives, we just happen to share a baby. There's a big art festival going on in Perth and she wants to go there and work. But she can't take a baby into the pot-smoking, communal life...'

'Wow, I never thought I'd hear you say that, Dan!' It seemed fatherhood had turned him into a sensible man suddenly. 'I'd have been more concerned about *you* taking a baby into a pot-smoking...'

'I've changed,' he said. 'Saff's an artist, she's really good, but when she's working, it consumes her...'

'You're the same, Dan, you're consumed by your business, the recipes, the ingredients, the origins of those ingredients. You've always been obsessed...'

'Yes, but it's an obsession I used to share with you. I've missed that, because Saff and I don't share the same passions. It's like we're both lonely when we're together... I didn't think that was possible, to be lonely with someone else.'

I remembered my marriage to Craig and nodded silently. But he didn't want to hear my diatribe on 'life with Craig' just now, he had enough on his plate.

'Sometimes I think she blames me for the fact she has a baby and can't just run off and paint,' he sighed. 'But we've both had to sacrifice our freedom… I just think she finds it harder than I do.'

Despite Dan now being a dad and having a 'babymummy' in his life, I still loved him, nothing would change that.

'I know this wasn't what you expected to find here, but we can still be together. I mean, how much difference will a part-time baby make to our lives?' he laughed. 'And she's gorgeous, but she is very independent.'

I laughed at this; I was slowly coming round to seeing Dan as a dad – a very proud dad too. I confess I also found it very attractive.

'I know it's not ideal that Saff and I share a place, but she's moving out next week to share with a friend, and after that you could stay there?'

'Oh God, it feels like you have a conveyor belt of women,' I said. 'Dead men's shoes aren't my thing really. Let's take a little time and see how things pan out before we dance on her grave.'

'Okay, but it's really not like that. There's only ever been you, Faye.'

We looked at each other for what seemed like ages, communicating only with our eyes, until I had to look away or I might kiss him.

'Look, why don't I just show you round Sydney?' he said in the slightly awkward aftermath. 'There's a wonderful place we could go for tapas and early cocktails, and this great little seafood joint down by the harbour, all those twinkly lights you love – and prawns to die for. We could go there for dinner, and then afterwards we could see the Opera House, plenty of photo opportunities, Madam,' he said, playing the tour guide. 'Oh, and before you say anything, I'll check the firework situation – not sure they're doing them tonight, but I could find you a sparkler,' he laughed.

'Oh, you cheapskate,' I teased, suddenly feeling lighter, happier. 'He promises me diamonds and I end up with paste!'

'No, only diamonds for you, babe,' he said, looking at me like he could see deep inside my head, like he wanted to possess me. He was probably about to say something wonderful, then stopped himself. It was clear from the eye contact that we felt the same, but neither of us was ready yet for the old intimacy yet. 'I've done an itinerary and we can get up early tomorrow and...' he started, suddenly morphing into someone resembling the old Dan, 'we'll do a thorough whistle-stop tour of the city in a day, I know you'll love it.'

'That sounds good,' I smiled, and he reached out and squeezed my hand, then pulled away.

We were a long way from being how we used to be, but perhaps we could manoeuvre our way round all this and work something out after all?

'So, why don't you get changed and I'll check the Opera House...' Mid-sentence, his phone rang. He looked at it, looked at me and then looked at his phone again as it kept on ringing.

'Who is it?' I asked, confused.

'Saff... Sorry, Faye, I have to get this. It might be about Clover.'

'Of course,' I said, gesturing for him to pick up. But I could see in his pained expression he was torn and when he answered, I felt like I should leave the room. This was a private call, but I was strangely fascinated to hear the way he spoke to her, what their dynamic was, so I went into the bathroom and pressed my ear against the wall.

It had to be done. I trusted Dan but was a little concerned that he might be adapting things slightly to keep us both happy.

'Shit, Saff... No, I can't. Look... I can't. You know I've taken tomorrow off to be with Faye,' he was saying. 'Yes, I know... I know, your work's important... Of *course*... yes. Of *course* I want to be with Clover, you *know* I do, but I was supposed to be with... Yeah... yeah... okay. No problem, no problem at all. I'll drop everything so you can just set off for Perth early... No, I told you I don't want Clover in that atmosphere, everyone drinking and smoking dope. No, I'll change my plans... okay,' he said abruptly, clearly not happy.

I gave it a minute, then wandered back into the room.

'Sorry,' he sighed, looking up, 'that was a bit difficult.'

'Difficult? Why?' I asked, feigning surprise. I didn't want him to think I was earwigging – which I so was.

'She has to go a day earlier. She wants to see the sunset over Ayers Rock.'

'Don't we all!' I sighed, feeling a little prickly that this woman was going to a) abandon her child a day early, and b) ruin my plans. I was bitterly disappointed, and for once my usual optimism failed me. Is this what life would be like if I was here with Dan? Would Saffron just take off every time she felt like it? If this was a taste of things to come, I doubted we'd even be able to make plans for dinner, let alone anything else. 'Hey, it's okay,' I said. It wasn't, but what else could I say? So much for this baby not having any impact on the rekindling of our relationship.

'Thanks for being understanding. I'm disappointed, I really wanted to show you round and now you know about Clover, I feel like a weight's been lifted. I was looking forward to having the day with you... was hoping we could be together. But I'll have to go back, so someone's with Clover. If I don't, Saff says she'll take her with her to Perth – I just don't think...'

'Honestly, it's okay, I understand,' I said. And I did. As one of the world's most active helicopter mothers, I understood only too well how he felt.

'I mean, this isn't going to go on indefinitely,' he added, picking up his jacket.

'What isn't? Fatherhood?' I laughed.

'No, I mean, as Clover gets older, things will change and she'll become more independent and...'

'Then she'll start walking and you won't be able to rest for fear she'll fall or hurt herself in some way.'

He shrugged, 'I guess. Are you upset, about the sightseeing?'

'I'm upset, but it's not just about the sightseeing. I'm angry with myself because I let you go... but then there's a part of me that wonders if this little girl might be good for you.'

'I think she is. I just feel like I'm finally growing up – but it's quite scary, I'm not gonna lie. But now you're here and you know the score and...'

'Yeah, but it's going to take some getting used to and I don't honestly know if there's room in your life for me too.'

'Oh, don't say that...' He looked suddenly crestfallen.

'I mean, you're juggling so many balls – the café, Clover, Saffron... and now me. I don't want to be another pull on your life, someone else in the queue of people to placate.'

'It's just a matter of time... Things need to settle.'

'Perhaps you were right and it is too soon for me to be here? You and Saffron need time to "uncouple" and I need time to get my head round this and decide what to do, not just for me, for everyone. I'm sure Clover is gorgeous, but even the loveliest baby in the world can come with a lot of pressure and stress and you don't need me on top of all that.'

'Faye, you're *just* what I need…'

That was nice to hear, but part of me wondered if he'd still think that in a few days' time when the reality of having me around had sunk in. This time we'd be different – we were in a different country with different problems. I just hoped we were strong enough to overcome whatever life had left to throw at us.

'Okay, we're going round and round in circles. I'm jet-lagged and emotionally exhausted, I can't talk anymore today or I'll stop making sense. This is all so weird for me to think about.'

'Yeah, I understand,' he said. 'This isn't the best time to make any big life decisions for either of us, I'll let you get some sleep.'

He leaned towards me and for a moment it seemed like we might kiss. Everything around us was still and quiet and I held my breath, but at the very last moment it seemed we both thought better of it and we hugged instead.

'I'll call you,' he said as he walked towards the door and opened it. Then, just before he disappeared, he popped his head back round the door: 'Faye?'

I looked up at him with a weak smile. I was genuinely tired and emotionally wrecked. 'Yeah?'

'Don't just go without telling me, will you?'

'No… Whatever happens, you'll be the first to know.' I smiled and blew him a rather half-hearted kiss as he closed the door behind him.

I lay back on the bed for some time just digesting everything that had happened today. It was a completely different scenario than the one I'd imagined here in this land of sunshine and koala bears. I'd hoped to be setting off for a late lunch now, cocktails, a walk round the Opera House, soaking up the light, the sunshine, the lovely Aussie voices. I wanted to stay awake and beat the jet lag, and a sightseeing trip with Dan would have certainly kept me awake – I'd been so excited about seeing Sydney with him.

My eyes began to droop, my body screaming for sleep, as my mind whirred on and on, and when, after an hour I couldn't relax into it, I knew I needed to talk to someone who was unbiased, wise and would give me good advice. So I called Emma. It was late where she was, but she answered straight away.

'Mum… Mum, are you okay?'

'I'm fine, fine,' I lied, trying to sound happy. Emma was my daughter, but also my sensible friend. So I told her everything.

'Oh, Mum, it all sounds a bit messy,' she said. 'I know it's stupid, but I never thought Dan would ever be with anyone else after you…'

'I know, I was *really* stupid and thought the same. I came all this way and he's sprung it on me – I'm not sure how I feel about it all.'

'He probably didn't tell you because he thought you wouldn't turn up if you knew.'

'Yeah, I can see that, but I thought I'd come here and be swept up into the middle of a new, exciting life. Instead I feel like I've been swept up into the middle of someone's bloody break-up.' I didn't add that he'd tried to put me off, told me to wait, but I hadn't listened. I didn't want to get into detail, I wanted good advice... and a little sympathy from my daughter.

'I feel sorry for him,' she sighed. 'He can't help it if he loves you and wants to be with you, but got himself tied up in another relationship.'

'Yeah, but I feel a bit guilty about them splitting up.'

'Don't. Look at it this way: To him Saff is like Dad was to you – your marriage was over, there was no hope and you were both unhappy. Dan's only doing what you did when you left Dad, leaving the person he doesn't love for the one he does.'

'Thanks for saying that, sweetie, it means a lot.' I smiled; I wanted to hug her, she saw things so clearly sometimes when I couldn't. There were times when I'd wondered if Emma understood my reasons for leaving the family home, abandoning her dad and then running away with a younger man. Back then, I doubted she had any concept of my unhappiness, but it seems she did, and she never held it against me – my daughter understood more than I ever realised.

'So keep on keeping on... Don't give up now, Mum,' she urged.

'But what do I do? Just sit here while they sort everything out and wait around like a vulture?' I asked.

'You don't have to do that. Instead of hanging around, waiting for them to sort things out, why don't you take some time out? Give yourself space to think, and give Dan and Saffron the chance to get their shit together...'

'Apart – their shit will be apart,' I half-joked.

'Yes, Mum, it's a phrase.' I imagined her rolling her eyes at this. 'Anyway, while they're "consciously uncoupling", to quote Gwyneth, why don't you leave Sydney for a few days and go see a bit of Australia?'

'I might... I might just do that,' I said. I was loath to do too much, but there was nothing to stop me getting out of the city for a while.

I put down the phone after we ended the call and felt calmed. Emma was right, this wasn't going to be solved overnight, and it hadn't been fair of me to turn up and expect Dan to have frozen in time. His life had moved on and I wasn't excluded from it, the whole thing just had a different shape now.

The jet lag soon kicked in and I turned off my phone, turned off the light and planned to nap a while. Perhaps when I woke things would be clearer?

I really had no idea what to do next, I felt like my brain had been wiped. I didn't want to be here without Dan, but I wasn't sure what this new future held. What the hell was I going to do? And was it even up to me, or Dan? There were two other people's lives to consider now.

I lay in the too-big-for-one-person bed, lost in a sea of anonymous white hotel sheets, feeling like a computer that has no hard drive. Everything I believed to be true wasn't.

After tossing and turning for a while, both physically and emotionally, I wandered into the bathroom, poured myself more water and gazed into the mirror. I looked like shit – even after all my planning and preening, the tan, the make-up, the dress, all intended to create the impression of slightly-older-but-still-got-it girlfriend.

Looking at my reflection now, I was more very-older-looked-like-she-never-had-it girlfriend, with swollen eyes from crying, hair frizzed up with heat, and my lovely blue dress inelegantly splashed with my own vomit. As I took off my clothes and left them in a heap on the floor, I padded back to bed and once more contemplated taking the next flight home. I was angry with Dan for not being honest with me, but I still loved him for all the other wonderful things he was.

I thought about the way he used to tell me I was beautiful, that I could do anything, the way he gave me confidence and made me laugh, and eventually cried myself to sleep, dreaming of Opera Houses, waffles, babies and puke – which just about summed up my first day in Oz.

Chapter Nineteen

Bush Oysters Down Under

I woke the following day, unaware I'd slept for fourteen hours until I glanced at the time on my phone. There were also about twenty texts and at least ten missed calls from Dan, which gave me a little sparkle but at the same time made my stomach dip when I remembered there were now four of us in this relationship. I had to take most of the blame for this: like Emma said, I was the one who dumped him and told him never to darken my doorstep again. I couldn't turn back the clock, it was done, and now I was filled with this overwhelming sadness and loss, because what we'd had was changed forever.

I turned the sound on my phone back on and just as I did, he called. I gave it a few seconds – I didn't want him to think I'd been waiting for this – also, I wasn't really sure what I wanted to say.

'Faye…' he started. 'Where've you been?'

'I was asleep, the jet lag finally got me,' I said.

That awkward silence filled the air again. There was so much to say, it was difficult to know where to begin.

'I'm sorry…' we both said at exactly the same time, then both giggled.

'No, Dan, you've nothing to be sorry about. I told you to go and live your life and you did. And I lived mine for a little while and then when it suited me, I thought I could step back into yours.'

'But it's what I want, I just need to sort things out. Can you give me some time?'

'Yes, I think it might be an idea if I left you to deal with things. I'm going to take a couple of days to explore – I fancy just heading out and seeing a bit of the area. I know you have commitments and I don't want to put you under pressure,' I said, knowing I also needed some time out to get my head round how I felt. 'I overreacted yesterday,' I added. 'I was tired and emotional and just never expected...'

'How *could* you expect something like this?' he sighed. 'If I'm honest, it took me a while to get used to the idea myself... Jeez, Faye, as upset as you were yesterday, it was a relief for me to tell you. I feel so much better now that you know.'

'Oh, I'm glad *you* feel better,' I joked. 'I feel like I've been in a spin dryer and my head's about to come off.'

'You know what I mean.'

'Yes, I do. It's madness, isn't it? When we met I was married and you were free as a bird, and here I am with my wings intact, rucksack on my back and I'm ready to fly. And there you are, changing nappies.'

'Yeah, it's a bit relentless, this baby thing,' he laughed, 'and she keeps wanting milk too, then she cries a lot and it's back to the nappy again... What's all that about?'

I laughed. 'Yep, it never lets up. No one tells you that being a parent means you spend the rest of your life looking like you need a shower, a night's sleep, and a strong drink... all of which you do. But you don't have the time, because your child always want something and their needs become the priority and that never changes.'

I remembered Emma as a baby, the loneliness of being at home with her all day and the never-ending cycle of nappies and feeding and sleeping. Emma had gone back to work when Rosie was a few months old and I'd gone through it all again, but this time it had been different. I loved caring for Rosie because she was my grand-daughter and I had the hang of it by then – but I didn't envy Dan going through it for the first time. I'd been devastated about Emma and Rosie leaving for Scotland, but I'd been surprised at how much I enjoyed only having myself to look after. A few times after they'd gone, I'd suddenly looked at my watch and thought about picking Rosie up from nursery, then remembered I didn't have to. And it wasn't the worst feeling in the world. Having had responsibility for much of my life, it was refreshing to be on my own, just me and wherever I wanted to go. And I was going to continue in that vein while I was here.

'I'm going sightseeing,' I heard myself say. I had some ideas about things I wanted to do and I didn't need Dan or anyone else to show me around. I'd become pretty independent since the end of my marriage and I had no intention of sitting in this hotel room waiting for when Dan was available. I didn't want him to feel like I was being unfair and punishing him, he had other responsibilities now and I was simply respecting that. 'I'll call you in a couple of days,' I said.

'No, not in a couple of days. *Keep* calling me.' He sounded a little hurt.

'Okay, I'll try. But Dan, I'm giving you some space. I know you have a lot to deal with and I want to do my thing too. So let's stay in touch and talk later in the week?'

He agreed, we said goodbye and I put down the phone, sad he wouldn't be with me, but excited at the prospect of discovering Sydney on my own.

I stood by the window of the hotel room looking out over concrete and glass, futuristic buildings soared against a backdrop beyond was sea and sky, like two worlds colliding. Dan had chosen well, what a shame we couldn't have stayed here together as we'd planned. The silver lining was that, deep down, I'd always known he'd be a good dad. His mother's early death and his brother's illness had made him run away from pain and responsibility, yet the love and guilt he'd felt had pulled him home. Now, Clover's presence was the grounding he needed; he would stay in Sydney and build a life with her. I had no idea about the role Saffron would play in Dan's day-to-day living. It didn't sound like love, but as he said, they shared a baby, and that was forever. It made me think about my own role in his future: was this something I wanted? Of course I loved Dan, but now he came with so much baggage, it wouldn't be the life we'd planned. There would be no climbing into a VW van and spontaneously heading off up the coast. I knew what life was like with babies and their equipment. And even if he and Saffron managed to extricate themselves from each other's daily lives and he and I had a chance, did I want to give away my hard-won freedom to look after another baby?

Because that's how it would be. To be with Dan would mean being a stepmum to Clover and she was only a few months old, which meant I'd be in my sixties before she was off our hands. I could see that it would be easy to grow fond of little Clover – she was just a tiny baby stuck in the middle of all this adult mess – but her mother was a different matter. I was finding it hard to like Saffron from what I'd heard so far; it seemed she didn't want the responsibility of a child and was happy to hand her to Dan and run off with her bloody easel the minute things got tough.

There was a lot to think about, and this time I wasn't going to put myself second, or third down the line when I made my decision. I thought of Mandy, who told me to 'go for it, bitch', and I thought yes, this is going to be about what I want – and in Mandy's voice, I heard myself say, *this time it's all about me, bitch.*

I started by getting dressed – faded jeans and a blue T-shirt that showed off my tan. I'd imagined myself wearing these as Dan and I explored the Opera House, but now I'd just do it alone, and I headed off into the blazing white sunshine.

I found a small café, where I had the best eggs and bacon I'd had in a long time – soft, rich-yoked eggs, crisp, salty bacon and a gallon of coffee to see me through the morning. I felt okay, not brilliant, not Amazonian yet – but okay, I was getting there. I'd wasted half my life because of a man (thanks, Craig!) and I wasn't going to waste this trip because of another. I would discover every-thing, hold cute Koalas, watch kangaroos, enjoy the galleries, the beaches and the food. And I'd do it all alone – again. But I counted my blessings: I was bloody lucky to be here in this beautiful place of blue skies and white sunshine. I wasn't going to feel sorry for myself, I was going to make the most of doing what I wanted to do when I wanted to do it.

I spent the next couple of days planning my time and reading all about Australia from a sunlounger on Bondi Beach. Tough job, but someone had to do it! I devoured the delicious descriptions of 'the gastronomic allure of Melbourne', along with photos of stunning roadside vistas of the ocean. I was excited about discovering these new places, but it was tinged with heartbreak and a good old dollop of wet, ugly crying thrown in when I was alone in my hotel room. But I was ready for my next adventure and I would start by doing a dive. Yes, me, Faye Dobson, a forty-six-year-old gran from the Midlands, was going to go diving off some coral reef somewhere in Sydney. I wasn't sure of the details yet, and hadn't a clue where to start, but that was part of the fun, wasn't it?

The 'Diving Day Course' was booked up until later in the week, so I reserved my place and decided to stick around the hotel a few more days and be a tourist locally until I could take to the water.

As I donned my factor 30 suncream, a large hat and set off for Sydney Harbour, I felt it was as good a starting point as any. I sent selfies in the sun to Emma, Sue and Mandy, telling them how wonderful it was. Emma responded by sending a kiss and a sunshine emoji, Sue responded by calling me straight away and informed me I had to act quickly because Leo was in Capricorn with several suns rising (or something like that). I told her about Dan and the baby and she said not to worry because my starry alignment was good for a love match. 'So even if things with Dan don't work out, there's a big love on the horizon,' she announced. 'You're young, free and single, the world's your lobster, love.'

'I don't know about the "young" bit,' I giggled. I wasn't sure about the lobster bit either, but fortunately I spoke 'Sue' and knew what she meant. 'Thing is, Sue, doesn't matter how single I am, I can't just forget Dan and fall in love with someone else.'

'You must be open, my love,' she said. 'You can't have channel vision when it comes to love – you have to let it in, and trust me there's a Leo with a big, fluffy mane waiting for you.'

I didn't fancy the idea of a man with a big fluffy mane, but thanked her anyway, put down the phone and received a text from Mandy in response to my selfie. She asked where 'Bruce' was, wanted to know how many times we'd 'done it' and posed the question, 'Have you handled any other bush oysters yet? After all you are "down under", if you know what I mean?' She added an emoji, which was frankly disturbing, so I turned off my phone for a while. My friends were lovely, but I needed some quiet in my head and talk of bush oysters and men waiting for me down under with fluffy manes wasn't doing it. I didn't want to think about love, or star signs, or sex… or Dan, which was where my mind gravitated to every few seconds. As much as I tried not to think about him and just get on with my day, the sight of a fair-haired man in jeans, or even a good sandwich made me think of him and I turned to mush. His accent was everywhere, his phrasing intruding on my lunch, my nap on a bus, my tour of the Opera House (the guide must have come from next door to where he lived because he sounded so like Dan it was pure agony to hear those raised inflections that made every sentence sound like a question).

As the days passed, I could hear Dan's voice in my head talking of the waves and though he wasn't with me, I would listen to his advice and go where he'd wanted to take me. I recalled him telling me about The Surf Pavillion, an old bathhouse on Bondi that had been there since the 1920s. 'It's beautiful, a bit of a historical landmark, you know?' I could hear him saying. I decided that would be my next stop; I packed my beach bag and set off for those famous waves.

So there I was, lying on a towel on the beach, my 'Diving for Beginners Guide' across my stomach, to prepare myself for the following day's dive. I was wearing my new, navy blue one-piece, not the string bikini Mandy had bought me as a 'going-away gift'. I wasn't sure what the laws were here, but in the UK, I would be in danger of being arrested for outraging public decency if I wore Mandy's offering. The sun was beating down, I sipped from a glass of chilled lemonade, and was beginning to think that life could be good again. I wasn't sure what form that life was going to take, but I was going to stop worrying about it – I couldn't change anything and when I next saw Dan we'd just have to see where we were. Then above the sound of the waves and the children playing, I heard his voice. But of course it wasn't his voice, was it? It was just another Australian guy with fair hair on the beach… with a baby?

He was manoeuvring the pushchair over the shifting sand. It wasn't a smooth ride for that poor baby. He was talking to someone as he grappled with the pushchair and my stomach crumpled like wet tissue paper. It was definitely Dan, and he was walking towards me.

Chapter Twenty

Sunlounger Stalking

I put on my sunglasses for disguise and also to enable me to really stare without him or his companion noticing. From my vantage point I couldn't see who he was talking to, and he hadn't yet seen me, but my heart began hammering against my chest. Oh God, I'd come all the way here from my hotel and was now on his side of Sydney, he might think I was stalking him!

I didn't know what to do – should I get up quickly, gather my things and rush off? Or should I style it out at the risk of looking like a twisted psycho? If I took my sunglasses off now he would know it was me, and I really wasn't ready to see Saffron, if she was with him. Perhaps she was back from Perth already?

I stayed very still, not moving, just letting my eyes follow him behind my sunglasses and waiting for the babymother to appear in my eyeline. Throughout everything that had happened, I'd found it hard to think of Saffron. I tried not to dwell on how young and beautiful she'd be. I knew Dan loved me and didn't doubt that, but like any woman, I wasn't completely secure about my looks, or my forty-six-year-old body. I didn't want to think too much about the thirty-something, firm-thighed babymother in my boyfriend's life. I certainly wasn't ready for the family tableau that was about to set up on the beach several feet away from me. As I looked on in my floppy sunhat and dark glasses, shuffling slightly in my sunlounger, I knew any minute now that woman was going to wander down the beach, a slinky-hipped dusky-skinned sun goddess who didn't know the meaning of eye bags, cellulite or mottled flesh. But she was about to witness it in all its glory.

I lay awkwardly, trying to see without being seen, and trust me, I was no spy. I had one foot in the sand to steady myself and one up on the lounger in an attempt to keep it balanced. I'd always had a thing for sunloungers – they represented such glamour in films and magazines: the beautiful, bronzed film star/model, gleaming limbs, pouting lips, sunglasses lowered slightly beneath lapping lashes. Sadly, I'd never achieved this 'look' and the only time I'd ever mastered the art of just sitting on one was if someone else held it down as I landed. Over the years they'd thrown me in the air, folded me in half and hurled me onto sand with no warning, usually just as I was dropping off. I'd already been 'man overboard' that morning when I'd whiffed the salty golden promise of fish and chips being carried past me by an unsuspecting child. Keen to follow the delicious smell, I'd turned rather abruptly, causing the sunbed to capsize and the child to scream, assuming some woman was about to rugby-tackle her for her lunch. After much apologising and explaining to her bemused but slightly concerned mother that I wasn't trying to fight her kid for chips, all was good. But one false move and it can be curtains for any kind of beach-body glamour, as I was proving now, straddling the bloody thing like it was a bucking bronco while trying to be discreet.

Dan was now setting up camp with his baby only feet away, far too close for comfort as I waited and waited for Saffron to appear with her no doubt heartbreakingly beautiful body. But her gorgeousness was the least of my problems. As I'd banged on about us both needing time and space, it would look weird me sitting here apparently on the exact spot where he came to sunbathe. I felt so stupid. I would look like such a weirdo stalker if he saw me, so I waited until he was about to take the baby from the pushchair to make my escape. As he picked her up, he kept talking and I realised, to my great relief, he wasn't speaking to Saffron or any other adult – he was speaking to Clover. And suddenly, in spite of being in the wrong place, I was melting slightly at the sound of his voice, gentle and loving, the Dan I knew. I caught snatches of the conversation – he was telling his baby daughter how he learned to surf on this beach. I smiled at the sweetness of him: this baby couldn't even sit up yet and here he was, telling her all about how he and her uncle were permanently in the water growing up. I wondered how he was really coping after his brother's death; he kept it in, but I knew it cut deep.

'You're going to be just the same, Clover,' he said, 'a little water baby.' He held her in his arms, looking from her face up to the great expanse of white foam rising up above the beach. And as much as I wanted to grab my things and run away, my feet wouldn't let me, my whole body was arguing with my mind. My heart was saying, 'Stay a while, watch him, we don't know what's going to happen – he doesn't know you're here, enjoy this moment. Look at that gorgeous baby, she's just like a dark-haired version of him.'

I was trying to dig the leg of the sunlounger into the sand while observing this poster of fatherhood and, at the same time, imagin-

ing what our child might have looked like. But losing focus for a
moment, I pushed too far into the sand and, like a dog burying a
bone, I found myself going too deep, too soon. I tried to grab onto
the sunlounger next to me for balance, but that tipped and before
I knew it, I was face down with the bloody thing on top of me.
I instinctively screamed with surprise and within seconds several
people had run over to see if I was okay. I insisted I was, and willed
them to bugger off because they were drawing attention to me, and
I could see from under my sunglasses, now skewed as they'd hit the
deck, that Dan was glancing over at the kerfuffle.

I then saw a look of recognition on his face, while fighting off
some man who was trying to lift me up off the sand.

'Thank you, but I'm fine,' I was saying as Dan approached,
holding Clover, to see me being mauled by well-meaning strangers.

'Faye, is that you?'

I was desperately clambering to get up without help and I was
painfully aware he was addressing my upturned arse. It wasn't a
look I'd planned.

'I'm fine, really…' I was insisting to all the do-gooders, who
apparently came out of the woodwork here the minute a girl tripped
slightly. 'I haven't had a heart attack, I just fell off my sunlounger,'
I said with some force.

'You certainly seem to be attracting the crowds…' he laughed.

I nodded, wiping sand from my face, which had stuck to the
suncream – I must have looked like a bloody sand sculpture.

'What are you doing here anyway?' he asked.

'I'm looking… I mean, I'm watching the sea. Not you, I wasn't
stalking you or anything… I wasn't looking at you. I hadn't even

noticed you... Oh, it's you, there you are,' I said, nonsensically. 'I came to see the beach, not you or your baby's mum, so don't even think that.'

'I wasn't.' He seemed vaguely amused. 'I didn't mean what are you *doing* here? I just didn't think you'd want to sunbathe – you said you were going to see the sights, The Opera House and...'

I straightened out my sunlounger and stood near it; I wasn't letting that bucking bronco beat me again.

'Yeah, yeah, I did. And I have, but I just wanted a day on the beach and you'd told me all about the pavilion,' I waved behind me in the general direction, trying to hold in my stomach as I spoke, '... and the waves like skyscrapers...'

He stood there, holding the baby, just looking at me, and I looked at him and for a moment it felt like the sea stopped moving and everyone around us was still.

'I'm touched that you remember,' he finally said. 'But you never called me... You should have called me and we could have come here together.'

'You know why I haven't called you, I want you to have the chance to work out what you're doing without me being around.'

'But I like you being around.'

'So, this is Clover?' I said, keen to move on. It didn't feel appropriate yet for either of us to be saying nice things to each other. I wanted to be sure that he was sure and that everything was settled with Saffron before anyone declared undying love.

'Yeah, this is my baby girl.' He turned her towards me and I looked into this perfect little face with huge brown eyes.

'She's beautiful,' I said, feeling a little catch in my heart. I fell easily for babies, but this one was special: she was Dan's baby. I gently stroked her soft, warm cheek and suddenly felt a deep pang for what might have been and what never could be.

'Would you like to join us?' he asked, gesturing over to the 'baby camp' he'd set up.

'Oh no… Thanks, I have to get off, I'm meeting someone,' I lied, pointing vaguely up the beach. I wasn't ready to sit there playing happy families, I felt like the other woman. The interloper. I just didn't belong here.

He seemed disappointed that I wasn't staying and shrugged without taking his eyes from mine.

'So… I'd better go…' I said, gesturing again up the beach in an attempt to make it look like I had somewhere to go. So we said awkward goodbyes, no hugs, no kisses, and I just picked up my bag, wrapped my sarong around me while still holding in my stomach and smiled, wandering away. I suddenly realised that as well as leaving my upturned sunlounger and scattered towels, I'd also stupidly left my flip-flops but rather than go back for them, I just kept walking. I'd made my exit, I couldn't go back, so I tried in vain to walk straight and smoothly on the hot sand. I wanted him to see flowing blonde hair and a smooth glide on brown legs, but I may have yelped and jerked a little. And I was horrified when he turned up at my side, Clover in one arm, my flip-flops in the other.

'You forgot your thongs,' he said, and I thanked him, popped them on and set off again, smiling and waving and holding my stomach in – all at the same time. He was standing there watching me go and I felt awkward. I was a mess, I didn't know what to do. Eventually, when I hoped it was safe, I glanced back, but he was now involved with Clover – I'd almost forgotten that you can't concentrate on anything for long with a baby in your arms. I was thinking about his face as I waltzed up the beach, then realised to my horror I'd left my purse, with money in it!

'Christ,' I muttered to myself, as I gave a sideways glance back, just as he looked up at me in the distance. He waved and I waved again – I couldn't go back there now, I just had to keep walking and hope that by the time I returned to the scene of the crime he'd gone – and my purse hadn't. He wouldn't stay out in this heat too long with a tiny baby anyway, so I walked for another ten minutes, then slowly headed back.

As I approached the area where I'd been sitting, I could see he was still there. The touching silhouette of a man holding his baby, the sun high in the sky, against a wave wall of turquoise sea. He hadn't seen me, but if I turned and left, he might see me walking away and that would look weird – he'd really think I was stalking him then.

When I arrived at my sunlounger, I checked to see my purse was still there, which it was, thank God, and saw Dan was busy with Clover. I reckoned I could stay a while and just look at them discreetly from behind my sunglasses. It was a little creepy of me, I'll admit, but as a new family had now settled on the beach between us, I didn't think he'd be able to see me straight away, and he had his hands full with Clover. So I watched as he played with her and I tried really, really hard not to fall in love with him all over again. I wanted him, but did I want what he now brought with him? I watched as he attempted to extricate her blanket from the wheel of the pushchair, and in doing so nearly planted her face down in the sand. This made me agitated and I had to stop myself from shouting 'Be careful!' I tried not to look, but had no choice; I so desperately wanted to help, but he would be so weirded out if he thought I'd come back unannounced and was observing like some obsessed psycho. I wasn't. Honestly.

I watched as he sat staring up into the sun, and continued to talk to his baby, whose sunhat had now fallen off and the mother in me was taking over from the obsessed psycho and becoming even more anxious. I tried to look away, told myself it was none of my business, this was Dan and Saffron's baby, not mine – but my eyes dragged me back. He was now juggling with a bottle of baby milk in one hand and Clover dangling in the other. This guy who could ride the highest waves, climb treetops, jump into streams, and even make the lightest sponge wasn't quite as dexterous with a baby. From my discreet vantage point, disguised behind floppy hat and sunglasses, I saw he'd just dripped milk onto the baby's now sun-exposed head. I was itching to just go over there and take Clover off him, like some TV supernanny, and tell him exactly where he was going wrong. But that would be even weirder than me silently stalking from my wobbly sunlounger, wouldn't it? Then I spotted that thing all mothers know only too well – an induction into motherhood that happens swiftly and without warning: projectile vomit.

As this babycare car crash unfolded, I could see his helplessness and, sensing danger for the baby, suddenly found myself up and over the hot sand and by his side, beckoning assertively with my arms and shouting, 'Dan, Dan, give her to me!'

He'd just been surprised by the trajectory of vomit on his chest and shoulders and was now even more surprised to see me lurching over him and demanding he hand me his baby. I felt like some sinister Mary Poppins, turning up out of nowhere, but I couldn't help myself.

The vomit was now congealing on his T-shirt, the baby was screaming, and there was milk everywhere.

Wordlessly, I gestured again for him to hand me the screeching Clover and he looked from me to her and lifted her up to me. I took her, and at the same time grabbed a muslin square that was in the storage part of the pushchair.

'Oh, I wondered why Saff had left those in the buggy,' Dan said, standing up. 'Now I know.'

Clover had stopped crying, and was looking up at me, her eyes trying to focus, as I automatically rocked her gently. Dan wiped himself down and headed for the water to wash away the baby detritus as Clover and I looked at each other.

'Well, you picked your timing, didn't you?' I said to her, losing myself in her big brown eyes. It's a cliché to say rosebud mouth, but that's just what it was, a little pink rosebud. It reminded me of Emma when she was a baby – the tiny, upturned nose, the unbelievable lightness when you lifted her from her cot. And the unbelievable heaviness of a full nappy, I reminded myself, trying to focus less on the wonderful bits and remember just how hard this baby journey was.

'How did you do that?' Dan's voice suddenly cut into my thoughts.

I looked down. 'I've done it before,' I smiled.

'Sit with us,' he suddenly said. 'I want you to get to know Clover.'

That's what I was scared of. I was already beginning to feel that connection, where you want to protect them from anything and everything. I was perimenopausal, not maternal, how on earth was this happening? I couldn't let myself fall for her, she wasn't mine to love.

'I won't sit with you, if you don't mind. But I think she's too warm, you need to get her out of the heat for a bit.' I was feeling her forehead, looking around for somewhere he could take her under shade.

'Oh right, but she's got cream on,' he said, like that was all she needed. 'Factor sixty, total sunblock,' he offered.

'Yeah, that's great, but it won't keep her cool. It doesn't matter how much sunblock you put on, you have to be aware of a baby's temperature.'

'Oh, Saff said to find somewhere sheltered, but I thought she was fussing.'

'Well, she wasn't,' I said, hating her and envying her and agreeing with her all at once, this woman I'd never even met. 'There's more to having a baby than sitting her on a beach, telling her all about your surfing prowess,' I smiled.

'How long have you been watching?' he said, smiling.

'Watching, me? I wasn't... I'm not some stalker, I just caught sight of you as I... Look, it was long enough to know you needed rescuing. Just get her in the shade so you're not in trouble if Saffron turns up,' I said, pointing to a coffee shop in the distance.

'Saffron's not here, she's in Perth, remember? It's my time with Clover.'

'Oh well, whatever,' I said like it didn't matter – when it so did. I was just double-checking.

'I can't get all her stuff and carry her too,' he said. 'Will you come with us to the coffee shop so I don't drop her?'

I knew he was just saying this to make me go with him. Thing is, I really wanted to hold her a bit longer. I liked the feel of her babyness, the smell of suncream and soap – I also wanted to look into his eyes. So against my better judgement, I agreed to help him.

I set off quickly with Clover, keen to get her out of the sun as soon as possible, effortlessly picking up my bag, sunglasses and guidebook, and throwing my towel under my free arm along the way. I'd got this. I held her gently, she was so precious, and I looked at her again, marvelling at her perfection, her lightness. It seemed like yesterday that Emma and Rosie had been as tiny as this.

Dan followed us with the buggy and baby paraphernalia and in the few minutes it took to walk to shelter, I felt a rush of love and nostalgia. It surprised me to feel such strong emotions. And had I been younger and things had been different, Clover might have been mine. I'd always wanted another child, but it had never happened again for me and Craig, because babies just turn up sometimes – or not. As a mother of one you only get to do things once, and because it's your first time the worry smothers much of the joy. But a second child, or a grandchild, comes along and shows you just what you missed, and holding this little one was making me miss my own.

Arriving at the coffee shop, the air con like cool water on our faces, I sat with Clover in my arms and waited for Dan. It was odd to see him earlier, the free-spirited surfer boy now a slightly fretting father. But his smile when he saw her, that wide-open dimpled sunshine smile as he looked into her face, almost broke my heart.

'Daddy's here,' I said, surprised at the tears springing to my eyes. The tenderness in his voice, the softness in his face – this was a Dan I'd never seen before and it was quite lovely. No more carefree drinking, no more running away, I thought, as he touched her cheek and asked about her temperature. 'She's cooler now,' I said, touching her forehead. 'But this is a completely new look for you,' I smiled, pulling out a chair for him as he returned with the buggy, almost running over a woman's sandalled feet before parking it awkwardly.

'Yeah,' he laughed, taking out more muslin squares and putting one on his head. 'The ladies love the whole dad image,' he said, modelling it.

'I'm sure they do,' I laughed as he wiped his face with it, then offered the now-sweaty square to me.

'No, thanks,' I smiled. 'Do you really think either me or Clover would want that after you've wiped your hot grimy face with it?'

He looked at it and laughed, slightly breathlessly, obviously tired from pushing the buggy in the heat.

'You've got erm... some sick on your... chest,' he said, vaguely pointing in the direction of my left breast.

'Not quite the look I was after,' I laughed. 'I think there's a definite theme developing for me on this Sydney trip, isn't there, Clover sweetie?' I said gently into her face. I swear she smiled at me. 'Dan, look... she smiled,' I said.

'Yeah, you're a baby whisperer, Faye. I can't get her to be quiet like that once she starts that screeching thing.'

'You're a new dad and babies can often sense the panic. It makes them panic,' I said, unable to take my eyes from her.

Dan's phone was now ringing: 'Oh shit, it's the café...' he said, picking up and having a conversation with someone about a delivery of seafood. 'You need to speak to Shane at the docks,' he was saying. 'I can't... I'm with Clover and I... Oh, look, I'll do it, just get on with the service. I'll sort it.' He clicked off, then turned to me, 'It's the café, they…'

'Yeah, I know, seafood order…'

He nodded. 'The crayfish have gone awol, I have to ring…'

'Shane?'

He laughed. 'Yeah, won't be a minute,' he said absently, and punching numbers out on his phone, he walked out of the coffee shop and stood outside to have the conversation. Meanwhile, I sat with Clover in my arms as she slept, and watched as Dan waved his arms around outside and had what looked like a very intense conversation with Shane about lost crayfish. This went on for some time, and I sat there – literally, holding the baby. And I suddenly had a moment and wondered what life with Dan would be like now. The joy of my relationship with him was that it had always been a little selfish – we'd enjoyed decadent weekends away, we indulged each other, spent time caring, loving. This would now be a very different life than the one I'd envisaged, and if I wasn't careful, I would fall for this little one. Looking down at her, I asked myself if this was what I really wanted.

Eventually Dan returned, and after some small talk about crayfish, I gently, and reluctantly, transferred Clover back to him.

'What are you doing?' he said, like I'd just handed him a ticking bomb.

'Returning her to her daddy, I don't want to get too attached.'

'Please, Faye… get attached. Get so attached that you stay here forever and even if I can't make you stay, she will.'

I felt a little shimmer of pleasure at the word 'forever', but at the same time I was aware that this wasn't the forever I'd planned.

Dan smiled. 'Lemonade?' he said, and I nodded, as he called over the waitress. She seemed a bit surprised to be beckoned over as there was a big sign saying 'order at the counter' and was about to inform him of this when I saw the change in her face as she looked into his eyes. I could see her transform before me, from stroppy jobsworth to waitress princess, immediately under his spell.

Look away, love, I thought, but it was too late, before she knew it she was taking our order and rushing off for iced lemonades and cake, going above and beyond the call of duty and also warming a baby bottle for the beautiful man on table four. She didn't even notice me, until she returned with the milk and lemonades, and told Dan longingly he was so lucky to have such a beautiful baby. I could see the confusion on her face as she finally took me in. The baby was darker-skinned than both of us but I wondered if she felt I was too old to be the baby's mother... or Dan's partner. *There you go again*, I thought, *old insecurities slowly emerging* – this wasn't the real Faye, but sometimes the odd residue from the past still needed wiping away. You can make changes to yourself and your life, but you have to be vigilant or they come marching back and there were still occasions when I felt too old, too fat, too insignificant. I guess a lifetime with indifferent Craig and his perfect pipes had taken their toll.

'So you're thinking about diving?' Dan said, looking at the guidebook propped in my bag. He was handing me the bottle, which I took and automatically went into mother mode again.

'Yes, I figured that I'm here, so I might as well make the most of it. I was thinking about a trip to Melbourne too.' I was concentrating on Clover's feeding.

'Melbourne?' he said, just as his phone pinged a text and took him away again. 'Oh, Shane says the crayfish are en route,' he smiled.

'Hurrah for the crayfish,' I sighed, as his phone pinged once more.

'Oh, it's Saff... She's delayed, not sure when she'll be back now. That's a shame, I was going to ask if you fancied dinner.'

'Never mind,' I said, not resenting the baby, but feeling a bit miffed that Saff had done me out of an evening with Dan.

'No, we still could. We could get a takeaway, eat it at the flat...'

'Will Saffron be there?' I asked, thinking what an awkward threesome that would be.

'Yeah, when she eventually gets back. I have to stay with Clover until Saff gets back. Saff'd be okay with you being there.'

'*I* wouldn't,' I said, looking down at Clover and shutting this ridiculous idea down before it seeded. After a few seconds I looked up to see he was texting. Bloody hell, it was worse than being with Emma! I felt like just walking out, and was about to do just that when he looked up and remembered I was there and he tried desperately to get back to where we were, pre-text.

'So, Melbourne?' he asked.

'I hear there are great restaurants,' I said, calming down a little. He couldn't help it if work and Saffron needed to contact him, he had a full life, and when he was in the UK, he only had the deli and me.

'Yeah, the restaurants are amazing... Melbourne's become a real gastronomic hotspot. Some of Australia's best restaurants are there,' he said, suddenly coming alive. 'There's this amazing drive along the coast, all the way from here to Melbourne – we did it once with my parents,' he sighed. 'I was only a kid, but I'll never forget it. We went swimming at Hyams Beach, it's got the whitest sand in the world and we stopped off at the forest at Victorian Alps,' he smiled at the memory. 'Oh, and we saw fairy penguins on Philip Island... Amazing!'

That sounded perfect, and for a microsecond I allowed myself to think of the two of us driving down the coast, top down, the wind in our hair.

'I wish I could come with you,' he started to say.

'Yes, but you've got so much else going on... I don't suppose you have the time,' I said, hoping against hope he did.

'No, I guess not.' There was a shadow of disappointment across his face. 'I can take a few days off with some forward planning, but can't really leave Clover,' he added, sipping from his lemonade and looking around the café. 'Saffron's all over the place at the moment. I don't know what's got into her. We did a rota and everything, but she just keeps going off.'

I nodded – I didn't want to get into a conversation about Saffron or her fitness to be a mother, it wasn't my call. But hearing about her made me feel even more protective towards Clover.

'It's nice here,' I said, changing the subject. 'Is your café bigger than this?' I was still a little hurt that he hadn't taken me there when I'd arrived. I understood why now, he wanted to tell me about Clover first, but I still felt excluded from his dream, his life. There was a distance between us and while he was still coming and going from the same apartment as Saffron there always would be, because I couldn't go to his home. I'd been in Sydney for almost a week now and I'd seen neither his home nor the café.

'Our café's bigger, yeah,' he said. 'I'm really pleased, you know?' He was looking down at Clover feeding from the bottle I was holding. 'It's hard work, but I love it even more now this little one's here, she's given me a reason to keep going. Clover's gonna work there one day, aren't you, sugar?' he was touching her face as I held her, and my heart just unfurled like a flower filmed at speed.

'I told you about babies, didn't I?' I said.

'Yeah, they grip your heart with their tiny fingers and never let go.' His eyes were misty and I thought he might cry, so I put on my Mary Poppins voice so I didn't start blubbing. I'd made enough of a spectacle of myself in the short time I'd been here. 'Yes, and you must let her grow, decide what she wants from life, don't force her into your kitchen. She might be an artist like her mum, so let her choose,' I said, reminding both of us that she had a mother, and as cosy as this felt, it wasn't real.

He smiled, that old, twinkly smile. 'Yeah, but wait till she tastes my lemon cake, and my breakfast muffins... and we're working on this new kind of batter made with avos... She won't be able to stop herself.'

I smiled at him as he talked passionately about avocado batter, then looked down at Clover drinking her milk. She was so tiny, so vulnerable, so trusting of the woman who had suddenly stepped into her life. Would I stay, *could* I? Was it even my decision to make? I hated myself for even thinking it. I know how I'd feel if I was Saffron and I'd found out my former partner's woman had fed my child, sat drinking lemonade with him while batting her eyelashes and holding in her stomach. As for me taking care of Clover in the short time we were together, I hadn't done this in a territorial way, I did it because it felt like the right thing to do. I'd been amazed at my own feelings towards this little bundle, but I was also aware I mustn't lose my heart to her. Nothing was built in stone for me and Dan, our foundations were shaky, and if, for whatever reason, we couldn't be together, I didn't want to be hurting over Clover along with my heart breaking over Dan. I tried to stop myself worrying about what was going to happen in the future; I had little or no control of it. All I could do was make the best of my time here and hope things worked themselves out for the best.

'I'd still love to see the café,' I said, looking up from Clover's soft, rounded cheeks, warm and satisfied from the milk. I gently sat her up and began rubbing her back, just like I had Emma and then Rosie, a rush of the past coming in and filling me with such sweetness I could taste it in the air. Once you have a baby it's like you're programmed to understand them, know what they need when they need it. And here I was, just doing what came naturally and thinking nothing of it while Dan looked on in awe.

'You're amazing with her,' he sighed.

'And so are you. Don't forget, when she gets a bit older you'll come into your own, you were wonderful with Rosie.'

He smiled just thinking about her and I told him all about her latest boyfriend and how she'd recently considered 'speed dating' as she'd seen it on TV. Dan laughed loudly at this. 'Are you in touch with her here?' he said.

I nodded. 'Of course. I had a text this morning asking for a boomerang and a koala bear,' I laughed.

'Is she still into Dora the Explorer?'

'I think she's moved on to *The Real Housewives* now,' I joked. 'They grow up so quickly.'

'I miss Rosie,' he said wistfully. 'Can we Skype her some time?'

'Yeah, of course,' I said, knowing Rosie would be over the moon to see Dan again. As was I.

'What are you doing tomorrow?' he asked, and I told him I was going diving.

'Oh, babe, I wish you'd waited until I was free. I wanted to take you to this reef…'

'I know, but I wanted to do this and the way things are you might never be free. You've got the café and Clover and I just feel while I'm here I need to do stuff.'

'Fair enough, you don't want to be hanging around waiting for me,' he said, checking my face, hoping, I think, that I'd contradict him. But I didn't because he was right. 'So, are you free the day after tomorrow?'

'Yeah… I think so.'

'I'll call you, let's do something?'

'That would be nice,' I said honestly.

'But that's two whole days away,' he sighed.

'We waited over a year, Dan, I think we can do another two days.'

Sitting here with him, holding his baby, I had to ask myself if either of us was ready for this. He was so busy and I was determined to grab some me-time. I wanted a simple life. But Clover changed all that. I don't know why I felt like I'd been cheated out of something, because it was my own fault he'd gone and got himself another life. But I was frustrated – he'd suddenly become a business owner and father at a time when I had no commitments.

There was a silence as Clover began to fall back to sleep in my arms, and Dan leaned forward and touched my knee. I felt the frisson, the weakening in my bones, but moved my knee away from his hand, and he took it back, injured.

'Faye… I've been so scared of losing you. I've lost you before and I didn't want to go through it again. I understand if you'd rather be on your own. You were married for a long time, maybe you're not ready to settle down yet… ever?'

I shrugged. 'I *want* to go diving, go to Melbourne, I *want* to see Australia,' I said, reminding myself to stay focussed and not allow his eyes to sway me. 'I am in the rather lovely position of only having to think about me, and I like it.'

'It doesn't mean we can't be together.'

'It's not just about you and me anymore, Dan, it's about this little one,' I said, gazing at Clover, whose facial expressions suggested she might be filling her nappy. I almost laughed – here we were talking about our feelings and what we wanted from life, while she carried on her bodily functions. Babies always put things into perspective. 'Anyway, enough of talking about me,' I raised my eyebrows and smiled, at myself as much as anything else. 'This baby has far more important things for Daddy to deal with just now.' I gently handed her back to him.

'You're not just going… we need to talk.' He looked hurt.

'We will, but you've got a nappy to change and a baby to look after. It'll soon be her bedtime, we can't just sit and talk until the sun goes down.'

'Okay, so come to the café the day after tomorrow,' he said. 'I'll be working, but I'll make sure we have some time together and I'll cook specially for you.'

I smiled and stood up and bent down to kiss Clover on the head – she smelled like heaven.

He looked up at me as I stood again.

'I'm not kissing you on the forehead,' I joked.

'I was hoping for something a little more,' he teased.

'Keep hoping,' I winked, and picking up my guidebook, floppy hat and beach bag, I walked out of the coffee shop, leaving a now rather grizzly baby and a harassed father in my wake.

I couldn't stay any longer, it was all beginning to feel rather lovely and I needed to work out what was happening between us. I also wanted to confirm everything that was happening between Dan and Saffron, and as much as I didn't want to meet her, if I wanted to be with Dan it was inevitable that I would have to.

I tried to sashay down the walkway, remembering Sue's instructions to imagine I was a strong, sexy Leo and ruler of the stars. So I strutted like Uma Thurman in *Kill Bill* (minus the yellow jumpsuit and samurai sword), knocking people out of my way. A poor woman almost ended up falling over, but thankfully, I caught her, apologising profusely as she gathered herself together, looking very scared. It seemed I had Uma's walk, but not her grace. Thankfully, I spotted a cocktail bar, and going straight in, channelled Uma and took a perch at the bar and ordered myself a mai tai. After which I felt pretty positive. Nothing like a good old shot of alcohol to make one see things differently.

I'd had a child in my life since I was eighteen years old, and then a grandchild. They were, and always would be, the best things in my life, but handing that nappy-filled baby back to her father made me wonder if it was time for a proper 'baby' break. I had some time now to enjoy my freedom and take a rest from looking after children, but did that make me selfish?

As I mused on this and sipped my second delicious cocktail, Dan wandered past. He was pushing the buggy, and I noticed his head was down, and immediately assumed he was feeling bad because I wasn't there... But he was just leaning down, talking to Clover. I smiled at my own arrogance, to think I was all that mattered to him. He was laughing with her now as he gently wiped her face with a muslin cloth and I felt another rush of love as high as those bloody Bondi waves and wished I could practise what I preached about bloody freedom. If I was so damn free, why did I feel like my chest had opened and my heart was hanging out?

Chapter Twenty-One

The Rampaging Pirate Meets Crazed Crustacean

Dan had told me all about his own diving experiences, the way the sea opened up to you once you were underwater and was like a HD film in colour. But I was going to live this myself, see things through my own eyes and have an amazing time away from hairdressing, essays and even childcare.

I was a complete beginner when it came to diving, though having listened to Dan's stories, he'd made it sound fun and easy, so it had become another thing on my living list and I was eager to tick it off. I wandered into the diving school that morning and explained to the friendly guy at reception that I'd made a booking online. The guy was laid-back and smiley, and when I told him I was a beginner, he said, 'Fair dinkum,' and handed me some paperwork to sign. I'd paid online for an hour's tuition followed by a beginner's boat dive, which wasn't cheap, so I had to do it now or lose it.

'Will we be diving from one of the boats out there?' I asked, pointing to a clutch of lovely white-sailed yachts out on the water, framed by the deep blue sky. I could see myself leaping off one of those and discovering a whole world underneath – I'd take photos of me in my gear and send them to all my friends. I smiled at what Mandy's response would be to a photo of me in a bodysuit made of rubber. The friendly reception guy said his name was Ken and he was the dive master, which made me think of Mandy again – God only knew what she'd make of that. 'I'll take care of you,' he smiled, and despite his big strong arms and no doubt expertise at twenty thousand fathoms under the sea, I suddenly felt very nervous. I was actually quite alarmed when he stood up and said, 'Come with me and I will show you the sea,' like Poseidon himself, not the dive master of 'Starfish Enterprises – where diving is our game'. It hit me at this point what I might be letting myself in for, but I had to do this, I had to do something out of my comfort zone. I'd come to Sydney, which had been a big deal, but this was more personal – it was about me ticking another thing off my living list.

'Oh okay, but don't I need to be wearing rubber, or something?'

'It's a dive, not an orgy, lady,' he laughed.

I was embarrassed. 'Yes, I know, I wasn't expecting some S&M style get-together,' I tried to joke back. 'I don't need a gimp mask,' I laughed, but when he looked at me like I was some kind of nympho I decided not to elaborate and stopped talking. For once.

'You have your bikini on underneath?'

'Why?' I asked. Oh God, my conversation had given him the impression I was up for anything.

'Because you'll need to be in swimwear, you put the wetsuit on top.'

'Oh… I…? No.'

'You need to go and put swimwear on,' he said, like I was a madwoman. I just hadn't thought – it's not like I'd done this before, but I should have thought it through. I felt rather foolish.

'I'll meet you at the boat with the rest of the class, where I'll hook you up with your bondage wings and your bottom dump.'

I didn't know what to say.

He pointed vaguely in the direction of a large white yacht and told me to hurry.

'We leave in half an hour, lady,' he added, as I turned to dash back to the hotel, which was further than I'd thought and almost killed me.

I hurriedly put on my costume, threw my T-shirt and shorts on over the top and ran back across the warm sand to the water's edge, where the boats were, holding my sandals as I could run faster barefoot. As I got closer to the boats bobbing about in the shallow end, I was a little concerned as I couldn't see the boat Ken had pointed out, so I ran into the water for a closer look. I was very hot and breathless now and the top of my swimsuit was beginning to ride down, which could be difficult to manage once on board when I had to take off the T-shirt and slip into my wetsuit. A glance at my watch told me the fit of my swimsuit was the least of my problems as the boat was about to set off any minute.

My eyes scanned the decks for Ken, but there were so many boats and so many people wandering about, this was a nightmare. Eventually, I spotted him, but he seemed to be throwing anchor and about to leave and all I could see was the $150 I'd paid sailing off into the sunset. So I yanked my bag onto my back and thrust hard into the water, shouting, 'Ken, Ken, wait for me!' But he didn't seem to hear me, so I ran on, wading through the water, now thigh-deep, and calling for him to wait. I managed to get to the boat and scrambled up the side like a bloody pirate, shouting all the time for them to stop.

Ken didn't even turn as I called his name and tried to lurch over the side to get my feet on deck. *Wow*, I thought, *this is real diving*. It was certainly no pleasure cruise. But that suited this adventuress – this was the Faye that jumped off rocks and abseiled over mountains. I was a world traveller and didn't want to be treated like a soft tourist. Having said that, as I clutched at the side of the boat, my legs unable to make purchase on the side and moving like a giant frog, I did think some kind of gangplank might be in order.

'It's me… Faye, I went to put on my costume,' I was yelling, as I continued the frog-like advances up the side of the boat. But now Ken had got my dollars, his easy-going friendliness in reception seemed to have disappeared as he'd transformed into the hard dive master. I was determined though to prove I was no meek landlubber – Ken could push that throttle as fast as he liked, but this mermaid wasn't letting go, so I kept scrambling, like a rampaging pirate, until I landed with a loud bump in an exhausted, dripping, frankly frightful heap at Ken's feet.

I looked up, as he looked down. But to my horror, this wasn't Ken, this guy was in full hardcore sailor regalia. I attempted to rise by getting on all fours, but the weight of the water in my bag pulled me back down. I was now face down and dripping at the feet of a complete stranger, who seemed as surprised to see me as I was to see him. Meanwhile, I was aware the boat was now setting off at some speed. And I couldn't see anyone else on board.

The man who wasn't Ken was now watching me warily, like I really might be a pirate or some kind of sea criminal (if there is such a thing).

'Is this… the dive boat?' I asked. I was now climbing up his leg in an attempt to gain purchase and make it to my feet. He was looking down at me like I was some kind of crazed crustacean that had landed on him.

'No,' was all he said, as I slowly moved up him, taking a quick glance at the nearby table set with gold cutlery, fresh tropical fruits laid on silver platters and a bottle of champagne on ice. No, this clearly wasn't some scuzzy scuba-diving vehicle filled with beginner divers, this was a private yacht. And I'd just clambered aboard like a mad, middle-aged stowaway – and God only knew where this yacht was headed, but a quick check told me that land was getting further and further away.

The man helped me to my feet and as I continued to cling to him, called for someone to come from below deck, while I stood there in all my damp sea glory. My hair was now stuck to my head with salt and sweat, my shorts so wet it appeared I'd had some kind of exploding bladder incident. As if that wasn't bad enough, I was dangerously close to having a wardrobe malfunction as the top of my swimming costume was edging dangerously close to my breasts and I wasn't quite sure which problem to deal with first.

'I think I may have the wrong boat…' I started, as a young woman appeared from below decks. She was dressed in a spanking white kaftan, the dazzle of which was matched only by the diamonds on her fingers.

'Who are you?' she said, in a French accent. She looked terrified and moved her perfectly manicured hand to her mouth in horror. She'd clearly never seen a wet, working-class person on her yacht before.

'I'm on the wrong boat,' I explained. 'The wrong boat,' I repeated, slightly louder, like this would help if English wasn't their first language.

At this point a man appeared, equally horrified, equally French. Then I realised the champagne breakfast must be for these two, they were obviously about to have a romantic meal, alone at sea. But guess who was coming to dinner?

Eventually another, older man appeared. Oh God, was there a long line of people coming out to witness my latest humiliation? I felt like the curious catch of the day.

'Where did you come from?' he asked. To my relief he spoke English – with a delicious French accent, I noticed, despite my plight.

'England,' I said, stupidly.

'You swam a looong way,' he chuckled.

'No, sorry… I came to holiday with my… Well, the man I was going to spend time with has a baby and it's all…'

'Complicated?' he said, looking bemused, as everyone else looked on, waiting to see what I did next – like I was the on-board entertainment.

'Something like that. My name is Faye… I'm staying in Sydney… I thought you were the dive school.'

'No, we're not,' the young woman said, clutching the young man for safety, like I was some mad marauder she needed to be protected from.

'Sorry… The thing is, I need to get on the dive boat. I've already paid for the lesson, you see.'

'Ah… I'm so sorry, Faye, we can't turn around, we have planned the route, we're spending the day at sea,' he said as I looked forlornly behind me at the land disappearing rapidly. 'We book the crew, the team… we can't just go back now.'

'I'm so sorry,' I said, dripping saltwater all over the lovely white decking. My costume was doing strange things and seemed to have gathered water around the front of my groin, which was giving the impression that I had a large tummy and no bladder control. From the bemused look on his face, I was sure he thought I was standing there talking to him and blatantly weeing at the same time. The woman let out a little yelp and took a step back, her hand clutching her face, horrified at the spectacle before her. I felt like a wild sea beast.

'So please, use the facilities…' the older man said politely, averting his gaze from the Niagara Falls between my legs.

I smiled and moved my legs to walk, desperate to at least escape this awkward gathering, but the sound of gushing water and his graciousness made me feel like a wild sea beast.

'There are towels and a robe in the bedroom,' he gestured towards the cabin below. 'François will give you what you need.' Ah, so the man who wasn't Ken was François.

I apologised profusely, too much really, because the more I spoke, the longer I gushed water onto the decking, while the woman turned a dangerous shade of puce – I doubted it was seasickness. François meanwhile stood at a safe distance before taking me to the bedroom downstairs, where I was to avail myself of my wet clothes.

The room was amazing, and hard to believe I wasn't in a five-star hotel – the cabin was huge, the bed was king-size and the fittings in the en suite were gold. It was surreal to find myself in this beautiful room on water, especially as I was expecting to be aboard a sea-worn diving boat strewn with flippers and bondage wings (whatever they were). I gazed around as I slowly took off my T-shirt and shorts. I felt really weird about taking my costume off, though – I was in a stranger's boat on the high seas and being naked wasn't on the agenda. Despite the spectacle I'd created on deck with my errant costume and the waterfall between my legs, I had some dignity left. So, deciding to keep it on, I pulled up the ill-fitting costume around my bust and tried to manoeuvre the now-baggy groin area that had inexplicably filled itself with water and given everyone on board the impression that I was incontinent.

François had left towels and a robe on the bed, so I dried where I could and quickly wrapped the robe around me. I think the older man took pity on me because once I went back up on deck and François had taken my clothes to dry, he invited me to have brunch with them. The couple didn't seem too excited about this, and moved way up the banquette seating so I didn't contaminate them.

I couldn't believe it: here I was sitting in a bathrobe with three Parisians, dining on champagne, eggs Benedict and tropical fruit. I was speeding to an uncertain destination with a boatful of strangers and felt like I was starring in my own Agatha Christie novel. I smiled awkwardly at my hosts and the man whose legs I'd climbed, who seemed to be a waiter – and wondered just who was going to be murdered first. The way the Frenchwoman was staring at me, I was pretty sure I knew the answer to that. It was me – and the murderer was Madam Kaftan on the boat with the oyster fork!

Chapter Twenty-Two

Fluffy Manes and Seafaring Cleavage

As the journey wore on, the champagne thankfully relaxed us all. And the young couple shared basic information in broken English and I discovered that they were Parisian and on honeymoon. The older man, Pierre, a handsome, well-preserved fifty-year-old, was the woman's father, and owned the yacht.

'Angelina and Michael have come to visit me for the day, they are travelling,' he explained. 'I'm showing them the coast before they head off to Fiji – I *won't* be joining them there! Who wants parents on their honeymoon?' he chuckled at his own joke, so I laughed along heartily, the champagne soothing my nerves. 'She is the light of my life,' he said, almost under his breath, smiling fondly at the pretty young woman, who only had eyes for her good-looking groom. She seemed to have forgotten my earlier entrance, and was clearly bored of me by now.

I tore politely at my croissant and sipped more champagne as the honeymoon couple opted out of conversation and began canoodling at the table. I smiled awkwardly at Pierre, not sure what to say – and clearly the consummate host, he picked up on this. Moving the conversation skilfully on, he gave me his full attention.

'So you've come all the way from England?'

'Yes, I've always wanted to see Australia.'

'Me too. I live in Sydney now, and I'm happy – but sometimes I miss home,' he sighed.

'I can imagine. Paris is an amazing place, I can understand why you'd miss it,' I said, feeling a little pang remembering the last holiday Dan and I took together. 'I don't have family at home now and I'm wondering if my future lies somewhere else… here perhaps?'

'Here is good,' he smiled, rubbing the dark silver bristles on his face. He looked good in the white open-necked shirt which contrasted well with his deep tan. I also noted he had longish hair in a ponytail and thought about Sue's astrological prediction about a man with a fluffy mane waiting on water for me. But I soon shook this thought from my head – I was here in Sydney for Dan, it was just the champagne and seawater that had gone to my head.

'I think you have to try different places the way you try on a suit – live in them for a while, see how they fit and wait for your heart to tell you,' he was saying, as our two dining companions discreetly left the table. The way they were kissing and clinging to each other I could only guess why they were going below deck.

'I like the suit philosophy,' I smiled, catching his eyes grazing my cleavage then returning quickly to my face. I could see he appreciated what he saw and, what the hell, it gave me a frisson. I still had it then? 'So what was it that made Sydney fit for you, what made your heart say yes?' I asked, intrigued by this man who'd wandered halfway across the earth to find what he was looking for.

'I think it was more, as you say, where my heart *didn't* want to be.'

I must have looked slightly puzzled at this, so he went on to explain.

'My wife,' he started, 'she died in Paris and my heart can't stay there... It hurts too much inside my heart.' He made a fist and gently touched his chest.

'I'm so sorry, you are young to lose your wife.' I was genuinely moved. However much it had hurt to say goodbye to Dan, saying a permanent goodbye like Pierre had to was unthinkable.

'Yes, and she was young too, only forty. It was a few years ago now, but it doesn't get any easier.' His eyes glistened and I could see how deeply he was feeling. I thought of Dan and his brother and the impact death has on the living, shaping our lives, our futures, leaving its indelible mark on our forevers.

Pierre went on to tell me how he'd met his wife in an art gallery on the Left Bank and how she looked like a film star and the look on his face as he spoke brought tears to my eyes. I kept thinking how lucky she was to have someone who cared about her like this, but what made me want to cry was the knowledge that I'd had that too and I'd thrown it away.

'I'm touched by your tears,' he said, handing me his napkin (I wanted to blow my nose, but decided against it). 'You really listen, Faye. People don't listen to each other any more, you're very special.'

I smiled and sipped on my champers, feeling very comfortable in this man's company and enjoying the delicious breakfast. We stayed at the table and as the sun moved around, I discreetly lowered my towelling robe so I could allow some sun on my shoulders. I would be sun-kissed when I saw Dan the following day.

I continued to listen to this lovely man's life story and he'd just got to the sad bit when I looked down to see my costume had slipped. The top half had come down over my breasts and I was completely topless! I screamed and grabbed my breasts, which made him jump, and reaching for my napkin attempted to cover myself. I apologised profusely and at his polite suggestion headed below deck to manage my errant décolletage.

Once alone in the magnificent bedroom, I took away the napkin and stood in front of the full-length mirror. It looked like something from a bad porn movie. On closer inspection, I realised that in my hurry that morning to put on the swimsuit I'd put it on back to front. This explained the low top from which my breasts had unleashed themselves and the baggy groin, which was meant for my bum. My face was hot with embarrassment. God only knows how long I'd been sat there like a bloody porn star, breasts swinging in the sea breeze, tearing at croissants seductively. Pierre's eyes hadn't *grazed* my cleavage, they'd been knocked out by my naked breasts – oh the shame!

I changed the costume around and, mortified, returned to the table, where Pierre was smiling politely like I hadn't been topless for the past hour. I tried to think like Mandy, who did this regularly, as a welcome greeting to strangers in nightclubs, to make myself feel better, when actually I was mortified.

I apologised again and tried to explain, but once I'd started talking about my breasts and gesturing towards them, he looked confused, like I was inviting him to touch them, so I decided to quit while I was ahead.

Once the boob-flashing incident was put to bed, he asked me about me, which was nice.

'Oh, I was married to a man who loved the smell of drain cleaner, he sniffed it like some people sniff glue,' I sighed. 'We drifted…'

'And now?'

'Now? Oh, where to begin? To cut a long story short, I left my husband four years ago, fell madly in love with a younger man. We ran away, came back, then I rejected his marriage proposal, he left to come here and twelve months later, I followed him and here I am. I know, mixed up, eh?'

He shrugged. 'Faye, love is always very mixed up, that's part of the joy. If it was simple, we wouldn't want it – us humans tire of love too quickly,' he sighed, and I suspected he'd had his share of disappointments in love since losing his wife.

Before I could probe further François arrived with hot coffee, which Pierre thanked him for, and then poured as I watched him hold the cup gently, offering me cream and sugar like it were gold. He had this way of making you feel special, cared for, like he'd look after me, and it reminded me how I used to feel about Dan when we were together. Now, it felt different with Dan, slightly overwrought, stressful, and I worried because I'd pushed him away, he'd learned to live happily without me. If he had, then I couldn't stick around, but watching Pierre pour my coffee with such care and attention made me sad. If Dan weren't in my head and my heart, this might have been the beginning of something lovely here in the sunshine with this man who wanted to please me.

'So, what do you do?' I asked. Judging by this yacht I guessed he must be a millionaire.

'I made my fortune selling Lithuanian hair dye to the UK market,' he smiled, taking a sip of his coffee.

'Small world!' I gasped and was quick to explain how his products were working on the ground. I told him how none of us could read the names of the hair dyes and how Sue had originally christened them all with her own interpretive names that had stuck even after she'd left. He loved Sarcastic Scarlet the best, it made him laugh out loud – but then he looked straight at me and said, 'This is fate.'

'What?' I said, realising we were alone, and Pierre had his hand on mine. Then I recalled a film starring Nicole Kidman stranded on a yacht in the middle of the sea with a madman and quickly moved my hand away.

Pierre immediately apologised and became 'corporate', explaining that he was keen to visit the salon personally.

'The new owner will be delighted if you call,' I said, giving him Mandy's number, knowing she would be able to handle this French millionaire with style, and probably finish off what I'd started with the topless greeting. One could only imagine what his impression of English women would be based on his encounters with me and Mandy.

The sun moved across the sky and we continued to talk about everything and anything. And later, we enjoyed a light afternoon tea with more champagne and Pierre offered to show me the best sunset in Australia. I hoped this wasn't a euphemism and smiled; I was comfortable with him but also aware that I was literally captive on his boat and being a keen watcher of crime dramas I could see how this might end on TV or film. But Pierre's hospitality was generous and extravagant, and by now it was clear he was quite captivated by my working-class stories of day-to-day life in a British hairdressing salon. Things were lost in translation when I tried to explain Mandy's slutdropping but decided to draw the line on 'Vajazzle Week' – he'd heard enough. He was drinking in everything I said and, I have to admit, I was flattered by his undivided attention, because since I'd arrived in Oz, I'd felt like more of a hindrance to Dan.

Unlike Dan, Pierre wasn't constantly being called and texted by his baby mama, he wasn't rushing off to change nappies and no one's temperature needed to be constantly checked and fretted over (by me as much as Dan). Yes, sitting on a yacht with a millionaire was truly relaxing after being with Dan and Clover the day before and it made me wonder all the more about whether there was room in his life for me anymore.

'This is lovely,' I said, relaxing into it and gazing around as Pierre pointed out landmarks in the distance. The sky was blue, the sea was all around us, there was no phone signal, no interruptions except once or twice from François, who merely wanted to top up our tea/coffee/champagne and I began to think how lovely this life could be.

I glanced over at Pierre as he talked and imagined it was Dan sitting in the open-necked shirt, champagne on ice, no phone signal, firm thighs in tight denim, blond, messy, sun-kissed hair… and I had to stop before I did something untoward.

A couple of hours later, after more champagne and the re-emergence of Angelina and Michael, I could once again see dry land. I wondered what my day would have been like if I hadn't washed up on this fabulous yacht and gone diving, as planned. I could go diving again, but this was a once-in-a-lifetime experience, and maybe, as Pierre had said, it was fate? My skin was tingling from the sun and sea air and I felt like I was saying goodbye to a friend as Pierre and I said our goodbyes on deck.

'Faye, you have made this day very special for me,' he said, holding both my shoulders and looking at me. 'Would it be pushy of me to ask what you are doing for dinner this evening?'

I wasn't expecting that. I mean, what are the chances of me randomly hijacking a millionaire's yacht and him asking me out? My immediate reaction was to say no, but I looked at him and realised I had no plans, and I didn't want to say goodbye yet. This didn't have to be anything more than just two new friends going to dinner, did it? I was a grown woman with my own life and I was alone in Sydney, the man I loved was with his baby, so why not? And besides, how could I say no as Pierre had been so kind and gracious about my unannounced and uninvited arrival on his expansive, sunny deck? So I said, yes, I'd love to meet up again and I gave him my hotel address.

'Wonderful,' he said, his face beaming. 'I'll pick you up at 8 p.m? Is that okay with you?'

I nodded, delighted at the prospect, but feeling a little guilty about Dan. The niggle of guilt grew when I returned to the hotel and picked out a dress I'd planned to wear for Dan. But he was busy, and if I'd learned one thing recently, it was that waiting around for other people isn't always the best way to spend your time on this earth.

So I dressed and sat on the balcony, wondering if I might be getting myself into something I'd later regret. I even considered calling Pierre and cancelling. I could tell him I wasn't well, that I loved someone else, but it would be presumptuous because I was only going out for dinner. He wasn't asking me to marry him, so what did it matter who I loved? And why not? I couldn't wait to tell Emma, so I called her from my hotel balcony.

'Oh, Mum, that sounds amazing and no, you're not doing anything wrong. It sounds like Dan has stuff to deal with before either of you commit to anything and I can't pretend I don't want a millionaire for a stepfather,' she said, laughing.

'Oh, it's not like that – he's lonely, his wife died. And I don't care how much money he has, I'm not interested,' I said, honestly. She seemed relieved at that and warned me to keep in textual contact with her throughout the evening.

'Remember that film with Nicole Kidman?' she warned before the signal went and I lost her.

It was now 7.30 p.m. and I still had the chance to back out of this if I wanted to, so I called Dan. I just wanted to try and speak with him, tell him what I was going to do and see how he felt about it. But it went straight to answerphone. I called again and again over the next twenty minutes, but still he didn't pick up. So I texted, saying how I'd been on a yacht all day and had an adventure I didn't expect and was now going for dinner with 'the people' I'd met. I know it was a lie, but I didn't want him to think I'd given up on us to dine with a French millionaire. But then I thought about how he'd slept with another woman not long after we'd parted and it made me pick up my clutch bag and head down to reception in my new floaty white dress.

Pierre arrived at the hotel on the dot in a beautiful big black shiny car and whisked me off to one of the best, newest, trendiest French restaurants in Sydney.

'You will love the lamb,' he was saying in the car.

I looked across at him; he was lovely, not traditionally handsome, but likeable, with kind eyes and a nice, gentle humour. I watched him as he spoke, pointing out various landmarks from our seat in the back, and I wondered, for a moment, just a fleeting moment, what it would be like to kiss him.

We arrived at the restaurant and climbed out of the car at an unassuming little place with a dark timber façade and linen curtains at the windows. Once inside, I was transported by the fragrance – pungent garlic and rosemary filled the air, with an echo of alcohol and roasting meat. It was gorgeous, and the place wasn't posh or stuffy, it was warm and cosy, like being at a friend's house. A rich friend, but a friend nonetheless. We were greeted like royalty and I felt like a film star on Oscars night.

We were seated at a very discreet table and within seconds the first good bottle of red arrived, and later in the meal he even ordered some of the local Aussie beer, which was cold and delicious and perfect with the baked trout we'd ordered, silky against the crispy skin.

'How do you think they cooked this trout?' I asked Pierre, knowing this would be the first thought from Dan if he were tasting this wonderful dish.

Pierre shrugged. 'Who knows? But if you like, I can ask the chef and he can teach you? I could pay him to give you a lesson.'

'Oh no, I just wondered.' It was lovely of him to offer, but I didn't want a lesson, I wanted to talk. So many new flavours, I wanted to discuss each mouthful, talk about the ingredients, the recipes, like Dan and I always did. He would be working out the ocean flavours of the mussels we'd had to start, I thought to myself, as I sipped wine and watched Pierre instruct the waiter that he wanted 'the *vintage* champagne'.

He smiled across at me, and I waited for something, anything, a glimmer of recognition – that we were alike, we could relate. I felt nothing.

Later, the car came for us and we took coffee outside in a beautiful garden. He'd obviously arranged it specially because we were the only ones there. It was perfect, romantic – like something in a magazine, a film – the kind of place you dream of. He was looking at me: no phone, no baby, no one calling him from work to ask about the boiling point of sodding peas. And I couldn't have asked for anything more wonderful. So why, when I looked out onto the spiky green, the night sky scattered with stars, could I feel my eyes filling with tears?

'Faye, you are upset?' I heard him say beside me.

I shook my head. 'I'm so sorry, Pierre, I think I need to go back to my hotel,' I heard myself say in the beautifully manicured darkness.

He'd brought me to this beautiful place, the French restaurant with its cosy, delicious ambience. That night I'd tasted new flavours – and I'd also tasted old money and it tasted pretty good. It was an evening I would always remember because it was unlike any other in my life – and he was so unlike any other man. If things had been different, who knew what adventures I could have with Pierre, and who knew what kind of life that might lead to? But it turned out that I wasn't as free as I'd thought I was. And just by being here with this man I was reminded how much I still loved Dan.

All the flavours I longed to taste, the mountains I wanted to climb and the seas I wanted to cross would mean nothing if I wasn't with Dan. He was loving and funny and annoying and his laid-back vibe drove me to distraction, along with his infuriating inability to confront the tougher things in life. But I loved all of him, even the flaws – and as Pierre had said earlier that day, love wasn't simple, it was complicated and mixed up. It's what keeps us humans interested. Dan was the right fit for my heart and there was nothing I could do about that. Tonight, I realised, I was in the right place with the wrong man, and all the vintage champagne in the world wasn't going to change that.

Chapter Twenty-Three

Love, Lust or a Tropical Flush?

I woke the next morning feeling sad about Pierre, but glad I'd stopped anything before it started. I'd been flattered by the attentions of this lovely man and who knew what might have happened if things had been different? But that evening proved to me that I couldn't move on even if I wanted to. My heart was only interested in one man, and I had to try and see if there was enough love left on both sides to go for it and try and make things work. It wouldn't be easy, Dan was being pulled every which way, but perhaps if we could find a short stretch of time to be alone together without all the distractions, we could see if it was possible to get back to being us again. We'd both changed, but that didn't mean we didn't fit together anymore.

I gazed out of the window of my hotel room, contemplated giving Dan a call, then thought better of it. He was the one with all the life going on around him, I didn't want to call him in the middle of a breakfast service or just as Clover fell asleep in his arms. I knew how that felt from when Rosie was tiny – it was a nightmare to wake her suddenly.

I tried to stop thinking about him and Clover and collected the *Sydney Morning Herald* from outside my door, along with a continental breakfast. Sitting on the balcony with my coffee and croissant, I opened the Cuisine section to see Dan staring right back at me from his café kitchen. I wondered if the gods, or the fates (or even those rising Capricorns Sue had threatened me with) were trying to tell me something.

In the photo, he was standing with both hands on a kitchen counter, looking straight at the camera, master of his universe. The background was blurry, filled with running waiters and waitresses, a young, bustling place and, according to the love-struck journalist, was filled with the fragrance of baking bread and fresh herbs. How I longed to see him there. I felt like I'd been in on his dream from its early days, when we'd first met, and it seemed so unfair that I couldn't at least take a peek.

Described as 'the mega-talented owner chef', Dan was clearly flavour of the month in downtown Sydney – his cooking described as 'fresh, exciting' and 'tingling with aspiration and innovation'. The review was overwritten and flowery, but that's how Dan made you feel when you tasted his food – it demanded superlatives. He loved talking about what he cooked too – the way he spoke to me about food was as comforting as the food itself. His descriptions of Australian fayre were (apart from him) one of the main reasons Sydney was on my living list. I'd longed to taste his promises of the crisp, salty freshness of beer-battered fish and chips in Sydney Harbour, barbecued pork on the beach and chilled golden beers drunk by dying waves in a molten sunset on Bondi. And I felt a sting of sadness that we hadn't yet shared these longed-for moments together in Sydney after all. In fact, all we'd shared were fraught meetings, baby sick and lemonade.

I couldn't read beyond the first paragraph of the article declaring his genius – but I couldn't discard the newspaper either. Perhaps one day I'd be able to read it properly and be genuinely proud and happy for him, but at that moment I felt like I was outside the window gazing in, my palms pressed against the glass, my heart hoping for crumbs.

I put the paper away in a little pocket of my rucksack, realising the only way I could shake this off was to get away. Remembering what Dan had told me about the coastal drive from Sydney to Melbourne, I googled some car hire companies, but just as I was about to call one, my phone rang.

'Hey, it's me,' he said.

'Hey, I've just been reading all about this amazing chef who has a wonderful restaurant on the North Shore,' I said. My voice was light and smiley, but my eyes were damp, my throat stuffed with unshed tears.

'Yeah, it's great publicity for the café, we're really busy… so many bookings coming in since this morning.'

'Great,' I said. How I'd have loved to share all this with him.

'Are you still thinking of going to Melbourne?'

'Yes, I fancy taking the coastal road, looks good,' I said, continuing to fake brightness.

'So, when are you off?' It was hardly the response I'd hoped for.

'Tomorrow perhaps, or the next day. I just need to book a car.'

'Oh, you should come over to the café before you go. I'd love you to eat here. I talked about it often enough, didn't I?'

'Yeah, and the whole of Sydney's now talking about it,' I laughed, feeling like perhaps his invite was a bit of an afterthought.

'So, when should I come and see this "sparkling chef" in action?' I asked, still trying to show the smile in my voice, but not sure I was succeeding.

'Today? Now?'

'Oh, okay,' I said. 'Give me an hour or so, about three-ish?'

'Great, yeah, come after the lunch rush so I can give you lots of attention.'

I felt a frisson of excitement – I was going to Dan's restaurant, something he'd only ever talked about was real. Dreams do come true, I thought as I put the phone down and felt this rush of love, adrenalin and just a little bit of hope.

I had a long, relaxing bath, dressed in my new pink maxi dress, took time over my make-up, tied my hair back and set off. I took public transport to the restaurant and, arriving on the North Shore, I left the air-conditioned bus to be hit once more by that Australian sun beating down.

It was after three o'clock and I wondered at the 'lunch rush' as I walked into the still very busy café, teeming with people and smelling of steamy heaven. Within seconds Dan was at my side, taking my arm and leaning into me, whispering, 'Walk this way.' His mouth was too close to my neck, I felt his breath and I just wanted to pull his face down to mine and kiss him on the lips. Fortunately, I was momentarily distracted by a waitress carrying a fabulous dessert the size of the Sydney Opera House and was able to resist manhandling the chef.

He showed me outside, to a silver table sitting on pale wood decking. The view was spectacular, and despite my now quite extensive travels, I couldn't recall anywhere more stunning. It felt right, like I belonged here; I felt so much more at home here than I had in the fancy restaurant with Pierre. The air was fresh, and I looked out onto the kind of open vista of vivid blue skies and water I'd always imagined. The light was different here – brighter, more intense. Or perhaps it was just because Dan was there, pulling up a chair at the table and joining me? He called a waitress over and asked if she'd bring a menu and a bottle of white wine: Australian, of course.

'This is just beautiful,' I sighed. His eyes were on me, and I tried hard not to look back at him, because they would draw me in and I'd be lost.

He was silent, just looking at me as I looked out at the view. I made some small talk about 'sights' but he just kept staring at me.

'I've seen Sydney and I love it,' I said, trying not to lunge over the table at him.

'No, you haven't,' he said softly.

'I've seen the Opera House and…'

'Yeah, yeah. But you were supposed to see Sydney with me. You haven't seen all of it, there's stuff us natives keep secret.' He ran his hands along the table like he was checking for imperfections. 'There's still so much more I want you to see.'

My heart was melting and when the chilled bottle of white arrived and he poured us both a glass I gulped down half of mine to try and calm myself. I felt like my internal organs were on fire. It was either love, lust or a menopausal flush, what Sue would call a 'Tropical moment'. Either way, it wasn't pretty and I just knew my armpits were wet, which wasn't a good look.

I clamped down my arms and tried discreetly to lift my glass without showing them, which made me look weird.

'What are you doing?' he asked, laughter in his eyes.

'My armpits… you don't want to know.'

'No, I probably don't,' he smiled. 'Then again, some men might see armpits as a sexual thing?'

'Not mine at the moment,' I said awkwardly, my upper lip now covered in beads of sweat. I hoped to God I wasn't going to vomit again. This would be quite the spectacle on scrubbed decking surrounded by beautiful people in designer shades eating chi-chi sandwiches. 'So, I am very honoured,' I said, finally giving in to the armpit situation and lifting my glass, before wiping my upper lip with my napkin. 'Look at me, dining with the boss.'

He pulled an 'awkward' face.

'What?' I asked.

'Yes, I'm here and I'm going to spend as much time with you as I can, but I'm working. I tried to get the night off, but we're short-staffed.'

This was how it was going to be, and if I wanted Dan this would be our lives. And I was okay with that, because I'd realised since I'd been here that I'd rather have a bit of him than nothing at all.

'I'm fine alone – I'm a strong independent woman, remember?' I smiled. 'I'll just order and enjoy the lovely view,' I added, glancing at a rather good-looking man walking past.

Dan laughed and pointed both fingers to his eyes and back at mine. 'I may not be at the table, but I'll be watching you,' he teased. 'And cooking for you.'

I sipped my wine slowly, going for 'sophisticated allure', but I think my overheating body was probably blowing my cover and betraying me with the sweat and mottled red décolletage.

I remembered the first time Dan had cooked for me – he'd made fragrant chicken infused with Italian herbs and cooked with tomatoes on the vine. Then we'd made love on the kitchen table. I blushed now, thinking of it. He brought out the worst and the best in me, I was so liberated with him, *by* him, and I longed to be like that again, back in the place we'd once been together. The funny, irreverent comments, the childlike excitement, the pillow fights… the wonderful nakedness. I dragged myself away from my thoughts, they weren't helping my menopausal thermostat.

'Remember when I cooked for you the first time?' he asked, echoing my thoughts.

'Mmmm… the dessert was a little surprising,' I smiled, and he knew exactly what I was talking about.

'But *also* delicious,' he said, huskily, his fingertips now touching mine on the table. I wanted to take each one in my mouth but resisted and gently pulled my hand away.

He finished his glass of wine as he went to return to the kitchen, telling me he would send me the best on the menu.

'No pressure, no special treatment,' I said, as he got up to go.

He slowly moved around until he was standing behind me, his fingertips on my shoulders. It was gentle, but I could feel them so intensely, like we were sharing blood, flowing into each other. I was helpless to move, paralysed in my chair, the view ahead, blue upon blue with splashes of white, his fingers gentle, my legs empty of bone and muscle. I turned to see him, and he looked down at me slightly, just a glance, but it was enough to tell me I was going nowhere for the next few hours. I'd only had one glass of wine, but I felt drunk, almost unable to form words. I knew if someone had asked me to stand up I'd have fallen.

'I... I... You must get to work,' I blurted. 'I'm hungry.'

I looked up at him again and our eyes met and for one moment the blue world stood very still and I thought he might just lean down and kiss me. I closed my eyes and waited, wanting it more than I'd ever wanted anything, but when, after a few seconds I opened them, he'd gone.

Over the next couple of hours, he showed me his love in a different way, and it was almost as wonderful as I know that kiss would have been. He'd been gone about twenty minutes when a young waitress arrived and put before me a large, white bowl and I knew immediately what this was. It was a dish he'd cooked for me on Santorini – white aubergines with olive oil, garlic and lemon juice. 'The Greeks call it the Apple of Love,' he'd told me then while feeding me hot, sweet, juicy forkfuls in our huge double bed. It was just as good this time around and though we weren't in a double bed, surprisingly this felt just as intimate. Even with all of these people around me, I knew this was just for me.

A little later, he arrived at my table with a second plate. This time it was the first dish he'd ever cooked for me – fragrant chicken. I felt the blood thrum through me as I remembered how that evening had ended, and allowed myself to think about the two of us together again. In a big double bed. Dan came over and sat with me, serving us both from the large plate, adding a fresh green salad and fluffy rice. I looked down at my plate, then back at him; I didn't know what looked more delicious, Dan or the food. I picked up my fork, knowing his heart was on that plate, and with each mouthful I think I loved him just a little bit more. I didn't speak, just ate slowly, savouring every mouthful, watching him watching me and remembering the first time.

'Good?' he asked, when we'd finished.

'As delicious as I remember,' I said provocatively, and he smiled. 'Dan, I'm so proud of you,' I said, though it felt wrong, possessive. Was he even 'mine' to be proud of? Whatever, I wanted him to know how I felt, how he impressed me so much. 'The flavours, the way you put simple things together and turn them into magic, I'm in awe,' I added.

'Well, I think you provide a sprinkling of inspiration,' he smiled. 'Our snatched weekends in Europe, our time on Santorini – all the dishes are here, the menu reads like us.'

I was so touched by this, I didn't know what to say as he leaned over and grabbed a menu from a passing waiter and handed it to me.

Opening it was indeed like looking at our story, from the very first meal he cooked to garlicky, salty moules et frites – the last meal we'd shared together in Paris, delicious, yet bittersweet.

'Is there anything here you don't like?' he asked.

'No, nothing…' I said, and I wasn't just talking about the menu.

I knew our time together meant a lot to him, but I'd never imagined he'd base a whole café around our love story.

'Just like the Med and the Greek Islands, we can get the freshest fish from the market, and the fruit and veggies are the best here. I even have a kitchen garden out the back – remember that was part of the plan?'

I remembered.

'The cucumber was grown by my fair hand – organic, sweet…'

I just smiled and listened, basking in his sunshine.

'You know, Faye,' he said, leaning on the table, his hand propped under his chin, his face thoughtful, 'I've thought about you every single day, sometimes every hour, since we parted. And there have been days when I've just wanted to jump on a plane and be with you.'

I was clutching the menu to my chest, it felt like the most wonderful love letter anyone had ever sent.

'But then I'd look at Clover, and I'd think about the café. I'd think about home and how bloody wonderful it is to live somewhere the sun shines and I can earn a living from cooking all day and I knew the only way I could be with you was to remember our story through cooking.'

'And it's quite wonderful,' I said, leaning forward, eager to get close to him, to let him know how happy this had made me.

'How could I leave you?' he asked, like he was simply talking to himself.

I looked away from him and gazing into the early evening sky, I said, 'You did the right thing, you came back for your brother – and then this happened,' I gestured around the tables at the café. 'And then Clover and you did the right thing again.'

'I had no choice with my bro and I miss him every day.'

'You did have a choice – and you didn't run away, you stayed for your brother, and now you've made a life for yourself and your little girl. You wouldn't have any of this if you'd been with me, traipsing round Europe, staying in the grey UK, where the sun never shines. You'd always have wondered what might have been.'

'Maybe... Look, I know things aren't quite how you thought they'd be, how *we* thought they'd be. But don't be put off by all the extra baggage I seem to have acquired,' he smiled. 'My life's better with you than without you.'

I sighed, looking up at him, meeting his eyes.

'It is what it is – I love having you in my life,' he shrugged and stood up suddenly. 'Dessert?' he asked, swiftly moving on.

'A rhetorical question, surely?' I laughed, glad to stop talking about us and moving on to something loaded in chocolate and sugar. I watched him walk away and thought about how tough things had been for him, dealing with loss and then an unexpected arrival. And now me, turning up in his new life expecting him to be preserved in ice, waiting for me, unchanged. A lot had happened, everything was different – but I loved him just the same.

A little while later, as the sun began her orange descent into the water, a waiter brought me a plate with a dome of lemon sponge topped with passion fruit parfait. Drizzled with lime and rum cream, with a coconut tuile sail and a scattering of lavender, it looked so beautiful. The first mouthful took my breath away – it was tart, yet sweet, an explosion of fruit in my mouth, followed by the crunch of coconut. This was 'our' lemon cake, a deconstructed Australian version, but lemon cake nonetheless.

Dan's food was everything he'd talked about and more. He'd always been able to cook, but here it was as though he'd finally found himself. The fragrant lavender was probably from his kitchen garden, the lemon sponge so light and airy and so obviously made with his mother's secret ingredient – love. And underneath it all there was no denying that there was us. Even though he'd flown across the world and I'd told him let me go, even though he'd found Saffron and welcomed Clover, I'd been in his heart and in his food all along, just like he'd been with me. But that didn't mean that things weren't still beyond complicated.

I'd been alone for almost an hour and was just wondering if I should offer to pay and leave. Dan was at work and I might be in the way. We hadn't yet confirmed my status as girlfriend or ex or wannabe and until we did, I wasn't sure where I fitted in. I tried not to think too much about where Saffron fitted in either – according to Dan she was his ex and they'd never really been together properly. But I was aware I was in denial; I didn't ask too many questions, I didn't want to meet her – that way I could pretend none of this had happened. I was whisked away from these rather unwelcome thoughts when Dan suddenly appeared at my side. I looked up expecting to see another chapter in our story, but instead he was holding a sleeping Clover, wrapped in a fondant pink baby blanket. I guess she was the final chapter.

'Oh, you've brought me petits fours?' I smiled, and he rolled his eyes and smiled back.

'Saff's just announced she's got to go to Canberra for a few days, so has handed me this surprise bundle.' He looked down and his face softened. 'I don't mind though, I miss this little one when I'm not with her.'

'Oh, Saffron's been here?' I said, slightly uneasy to think she might have seen me, but I hadn't seen her. Another reminder that she existed, that this 'limbo' situation existed between us, the outgoing girlfriend, the incoming ex – it all felt so weird.

'Just. She had to rush off – her friend was waiting, he's driving her.' He sat down, still holding the sleeping Clover. She looked gorgeous: baby cheeks, a soft mop of black curls beginning on her head.

'Good job you weren't fraternising with me when she arrived,' I said, unable to resist a little probe into the situation. He was trying to pull out a chair while clutching Clover and I gesticulated for him to hand me the little pink bundle. 'She's definitely gone?' I asked, before taking Clover from him. 'I don't want to upset her by holding Clover. Does she know I'm still here in Sydney?'

'Of course she does.'

'And you're absolutely sure she's okay with you seeing me?'

He nodded and, pulling his chair next to me, we both looked down at Clover as I stroked her hair.

'Oh God, I bet she hates me. I would if I were her,' I continued.

He nodded again, which didn't reassure me. 'I guess she's always seen you as a threat. I talked about you a lot, but then again she's not jealous, she doesn't care enough to be jealous.'

My fear that Saffron was about to leap from behind a bush, *Fatal Attraction* style, and try to strangle me was only slightly tempered by the look on his face.

'You never told me she saw me as a threat,' I said, wondering what else he might not have told me. Was their break-up messier than he'd led me to believe? Was I the reason?

'She said I was obsessed and the only way I'd get over you was to go back to you.' He was folding and refolding a napkin with great concentration, then he looked up at me.

I felt so guilty. 'Oh God, and now me being here has ruined everything for you as a family.'

'No, it isn't like that. Saff was always hung up on her ex... He's back on the scene now too. Funny how we both kinda clung to each other back there for a while, both waiting for our exes to come back. If Clover hadn't happened, Saff and I would just have been a few lonely nights.'

I wondered again what she was like, what made her tick. I didn't feel comfortable talking about Dan and Saffron, but I had to know about her, about them.

'You're so vague about Saffron.' (I couldn't call her 'Saff' as he did, it felt too familiar.) 'It's as though she doesn't exist as a woman, she's just Clover's mum.'

He leaned back in his chair and ran his fingers through his hair, indicating he clearly didn't want to get into this. 'I don't mean to talk about her in that one-dimensional way, I suppose it's just how I see her.'

It was getting late, there were no other diners out on the decking now, just the two of us and Clover and it seemed Dan had clocked off.

'Did you ever love Saffron?' I asked, holding her baby in my arms.

He sat for a while, his head in his hands. 'It's all so complicated, it's like when you were with Craig and you met me and felt like you should do one thing, but wanted to do another. It was all okay until Clover – I didn't feel like I had to make any choices, but a baby changes everything.'

So they'd really never had their love story and even having this beautiful baby together hadn't changed that.

He leaned forward and put his hand on my arm as I held his tiny daughter. It felt strange, but lovely, like a complete circle – then I reminded myself that Clover was another woman's child, I didn't belong in this circle. I knew what I wanted – I wanted him and this life more than anything – but I wasn't sure it was mine to take.

'Stay,' he suddenly said into the silence. 'Please stay here in Sydney with me?'

How long had I wanted to hear those words, and how happy they made me, but...

'I don't know. Things aren't the same – you and I are both at different stages in our lives. How can it work, Dan?'

'Who knows? There aren't any guarantees, you know that, but we've got to take the leap, that's all being in love ever is.'

Hearing him say he was in love with me made my heart lift a little but at the same time I had to be rational, it wasn't just about us.

'I feel like it's a huge leap. I'd be living here in your life and...'

'Faye, I lived in yours. It's your turn to make a decision to stick or twist.'

He was right, but there was so much more to consider now. For a start there was Clover, lying in my arms, who knew nothing of the conversations going on above her sleeping head. This little child was completely unaware that her life was in our hands, a good part of her future could be decided tonight.

Saffron and Dan had both been caught up in a lovely accident, their lives forever tangled. Was I able to make a life for myself in this web? In the ashes of his relationship with Saffron, was there a future for me and Dan?

'I need some more time to think, Dan. My decision's not just about us, it's about this little one.'

'I understand, but I want you in my life, Faye, in *our* life.'

As I gazed out into the darkness now scattered with stars, Dan went back into the café and came out again with Clover's buggy. He

gently took her from me and settled her, covering her in an extra
blanket; though it was still warm, the breeze from the water was
fresh. He handed me a throw from the back of one of the chairs and,
pulling Clover's buggy towards us so we could see her, he pulled his
own chair closer to mine.

We sat in silence for a long time, the lapping of the water, the
fading goodbyes cut by clinking of glasses as customers left and staff
cleared up. Eventually even that faded, and when the restaurant
manager wandered outside looking for Dan, she smiled.

'There you are. Do you want to lock up tonight?'

Dan nodded. 'Yeah, thanks, Amy, it's been a good night. Busy,
eh?' he said, putting the restaurant keys on the table and taking a
good look at me. 'Oh... Sorry, this is Faye, she's my... girlfriend.'

Amy smiled. I fizzled. I loved the sound of the word on his lips,
it made me feel like singing 'Hallelujah'. Loudly. But I didn't – Amy
might have judged.

'Liking the weather here, Faye?' she asked, looking me up and
down.

'Lovely,' I answered, glowing at the fact he'd introduced me
properly, no hiding, despite the fact that I wasn't sure what that
meant anymore – what did the future look like as Dan's girlfriend?

'Can't believe how he's transformed this place,' she looked at me.
'The grub's fair dinkum too, eh?'

'Yes, he's very talented.'

She nodded slowly, and giving him a wink, she said goodnight.

After she'd gone, I looked at Dan. 'So I'm your girlfriend?' I said,
sounding like a teenager.

'Do you mind?'

'No, I like it – just need to get used to it again.'

He picked up a corner of the throw around me and pulled it over my shoulder. This brought his arm across me and his face closer to mine, and I just knew he was going to kiss me, and as his lips came towards mine I eagerly anticipated the kiss and went to meet it. This time it was real and full of meaning. This was Dan, who could be himself with me, who had nothing to hide anymore, and I was ready to take it all on. Yes, I could do this, I could be with him here and we'd work through the rest: we'd find a way.

I folded myself into his arms, now lost forever in each other, nothing but us and the big, black sky. I felt like I was floating, a feather, free and light, all the guilt blown away on the cool evening breeze. Then, suddenly, a splutter and a cry emerged from the now-thick darkness. My heart clenched, we weren't alone, and Clover was hungry! We pulled apart quickly, both flipping back into the moment and laughing at the baby's impeccable timing.

'I don't think she approves,' I said.

'I think she's cool with it,' he laughed, reaching into the buggy and plucking her out.

I watched him lay her gently in his arms as he pushed a bottle into her mouth, but she rejected it, spluttering and objecting quite fiercely to being fed this way.

'She always does this…' he sighed. 'She's hungry but she won't take the milk.'

I got up and gently took the milk bottle from his hands and he watched me as I rubbed the teat on Clover's upper lip to let her feel for it with her mouth. She immediately took the teat and was soon suckling away, her eyes barely open, full-on baby tantrum swiftly averted. Dan was still looking at me as I sat back down in my seat, and the look on his face was admiration and pure love.

Later, as he walked me to my taxi, we took the long way and kissed again on the quayside. I loved our kisses in the dark, enveloped in night; I could erase the parts I didn't want to see and told myself we were both free to fall in love again.

I climbed into the taxi reluctant to leave him, and he made me promise I'd meet up with him the next day. He wasn't working until late so suggested he and Clover show me some more of Sydney.

'We'll go off the tourist trail, take you for a picnic,' he said, shutting the door of the cab. I liked the sound of that, it's how I imagined being in Australia would be like, and I wanted this so much – even with our baby chaperone.

I waved through the window as he stood on the kerb with Clover asleep in her buggy, a wonderful tableau.

Walking through the hotel lobby and taking the lift, I wondered how Saffron had given him up so easily. And as the lift shot upwards, my stomach formed tight little braids of love and lies – and everything in between.

Chapter Twenty-Four

Freshly Shucked Oysters and Tongola Billy

'Can you believe this day?' Dan said as we settled down on the water's edge at McKell Park, on the shores of Sydney Harbour. It was indeed another beautiful day in paradise and he was showing me how the locals spend their time off. People were swimming in the harbour, barbequing on the grass littered with picnic baskets and packs of raw meat. Children filled the air with whoops and laughter and dogs barked excitedly under this amazing sun in this special place.

'It's a secret sanctuary,' Dan said, then smiled to himself, as a child ran over his feet, followed by a yapping dog, 'that the world and his wife, kids and dog knows about.'

Grassed landscaped terraces stepped down into the harbour from manicured gardens. Magnificent mature trees surrounded the area, and if it wasn't a Sunday, I'd imagine it really could be a secret sanctuary.

'It's just beautiful,' I sighed, watching Clover on her blanket, kicking her legs, tightening her little fists. *Enjoy this time, baby girl*, I thought, *because it's only now you're really free.*

'Yeah, it's one of my favourite places, you can get married here,' he shot a look at me. 'I always thought about this place… you know, when I asked you…?'

I felt suddenly awkward, still angry with myself for saying no, for breaking his heart – but knowing at the time I'd had no choice.

We let the silence fall, and like pink balloons disappearing into the bluest sky, my sadness and regret was swallowed up. I looked out onto lush green meeting the blue of the water, and instead of thinking of the wedding that never was, I dared to hope. A warm Australian spring, the purple sea of jacaranda trees, sun shimmering through their lavender-hued lace, and a couple, hand in hand. I saw only silhouettes in my head, but it was Dan and I laughing in the sunshine, running to the registry office, me in a white dress and short veil, both in flip-flops, a bouquet of wild flowers caught in my hand. But almost as soon as the image was downloaded, I wiped it from my hard drive. I couldn't ask for this – I'd had my chance and had to let it go.

'I wish things were different, that you'd waited,' I said.

'For what? For ten, twenty years or never? You told me not to wait… You said it was over, Faye.'

'I know, I know and…' Then I realised he might think I was blaming him, that I resented Clover, or Saffron. 'Clover makes up for everything,' I said, holding a teething rattle she gnawed happily on.

'Yeah, but promise me you won't leave. Once I've had a chance to sort things out with Saffron…'

'Dan, let's just enjoy today and not worry about tomorrow.'

'I thought that was my line?' he laughed.

'It used to be. I think I'm chilling out and you're becoming more uptight in your old age,' I said.

He pushed me gently in reprimand, and as he did so, he caught my arm and pulled me towards him. We sat for a while and watched Clover, who was now sleeping, exhausted from the leg waving and arm stretching baby workout she'd just done on her blanket. I gazed around me at the sun peeping through the trees, the birds singing, and Dan here with me, his baby sleeping – and I wished life was always this simple.

'So, let's get this picnic started,' Dan suddenly said. Food was always his best way of communicating, and as he brought out of the basket a beautiful olive-studded loaf, cheeses and charcuterie, I felt loved.

We ate slowly, savouring the soft, doughy bread, with salty olives, and the cheeses were delicious.

'Taste some of my Tongola Billy,' Dan said provocatively, with a twinkle in his eye. I could only imagine Mandy's reaction to that offer if she was within hearing distance, I'd never live it down.

'You Australians are so coarse,' I giggled as he proffered a lump of farmhouse cheese apparently made from 'the milk of thirty organically reared Toggenburg goats'.

'You can tell it's made by Swiss expats,' he said as we munched on the strong, nutty cheese, 'such a strong rind formation.'

'I've missed that,' I smiled, looking into his eyes.

'You've missed strong rind formation?'

I laughed. 'No, I missed you banging on about where the food comes from, which goat, which patch of land... I've missed it.'

'I've missed you,' he said, and this time when he reached for me I let him put his hand on mine. It sent a tingle through my whole body, and I knew we couldn't go on like this because I was starting to sweat again. I longed to say 'I missed you too' but I didn't want to turn the day into a misery fest where we both looked back with regret.

'I made cake,' he said, later, when I was so full after all the cheeses I could barely think about cake. I said *barely*. He brought out a plastic box, and inside was the palest, lightest lavender sponge, smothered in rose icing and crystallised rose petals. The fragrance of the rose and lavender hit me as soon as he opened the box.

'An English summer garden,' I sighed.

'Yeah… Makes me think of you, fragrant and delicious,' he said, cutting a slice.

I laughed, but my heart did a little dance as I bit into the delicious, light sponge. 'When did you have the time to make this?'

'Clover woke me at 5 a.m. and suggested we bake,' he said. 'I'm adding it to the café menu.'

'You're keeping the lemon cake though?' I asked.

'Of course, we'll always bake lemon cake… It's where it all started, you and me.'

I smiled, happy to know whatever happened, he'd always serve lemon cake, because it reminded him of us.

'This could have been our wedding cake…' He caressed my arm and I felt my eyes well with tears, the taste of the cake now overwhelming me, my feelings for him just filling me up.

'You have to stop,' I said seriously. 'You're making me feel sad, and guilty and…'

'Sorry.'

To my relief, Clover started to cry and he was distracted. She was obviously hungry, and her nappy needed changing. He was holding an empty bottle, a tub of formula, and a baby, and now he was trying to bend down and take a nappy from the bag under the buggy. Instantly, all thoughts of weddings and cakes were ejected from my mind as I went into action.

'Dan, you'll drop her,' I said, leaping up and gathering her in my arms just before she landed on the grass. 'Whatever you're doing, you make the baby safe first,' I added, like an overprotective midwife. 'You can leave her on the blanket while you do all that... She can't fall off a blanket on the ground.'

Disaster averted, I was laughing now as I held her against my chest, her tiny head in my hands, glad to have her safe as he pottered around, picking up baby wipes and balancing the tub of formula under his chin. Clover was yelling – she was frustrated, hungry, probably very uncomfortable in a wet nappy... and now the formula powder seemed to be escaping from the tub.

'Look, let me help, or this will take all day, and Clover doesn't have all day – places to go, people to see,' I said.

Dan was trying so hard, but it seemed the harder he tried, the more catastrophic he became.

'Why don't you take the bottle and the formula into the café, charm whoever's behind the counter to warm it for you? And I'll change her nappy,' I said, placing Clover on my shoulder and taking the nappy-changing kit from the buggy.

He watched me, as he stood by, surrounded by a light dusting of baby formula and a lot of muslin cloths. 'How do you do that?' he asked, 'you make it look so effortless... Is it a woman thing?'

'No, it isn't, you sexist pig, it's practice!' I smiled, as we trudged off towards the café, and civilisation.

I nudged open the toilet door and once inside began the process of changing Clover's nappy. It felt strange – the last time I changed a nappy was Rosie's, about three years before, and Emma's before that – I didn't expect to be doing it again. I chatted to Clover, telling her how gorgeous she was and how lucky she was to live here and how beautiful and clever she'd be when she grew up. Then I realised someone was in one of the cubicles and I felt a bit foolish. Whoever was in there must have thought I was crazy.

With Clover changed, we headed back into the park café and Dan had ordered cold drinks and was warming Clover's bottle as we settled down to join him. He went up to the counter for milk to go with the tea as I fed Clover, and through an ornate mirror on the wall, I spotted someone leaving the toilets. I was sure it was the woman I'd almost knocked over on the beach when I'd said goodbye to Dan in the coffee shop. I had to smile – Sydney was a big place, but we lived in such a small world. Seeing that woman reminded me how I'd felt that day and how different things were now. I was more composed, less hysterical, and Dan and I were closer, more relaxed with each other. And yet there was something still holding us both back, and I couldn't help but think it was the idea of Saffron. I found it difficult to think of her; I felt intrigued, but at the same time I felt guilty, particularly on a day like today when I was spending time with Clover... and Dan. I hoped he was right and she didn't care about him, but then again only she could confirm that and I found it hard to imagine anyone not being in love with Dan.

The rest of the afternoon flew by. We sat in the shade under the jacaranda trees, now violet in the late winter sunshine. I still found it hard to get my head around winter in July. If I stayed here, would I ever get used to living in a topsy-turvy world?

The late afternoon segued into early evening and we barely noticed. As Clover slept, we talked about Dan's ideas for the café.

'So, do you think you'll open another café?' I asked, and he explained that he and Shane, his business partner, were keen to open one further down the coast.

My plan was less ambitious and pretty straightforward: I was going to teach English literature to teenagers. 'I must be mad,' I sighed, 'but if I can convince just one of them that Shakespeare is relevant today then I can die happy. Oh, and that the syntax and diction Scott Fitzgerald uses is perfection; he conjures such terrible beauty – a time of rags and riches, splendour and ugliness. The contradictions, the subtle nuances… Then there's Jane Austen, a copy of *Pride and Prejudice* would teach young women more than a bloody YouTuber…'

Dan laughed. 'Whoa, Faye! You're as passionate about literature as I am about cheese.'

'Mmm, I still have a way to go… That stuff you said earlier about thirty organic goats was the cheese equivalent of trainspotting.'

'You could teach here in Sydney?' he said, screwing up his face in the sunshine, suddenly serious.

'Yeah, but I'm a British citizen, I don't know how that would work – I'd have to look into visas,' I said, then realised that if we married, my status would be different. I changed the subject; I didn't want him to think I was dropping hints. 'Anyway, enough about me, tell me all about fascinating Australian cheese,' I teased.

'Such unique, exciting flavours… such culinary loveliness… I mean, the creativity, the imagination! Bruny Island "OEN" is washed in a mix of brine and a local Pinot Noir…'

'STOP!' I laughed, covering my ears, but actually quite interested. 'Wait… Did you say cheese *washed* in wine?'

'Yeah, then wrapped in the Pinot Noir vine leaves.'

'Yum!' *Oh my God, how had I never heard of this?*

'We have it at the café. When you next come over, you can taste it.'

I wanted so much to stay here with Dan in this bubble, pretending everything was fine, but I still felt we both needed time to think. And I couldn't do that when he was looking at me with his big blue eyes and Clover was being so cute, I was falling for her too.

'Yeah, I'll come to the café when I get back… I'm going to do the coast road drive.'

'Yeah?' He seemed a little deflated, but I ploughed on.

'Yeah. I thought I'd book a car and set off for Melbourne tomorrow,' I said, brightly, not allowing him to creep into the cracks and change my mind. He looked crushed now.

'It's not that I don't want you to go, but don't go,' he said. 'Or, if you do, what about the day after? I could come with you?'

'You've got the café and Clover.' This, after all, was what it all boiled down to.

'I know, but you're more important than the café. And Saff's back then, so I won't have to worry about Clover.'

'I want to make the most of my time – see as much of Australia as I can. What if you can't get time off?' I was still feeling strongly about not waiting around for anyone anymore. This was my time to put me first and get on with my life without working to someone else's schedule.

'I will – I will get the time off, even if I have to shut the place. You and I need this time together, it's important. I want to show you that we can still be us… and you and me on the coast road to Melbourne would be perfect.'

Being Dan, he was soon swept up in the culinary delights of this prospective journey and spoke lovingly of olive groves and freshly shucked oysters. I drew the line at his suggestion of emu and Parma ham-wrapped wallaby, which put me in mind of a bushtucker trial.

'That's what it is – bush tucker, eaten by the indigenous peoples,' he said earnestly.

'I'd rather have lemon cake,' I smiled.

'I'll bring some with us,' he grinned, just as his phone rang. It was the café. Again. He'd called them earlier to check things were okay, and now someone was calling him with a query about something or other. The café was always on the phone or on his mind, it was relentless, but he seemed glad to be at the park, and putting down his phone he said, 'I need to sort out the work-life balance, you know? This is how things should be.' He sighed, looking at me and reaching for my hand over his sleeping baby, who suddenly woke and began to cry. He rolled his eyes and looked stressed again and I thought how much we both needed to get away from all the pressures and spend time together just driving along that coast road to Melbourne. He was right, we couldn't work things out while we were apart, so why not try to do it together?

Later, we ate fish and chips in the harbour and watched the sun set, and when we'd finished, I leaned my head on his shoulder. He put his arm around me and we talked about our plans to go away for a few days.

'We'll go the day after tomorrow,' he said. 'I promise, nothing will get in the way, it's important to me.' And in the darkening skies, among a handful of stars and a shimmer of water, we kissed, and my heart lost its way, melting on my tongue, fragile as spun sugar.

Back in my hotel room that night, my mind wandered to the jacaranda trees, to Dan's blue eyes and Clover's brown ones. I thought of the three of us together, not a family as such, but we could become one – one day perhaps? I'd like to think I'd be there a little for Clover, to cuddle her, change her nappy, feed her. I wondered if I'd figure in her future? I could feel the softness of her baby cheek, like Emma's, and Rosie's. Would Clover also be one of my babies some day? I didn't know, but I couldn't bear the thought of not seeing her ever again. I'd already said goodbye to Emma and Rosie. All these babies, all these goodbyes, made my heart sore. This time, I was opening myself up to double heartache: loving Dan meant loving Clover, the two were intertwined.

I drank a long glass of cold water to take away the memory of Clover's soft cheek, of Dan's warm kisses. But when I woke the following morning, I could still remember them, and it was too late – I knew I always would.

Chapter Twenty-Five

Guess Who's Coming to Melbourne?

Two days later, after much texting and calling and booking, Dan and I were due to set off for Melbourne. Having begged, borrowed and temporarily promoted his staff, Dan had managed to get a whole week off. He'd done this in quick speed against all the odds and knowing how much the café meant to him, I felt this was a real act of love. It also showed me how much he still cared and wanted to make us work despite the new circumstances.

Dan was collecting me from the hotel at 9 a.m., and I packed my case and said goodbye. I wasn't sure where I'd stay on my return, but I wanted to see how things worked out in Melbourne and we could either plan the next bit together, or I'd head home. I didn't want to think about the second possibility though right now, I was too excited about our road trip – this was what I'd come here for, to be alone with him, to get back to where we were and at the same time start a new page. It had been impossible with all his commitments to even have a decent conversation, and anyone who's had a new business and a new baby will know if the business isn't on the phone, the baby's crying. I just longed for the peace to be ourselves again, uninterrupted.

I waited in the cool of reception for Dan to arrive, unable to sit still, feeling like a child waiting to go to Disney World. I was so looking forward to seeing him, like we were going on a first date, which in effect we were because this was a fresh start. We'd spent the last few days getting to know each other again and catching up on everything that had changed, and now it was time to see if *we'd* changed. I still loved him, and I knew he still felt the same about me, but this was the test, and if, given everything that had happened between us, we could take these few days to confirm our feelings, then we were on our way.

I was wearing my jeans and a white T-shirt, two gallons of anti-perspirant and a spritz of duty-free Chanel. I felt good, composed, happy, and thrilled to be heading up the coast to Melbourne, just driving together and taking in the breathtaking views. Sydney to Melbourne would take a few days, but we'd plotted a map and were stopping where we wanted to, whenever the mood took us. It was going to be instinctive, easy, no pressure – and Dan had even promised not to call the café like a bloody obsessive.

I kept glancing through the huge reception windows to see if I could see his hire car – all I knew was that it was white and convertible and that was enough for me. It would be just as I'd imagined, me and Dan flying down that coast road, the wind in our hair, sun on our faces.

When he hadn't arrived by 9.30, I wasn't too worried – he'd had to collect the car and fill it with petrol – so I distracted myself by texting Emma and Sue and Mandy and sending photos. Emma responded with 'You go, girl!' which made me smile and Mandy called me. It was 8.30 at night, back in the UK, and her opening line was 'Hi bitch, I'm having prinks.'

'Who's Prinks… What happened to Jason?' I said.

This caused her to roar with laughter.

'I'm having *Pre-drinks*… Prinks, you know? A few large ones before I go out?' she yelled down the phone. 'Oh Faye, you're such a daft cow!'

'Oh,' I laughed. It was good to hear her voice. No one else verbally abused me in such an affectionate way – well, thankfully no one other than Mandy actually verbally abused me.

'How is everyone?' I asked, feeling a little pang of homesickness.

'Oh, everyone's great. Mrs J has finally agreed to have a vajazzle… It's her fiftieth wedding anniversary and she's having the Eiffel Tower in gold nuggets. She's gonna surprise him on the night.'

'I bet she is,' I said, imagining the effect that Mrs J's seventy-year-old, nugget-encrusted 'lady garden' would have on Mr J's recent bypass.

'Oh yeah, and Camilla's bought a new vibrator – huge, the biggest one they do. Had it delivered to the shop, needed two men to carry it in. I opened it in front of everyone. One word – CARNAGE!'

'Oh Mandy, you're so naughty! Camilla didn't order it, *you* did, didn't you?'

'How do you know?'

'I'm bloody psychic – especially where you're concerned. Poor Camilla. Anyway, how's Jason?'

'Oh shit, Faye! Jase hasn't texted me all day, he's either found out about the other blokes, or he's dead.'

'Oh dear. How's Katy Perry?' I said, quickly moving on. Jason's lack of contact sounded like a complicated epic and I really didn't have time to hear it in all its explicit glory – I was more concerned with looking out of the window for signs of Dan.

'Katy Perry's good. She sleeps a lot and eats a lot and just chills with me every night, we're best buds. Oh, and Flick gave her a Porn-star Martini last Thursday, she bloody loved it.'

'Oh, I'm not sure cats should…'

'It's okay, Big Jess took her round the block to walk it off after and she didn't even have a hangover the next day.'

'Oh, that's a relief,' I said, wondering what kind of life Katy Perry was living now. Mind you, life with Rosie involved being force-dressed as Dora the Explorer and made to stagger round attached to a backpack all day. Swings and roundabouts really.

'I just hope Katy Perry stays positive, Faye. After Lady Gaga, I worry about the furries – one minute they're fine, the next they're depressed and suicidal – but Flick's going to give her counselling, so…'

'Great,' I said, trying not to think about what that might involve.

'Anyway, just wanted to make sure you were okay,' she said, and I was touched. Under all the bluff and bluster Mandy had a heart of gold and I thought of her like a daughter really. It reminded me that family isn't always about blood – sometimes we make families with the people we're with because we love them.

'You'd have a ball here, Mand – the weather and all the good-looking young Aussies,' I said.

'Bitch, I'd have a *few* balls!' she roared, laughing. 'Yeah, wish I was there with you, now downing that amber nectar and showin' those Bruces how to party.'

I couldn't even begin to let my mind go there.

'Talking of Bruce… Is he treating you well? Bet you can't get enough of his…'

'Yes, yes,' I quickly cut in – I didn't need a pornographic description of something akin to a bush tucker trial involving me and Dan. I felt weird talking about him after the revelations, and I wasn't about to impart the fact he was a new dad to Mandy. I still hadn't quite got used to the idea myself.

I glanced at the time: it was now almost 10 a.m. and my mention of Australian sunshine had started Mandy off on last year's cultural extravaganza in Kavos. 'Three words, Faye: me. pissed. On the beach. With two blokes… Hang on, that's more than three words, that's bloody millions…' Fortunately at this the signal went (I reckon we'd been intercepted by Interpol, her stories so lurid they'd shut us down) and I couldn't hear her any more. It was probably just as well, I may have needed to wash my phone when she'd finished her sordid tale.

Still smiling to myself at her antics, I wandered outside, leaving the cool lobby behind me and entering the shimmering heat. It bounced off the road and covered me in sweat, so after ten minutes I headed back inside, now feeling a little wobbly.

I decided to text Dan, but had no response. Was he okay? He was driving a car he'd never driven before, had something happened? I just couldn't imagine what was making him so late. Dan had really worked hard to get the time off, this trip meant so much to him – so where the hell was he? If he was held up, surely he'd let me know so I wouldn't worry?

I sent another text, just asking if he was okay, then paced the lobby for another fifteen minutes, wandering backwards and forwards, keeping my eye on the windows at all times in case he pulled up.

By 10.47, he was almost two hours late and I was beginning to feel sick. I'd had no breakfast because we were going to stop on the way – but the heat, an empty stomach and worry were always going to end badly for me. Then, at 10.48, I saw a white car pull up. I went to the window and peered through. It didn't look like a convertible, but I thought it might be Dan driving, so I went outside. I didn't want to rush over in case it wasn't him, but when the car started beeping, I walked across the road with my bags. As I approached, I could see he was getting out of the driver's side and smiling, which lifted me. I wanted to do a little dance, but managed to stop myself and just waved instead. He waved back while watching the road and beckoning me over when it was clear both sides and I ran across.

'Dan, I've been so worried,' I said, hugging him as he grabbed my bags and threw them in the boot. I was clinging to his arm, looking up into his face as he kissed me and opened the rear passenger door. I looked at him quizzically through my smiles: 'What are you doing?'

'I… Clover's in the back. Her baby seat has to be there but she sometimes gets a bit fretful if she's there on her own, so I was hoping you could keep her company. Just until she's asleep?'

'Oh, right,' I said, climbing into the back seat as he ran round the front to get back into the driver's seat.

'Where is Saffron?' I asked, assuming we were dropping Clover off to be with her mum. I peered over the side of her car seat into the baby's face and my heart melted a little.

'Saff's not back yet, she wants to stay on a few more days. I'm a bit pissed off with her, to be honest.'

'A *bit* pissed off?' I snapped, thinking how irresponsible this girl was being. 'I think that's very reasonable of you.' Then I stopped myself; it wasn't fair of me to criticise this woman, it wasn't my business – it was between the two of them. 'So who's looking after Clover while we're away?'

He looked at me in the rear-view mirror: 'We are, babe.'

'We are?' I looked back at him in confusion and then it dawned on me: 'Oh, you mean she's coming with us?' I was taken aback – this was meant to be our time, me and Dan alone together for the first time in a long while.

'I'm sorry,' he was saying, 'but the woman who usually looks after her when we're both working has her three young grandsons to stay this week, and I didn't want to leave her in a house with three loud boys who fight constantly...'

'No, no, of course not,' I said, reaching over the baby seat and touching Clover's head with the tip of my fingers, the very thought of her being exposed to three rough boys filling me with horror.

'So sorry, babe,' he was saying, his eyes meeting mine in the rear-view mirror as he indicated and pulled away. 'I know it's not what we planned... You're not too pissed off with me, are you?'

I wasn't pissed off with him, but I was disappointed and a little resentful of Saffron, who seemed to pick up her baby and drop her the minute something better came along. I'd really looked forward to this time alone with Dan and no distractions and bloody selfish Saffron had ruined things. So much for the wind in my hair and the sun on my face. So much for snatched kisses and his hand on my thigh as we drove along the open road. But then I thought about the innocent little baby on the back seat next to me who had no idea her mother had chosen to stay away longer and not rush back to see her. It made me ashamed of feeling disappointed; here was a baby who needed a mother and for the next seven days it looked like that was me.

'It's fine, it'll be fun with Clover on board,' I smiled at him in the rear mirror.

'Not quite the kind of fun we had in mind though, babe?' I saw the twinkle in his eyes and my heart did a little dance.

'Let's stop at the first pretty place for coffee,' I said, not responding to his comment. I wasn't sure what the hell the nature of this trip was now. It certainly wasn't going to be a sexual rekindling, but I was with him, so I'd take that. 'I've been waiting for you for so long I'm starving – make that a pancake stop too!' I added.

He laughed, no doubt relieved that I'd accepted our little passenger and was still up for the trip.

After about an hour, we stopped at a little coffee shop overlooking the beach and when we climbed out of the car we stood looking out onto the ocean. It was so quiet, save the squawk of sea birds floating high above in the endless blue sky. It was hot, but a slight sea breeze ruffled the air and I breathed in deeply, finally beginning to feel relaxed.

Dan was holding Clover, and I turned to look at them, taking out my phone for a photo: 'You two look cute, as Rosie would say.' I smiled and took a picture.

'Hey, Mum should be in that too,' a voice said. An elderly couple were wandering past and the woman was offering to take a photo.

'Yeah, Mum, come over here,' Dan laughed.

I awkwardly stood with them, no point in explaining to these strangers that I wasn't Mum, and just said 'Cheese' when she commanded me to.

'Thanks,' Dan said, as I took my phone back from her.

'It's no bother at all,' the lady smiled. 'You just look so sweet, the two of you standing there with your baby. Lovely little family,' she nodded, 'have a great day now,' and they were on their way.

Dan smiled at me and, taking my hand, we wandered into the coffee shop, where we ordered two stacks of mini pancakes that came with strawberry jam and whipped cream. Our coffees arrived first, and before he began his juggling act with a baby and hot coffee, I opened my arms and he gently placed a sleeping Clover in them. As she snuggled against my chest, I knew the real reason I'd wanted to stop was so I could hold her. I buried my face in her neck so I could smell her baby skin. Breathing it in took me back to my own babies and the smell was the fragrance of new happiness. As Dan drank his coffee and talked of the food we'd eat, the sights we'd see, I cuddled her, feeling that sweet baby warmth in my arms. There was no going back, I was hooked.

After our pit stop, or rather pancake stop, we carried on with our journey, driving along the road, long and winding, the vast blue ocean on one side and rainforests on the other. Dan took credit for all the beauty, boasting about how Australia had everything a person ever needed, and I knew he was pitching for me to stay. He didn't have to try too hard – the views spoke for themselves, and they beat a rainy day in the Midlands hands down.

Arriving in Jervis Bay, we stayed in a fisherman's hut and wandered the white powdery beaches, hand in hand. The original plan had been to scuba-dive here, where the water was aqua clear, but as Clover was with us, we wouldn't be able to.

'Sorry, babe, I promise I'll bring you again and we can do all the things we said we'd do,' Dan said as we sat on the beach.

'Without Clover? I don't think so. Miss Clover would have something to say about that,' I laughed, and I looked at him seriously. 'No, let's come back here when Clover's old enough to swim *with* us in that beautiful sea.'

He knew what I was saying and smiled, 'Does this mean you might stay?'

'I'm not sure, but I love it here... with you... and Clover,' I said, feeling excited and a little nervous about what I'd just said. My heart wanted this so badly, it was just my head that kept telling me I mustn't make too many promises just yet because I didn't have the full picture. I'd never met Saffron, I didn't know who she was; all I'd ever had was the rather basic sketch from Dan, who wasn't all that comfortable talking to me about her. I knew that until I met her and spoke with her myself, I wouldn't know her at all, and there was still a niggle in the back of my mind that she might still have feelings for Dan. If she did, then I wasn't sure it would be wise to take on some gladiatorial challenge for her baby daddy. But for now, I put Saffron from my mind as Dan suggested we take Clover in the sea, and nervously carried her to the water's edge, where the three of us sat in a little huddle, letting the water wash over our toes. This wasn't how I'd imagined the day to be – but with Clover there giggling as the water lapped her feet and me and Dan watching on, I realised that perhaps it was even better than the day I'd imagined.

Later, after Clover had dined, we parked her buggy by our table. I left the wine list to Dan as she was in need of winding and belched loudly as the sun set over the white beach.

'How romantic,' Dan smiled.

'Who needs oysters as an aphrodisiac when you have a belching diner at the table?' I laughed, as I manipulated her back gently.

The wine arrived and as I rubbed Clover's back, Dan sipped, and after each sip said things like 'baked apple', then 'lemon... citrus,' and so on. Then he leaned over the table and lifted my glass to my lips so I could share this with him.

'Tastes like an Australian sunset,' I smiled.

And when the oysters were brought out, he was equally vociferous. 'Basically, most places in Oz serve dead oysters, shucked and rinsed – but these are alive, the way they serve them in France. Just taste that marvellous salty liquor, the natural oyster juice,' he said, feeding one to me. It was delicious – cool and salty, like the seaside on a windy day – and in that lovely golden light, with the man I loved, the sea on my lips, a baby in my arms, I wondered if it was possible to be any happier.

Clover soon dropped off and Dan put her in her buggy, where she snuggled down.

'Make the most of this peace,' he said, pouring the rest of the wine. 'We won't get much sleep tonight.'

'Is that a promise?' I said, finally feeling like my old self, free to play with him.

'I was talking about Clover's colic, but now you mention it,' he smiled, and began to gently run his finger around the rim of his glass without taking his eyes from mine. 'Okay, I reckon we have an hour tops before Princess Clover awakens and screams the whole bloody place down. So what do you say to us paying up and heading back to our room?'

I nodded, my brain finally giving in to my body and telling me this was okay, I was allowed to sleep with this beautiful man and love him the way I wanted to.

So we hurriedly walked back to the room, speaking only softly, cursing a loud growling motorbike whizzing by in case it woke Clover, but miraculously, she slept right through it. Once in the room, we parked the buggy and left Clover there to sleep, while we kissed and lay on the huge bed in the middle of the room.

Dan's touch was as gentle and loving as it had always been, but I sensed the urgency, the need, and it wasn't just because he was against the timer of a sleeping baby, it was because like me he wanted this moment so much, had waited for it for more than a year.

He pulled my dress over my head and cupped my naked breasts, kissing me deeply. He pushed me gently onto the pillows and wrapping my legs around his strong, smooth back, I told him how much I wanted him, as he responded with panting groans. We were swept up in each other, rolling around the sheets, tangled up as we always had been, and always would be. After only a few minutes it was over for both of us, for now – we were so desperate for each other, we couldn't hold on.

'Nothing… no one has ever been like you,' he sighed, his eyes damp, his chest shimmering with perspiration.

I felt the same – it had always been more than sex with Dan, it had been a final confirmation of love, and a knowledge that we were right together and nothing was going to stop our tidal wave.

He got up, wrapping a sheet around him, and checked Clover. 'She's still breathing,' he said, relieved. 'I bet you think I'm mad, don't you?' he laughed, walking back to the bed.

'No, I think you're a parent,' I said, 'and those feelings are with you forever, it's like a wonderful curse. I'd still check Emma's breathing when she slept if she let me,' I joked.

He sat on the edge of the bed, his broad back strong and sinewy, his hair still thick and sun-bleached, and I sat up and crawled towards him, resting my cheek on his back, reaching around and taking him in my hand. He groaned again, and I knelt up, kissing his neck, sliding around and climbing onto his knee, pushing him inside me, his kisses hot, our eventual climax like a thunderbolt through both our bodies… but our mutual pleasure on low volume, so we didn't wake the baby.

The following day, we turned up in Pambula, a village on the far south coast of New South Wales. Dan had been keen to show me this place with its artisan bakeries and coffee roasters, stopping for lunch at Wild Rye's, where we had the Angus beef pies made with red wine – short, crisp pastry, hot, meaty, fragrant filling. Probably the most delicious pie I've ever had, and trust me, I've had a few.

Later, as we took a boat out into the Sapphire Coast to go whale watching, we congratulated ourselves on taking a road trip with a baby of just a few months. Our congratulations seemed a bit premature though when Clover projectile vomited. This managed to eclipse the spectacle of a huge whale – but a few muslin cloths and a bottle of water soon erased the mess. We missed the rare sighting, but I told Dan it was a good excuse to come back again, as he apologised and mopped himself up.

'And you really must stop apologising for Clover,' I said afterwards as we ate a late picnic on the beach – a delicious fruit bread from Wild Rye's with a divine local cheese.

'I just feel guilty – there's so much to see and so much to do, but we can't because of Clover. I know you don't mind, I just wanted to do so much, show you everything…'

'I'm with you and Clover – it doesn't matter about what we see, I'm just having a wonderful time,' I said, and I was.

Throughout our trip, Saffron stayed in touch. She called Dan every day to ask about Clover, as we fed sea eagles in Mallacoota, when we were walking through Croajingolong National Park, boating on the vast, tranquil Gippsland Lakes. For those few short minutes when he spoke with her I felt different, like my role was suddenly defunct. Our time together was wonderful, but for me, the very sound of Dan's phone caused a shadow to drift across the sun. Away from Sydney, we were in another bubble, a pretend family of three on holiday, but where would I fit in when the holiday was over and our bubble was burst?

It seemed my heart was now buried in two corners of the world that weren't home – with Rosie and Emma in Scotland, and Dan and my new love Clover in Sydney. Walking along the sweeping expanse of Ninety Mile Beach, I picked up shells for Rosie, and bought a necklace for Emma, and thought about how babies get their little tiny fists around your heart and don't let go.

And through all those sleepy seaside towns, national parks and long, white beaches where our feet walked on untouched sand I tried not to think of the future too much, because who knew what twists and turns fate had in store for us?

Chapter Twenty-Six

Sex on Bondi – Three Times

I felt a little deflated as we headed back to Sydney and reality at the end of our week's road trip. As much as Dan always seemed to push me forward, the circumstances swirling around us pulled me back. Our first summer in Santorini had been a watershed. I'd changed and went on to take my degree and start a new life, but he'd always been in the background, each step bringing me closer to Sydney, and him. And now, here I was being delivered back to Sydney, Dan rushing back to the café and Clover to Saffron. But what about me? I felt like I had when Emma and Rosie left, like I was alone and didn't belong to anyone or anything.

Dan and I made quick arrangements to catch up in a few days, and I booked two nights in a guest house in the south of the city. Dan had offered again for me to stay at his apartment, but as Saffron hadn't moved out, I couldn't entertain it. He'd suggested the guest house, which was run by an old family friend, who turned out to be a crazy thespian called Molly, who'd apparently just enjoyed a successful first week in *Mamma Mia!*

'Dan's friend?' she asked, screwing up her face to look at me in the doorway when I arrived.

I nodded.

'Fabulous, dahling!' she shrieked, opening the door wide. 'You're just in time for cocktails,' she announced as I followed her into the old Victorian-style house. It was huge, with leaded windows, big oak doors and a sitting room that reminded me of my grandma's parlour. There was a massive bar in the corner, where Molly now stood with a cocktail shaker. And three 'Sex on Bondis' later, she was lying across her chaise longue describing every aspect of her life and performances in detail. From make-up to 'amazing' scripts to the applause of the crowd, I felt like I'd been there. Eventually I managed to butt into her conversation and ask if I could take a shower: 'It's been a long journey,' I said.

I headed upstairs to my room and the en suite, where I stood under the hot water, the beat and lyrics of 'I'm Gonna Wash That Man Right Outta My Hair' thrumming through the water into my brain for some reason. Was I being stupid? Was I merely putting myself in the same life I'd had at home, where I'd settled into a routine with Emma and Rosie and they'd upped and left?

I stepped out of the shower, covering my hair with a towel and wrapping myself in a towelling bathrobe. I lay on the bed waiting for the sound of a baby crying – was she hungry, did she need me? No, of course she didn't, Clover was with her real mother now and I had to get used to that. I also had to decide where I stood with Dan. Yes, I loved him, but I needed more to make a life. I had to make my own plans and think more clearly about my own future, the one that didn't rely on anyone else, and where no one else relied on me. I wanted to teach English, and I could do that here in Sydney, or back in the UK.

I dressed and went back downstairs, where the Wi-Fi was better. I wanted to google some stuff and talk to Emma and see what she thought, but when I logged on to Skype, Rosie appeared on the screen.

'Hello darling,' I said, my eyes instantly filling with tears. I missed her so much and was homesick to the point of just getting on a plane there and then.

'Nana, I have been worried about you!' was her opening line, her arms were crossed, and she was wearing her Cinderella dress. 'I've been trying to conc... conctact you,' she said, not quite getting the word.

I smiled. 'I've been away for a few days, sweetie, with Dan.'

'Did you play video games with Dam?' She did a theatrical gasp.

'Er, no...'

'Good, because he only plays with me, Nana... You can't play too. Can I conctact him?'

'He's busy right now, darling, but we could Skype you...'

'When?'

Who knew when I was seeing him again? Having spent the most idyllic week together, he'd gone back to his life and he'd be busy with the café and I'd just be waiting. And waiting was something I didn't want to do anymore.

'Dan and I went to the beach...' I started. 'We took Clover, you know... the baby?'

'Without me?' she said, and her little chin began to wobble.

'Yes, but...'

'Nana, when are you coming back? I miss you!'

Now my chin began to wobble and I thought, *I just can't do this anymore* – and my heart broke silently in my chest.

My heart was telling me to stay in Sydney. I loved Dan, I always would, and in an ideal world, I'd stay here with him and Clover forever. But Clover belonged to somebody else, she didn't need me, whereas here was my own flesh and blood telling me she missed me.

I felt like I was in two places, stretched across oceans and flipping so easily from one to the other. How could I possibly choose?

'Oh darling, Nana doesn't know what to do,' I said into the screen at Cinderella, who was now painting her nails. 'Thing is, darling, I'm missing you, but I like Dan too and I miss him when I'm not here. I don't want you upset though, because that would be awful. Do you wish I was there with you, Rosie?' I asked, tears streaming down my face. I couldn't bear this, my granddaughter was suffering; she missed me terribly, she needed me and I could take anything, but not this. I waited for her to finish painting her thumbnail, and eventually she looked up, like she'd forgotten I was there.

'Nana...' she started, and I moved closer to the screen, holding my breath: was she distraught? Did she want me to jump on the next plane? 'It's bruddy green!' she said, holding out her bright-green-covered nails.

I laughed at my stupidity. Of course she missed me, but it was passing, temporary. Rosie was so young, she had her mum and Richard and her step-siblings, new friends at school and probably a different boyfriend than the last time we'd spoken. Rosie was fine... it was Faye I needed to think about.

I eventually said goodbye to Rosie, having gone through her portfolio of nail varnishes and planned her next 'look' for a party the following day. I spoke briefly to Emma, but it was late there, and she was trying to get Rosie to bed and I wasn't exactly helping, so I gave her a very brief rundown of the trip and said I'd call the following day.

I was just closing my laptop and wondering what to do for the rest of the evening when Molly appeared. 'Ooh, dahling, meant to tell you, someone's been here looking for you,' she said.

'Dan?' I asked, hopefully. Perhaps he'd wangled another night away from the café and was going to sweep me into his arms again?

'No... A woman, a looker too – God, what I'd give for a figure like that!'

'Did she give a name, what did she want?' I asked, the hairs standing up on the back of my neck. What I really wanted to ask was if she was carrying anything that looked like a weapon or a boiled bunny.

'Didn't say... Have you seen the review of my performance in *Time Out Sydney*?' she asked, throwing the magazine gently onto my lap like we'd known each other forever. I didn't want to seem rude so I made a cursory glance. The review swam before me and I tried to look impressed, but wanted to get back to the matter in hand.

I looked up, making like I'd dragged myself from the riveting review: 'Did she ask for me by name?'

'Who?'

'The woman who came here... Did she ask for me by name?'

'Yes, how else would she ask for you?' she laughed, like I was mad. 'She asked if Faye Dobson was staying here and that she had to talk to you and said she'd be back.'

'She said she'll be back?' I echoed, thinking of Arnie's catchphrase from *The Terminator*.

This was all I needed. I was exhausted from the trip, bereft without Dan and Clover, and now I had to face Saffron, 'the looker'. She was probably going to warn me off, tell me to keep away from her baby, stop playing happy families. I felt sick at the thought of this encounter. I couldn't blame her, especially as Dan, much to my annoyance, had put pictures of the three of us on our trip all over his Instagram. I'd told him it was rubbing her face in it, but he said she was 'cool' about me. He always said she was 'cool', but I wasn't convinced.

'She said I mustn't let you leave before she grabbed you,' Molly was saying as she mixed herself another Sex on Bondi.

'Grabbed?' I asked, my mind suddenly filled with visions of Arnold Schwarzenegger crossed with Glenn Close. What the hell did this woman want from me?

'Yes. Dahling, I'm not being rude, but do you have to keep repeating everything, it's quite off-putting?'

I ignored her comment. 'I think it might be Dan's girlfriend,' I started, 'I'm worried she might think I'm trying to take Dan off her.'

'Are you?'

'Yes… no… I don't know. I don't know what she wants.'

'Oh shit! I should have frisked her.' She stood up quickly, a little shaky on her feet from her latest Sex on Bondi, and came strutting towards me in an over-exaggerated stage walk. She stood over me, bent down into my face and said, 'Be careful, my dahling. She said she'll call back this evening, she could be packing heat.'

'Oh God, I bloody hope not!' I said, looking at my watch: it was 6 p.m. Dan would be busy at work now. I doubted he had any idea that his baby mama was rampaging the streets looking for me. I was feeling a little creeped out, and Molly wasn't exactly helping.

'We were together… before. He met Clover's mum after me…' I tried to explain.

She raised her eyebrows, then swept across the room holding her head. 'Faye, my innocent little angel,' she was waving her arms about now, 'this could turn into a crime of passion.'

'No, it couldn't… Could it?'

'Oh, my love, the cyclic nature of love and violence. Think of *Othello*: "Yet she must die, else she'll betray more men. Put out the light, and then put out the light…"' She was now wringing her hands rather alarmingly.

'Thank you, Dame Judi, but no one will be putting anyone's lights out tonight,' I snapped, pulling myself together.

She was about to embark on an overlong, overdramatised story, with actions and dialogue, when the doorbell rang, making us both jump.

'Is that the wronged woman?' she hissed, stepping behind the curtain. In her drunkenness, she almost fell and I'd have laughed if I hadn't felt like this might be the last few seconds of my life.

'Could you answer it, Molly?' I asked.

'You answer it.'

'No, it's your house.'

'It's *your* love triangle,' she said, trying to stand without wobbling, pursing blood-red lips and attempting to place her hand on her hip.

'Oh for God's sake, it isn't a triangle,' I hissed. 'Dan and I are together, it's all fine, she's… cool.'

One look at Molly cowering behind the curtains and it was clear she only wanted fake drama and was keen to avoid the real thing, so there was nothing else for it but to deal with this myself.

I stomped into the hall and saw the shadowy figure of the person who'd changed my life standing at the door.

'Saffron?' I asked as I opened the door to her.

'Faye.'

I nodded unnecessarily and resisted the urge to slam the door in her face just in case Molly was right. I'd been travelling all day, I'd had 'Sex on Bondi' three times and was feeling the worse for wear and I wasn't in any state for some confrontation over Dan.

'Would you like to come in?' I asked, and unsmiling, she stepped into the hall.

'Are you going to frisk her?' Molly hissed in a stage whisper. She was now at my side, clutching me like both our lives were in great danger.

'No, Molly, that won't be necessary,' I said. 'I'll take my... friend through to the kitchen, if that's okay?'

Molly gave Saffron a wary look as we walked to the kitchen, where I immediately shut the door before she joined us.

'Tea?' I asked, and Saffron shook her head.

I pulled out a chair, she did the same, and for a long time we both faced each other in silence across the kitchen table. I wondered if this might be the prelude to a weird arm wrestle. Instead of keeping this to myself, my nerves got the better of me and I shared this observation with her: 'Is it me, or does this feel like we're about to have some sort of arm wrestle?' I said, trying to lift the mood and take away the obvious tension in the room, but my sudden movement made her flinch and she frowned at me like I was attempting to scare her. We weren't off to a great start.

You might think I would have learned by now that the more I talk, the worse it gets, but I hadn't – and having given her the wrong impression (that I was ready to brawl), I was more nervous. So I just kept on talking.

'When I say that, I don't mean I *want* a fight. God no, that's not how I roll… Oh, I don't roll around or anything… in a fight, I'm just. Saying…' I added, as she continued to look at me like I was unhinged. By now I think I was – I'd been wound up into a tightly coiled spring by Mad Molly.

We sat opposite each other across the pine table in the cottagey kitchen with the big old dresser, which I suddenly realised she could probably bring down on me in one swift move. I put my palms face down on the table, which seemed to make her flinch slightly – I didn't know who was more scared of whom.

Chapter Twenty-Seven

A Crime of Passion and a Bottle of Gin

'So you came here to see me?' I asked, unnecessarily. 'I hope I haven't upset you... being here. I wanted to see Australia, Sydney particularly, so I thought I'd try and see a bit of Dan too... Not a bit of him, I mean all of him. Fully dressed... Like a friend, yes, just friends, nothing more...' Oh God, I was starting over again.

She looked up and nodded slowly, her beautiful eyes gave nothing away.

'Dan said you're cool with us... I wouldn't want to hurt you by just sweeping in and...' I started again, observing her perfect nails, long tanned arms, glowing skin. She really was an attractive woman, about Dan's age, perhaps a little younger, which made her at least ten years younger than me.

'Oh hey, I am cool. I know how it is. You two go back a long way...' she spoke for the first time.

'I don't know what Dan's told you.'

'Everything,' she said, and with that she fixed her gaze right on me and I felt myself blush.

'I need a drink,' I said, knowing a glass of something from Molly's medicine cabinet was the only way I was going to get myself and my nerves through this. I rummaged around in the cupboard and found a bottle of gin and some very old tonic – I doubted Molly ever diluted her alcohol, even her cocktails seemed to be a mix of spirits and liqueurs. I found two glasses and poured us both a large gin. 'Tonic?' I asked, and as she nodded, I poured. 'I just hope it's not going to kill us, I think it's been in that cupboard since 1963,' I smiled, putting her glass in front of her.

She sniffed the glass. 'Arsenic?' she said, and I laughed nervously and tried to reassure her I wasn't going to murder her, though I wasn't sure the same could be said for Molly's ancient gin.

'You're safe,' I said and added rather creepily, 'I'm not about to commit a crime of passion,' which kind of gave the impression that I might, so I tried to smile, but she just looked worried.

She took a glug of gin, then placed both palms flat on the table, like she was about to make an announcement. I couldn't think what she possibly had to say to me – then I thought, *if she's pregnant, I don't want to know. But if she tells me she is with child, Dan's, and it's happened all over again before I got here, then I'm going to finish this bottle of gin all by myself in two minutes flat.*

'Do you know Dan carries photos of you in his wallet?' she said suddenly.

I was surprised, a little pleased too. 'Really?'

'Yeah, he showed me on the first night we met.'

Presenting a woman with photos of your ex wasn't the greatest chat-up line I'd ever heard.

'He never lied to me,' she continued. 'He told me from the start that he was in love with someone else.'

'Oh, that must have been… difficult?' I said, thinking how strange this conversation was, and where exactly was it going?

'No, not really, I was still in love with my ex. Dan was a one-night stand… Okay, a two- or three-night stand. He's a great guy…'

'Yes, he is,' I nodded, waiting for Saffron's declaration of love.

'But I was never in love with him.'

Hallelujah, was all I could think. I wanted to leap on the table and sing 'Who Runs the World?' in my Beyoncé voice, but this would probably alarm given the circumstances, so I made do with a large slug of gin, which burned my throat and made me think it might not be gin after all. Oh, the irony of hearing this wonderful news while inadvertently poisoning myself!

'It should have happened once, I should have got dressed, left his flat and never gone back. But then we bumped into each other again. We were both drunk, he was upset and I'd just found out my ex was with another woman and it happened again. I saw him as a friend,' she added, gesturing to herself, resting her hand on her chest, covered in gold chains twinkling on bronzed skin. 'Look, this isn't about me and Dan, or you and Dan.'

'Oh?'

'No, it's about Clover.'

'Of course,' I said, my heart lurching, waiting for her to say, 'Back off, bitch'. 'I understand. I have a daughter – and a grand-daughter – myself. I'm a mother too, Saffron, and I understand that whatever us adults do, we have to consider Clover.'

'Clover was never going to be part of a cosy mummy-daddy life. My mum was a single mum and I know how hard it is, but I never wanted to stay with Dan, even though I sometimes wondered if I should.' She lifted her hand up as if to stress this. 'You were always there. You lay between us in bed, you stood beside him when we'd kiss, shared our bloody snacks in the cinema,' she laughed.

The idea of me metaphorically lurking in the background of their relationship wasn't comfortable to hear. 'Do you think you could have made a go of it if I hadn't met him first?' I asked.

'No, Dan and I don't work. We're friends who happened to get pregnant and we have to make the best of it. I was just trying to explain to you how much you mean to him… He says you're not sure what to do?'

'No, I just don't know. Dan keeps talking about me moving in with him, but I don't want you to feel like you're being pushed out… or…'

'God no, it's not like that! Thing is, I don't know what to do myself. I've been offered this artist-in-residence post for a year.'

'Oh, that's good, isn't it?'

'Yeah, but it's full-time. It might involve some travel around Australia and I don't know what to do about Clover. My ex – Kevin – says I should stay here and we should get married, and I should just get a job and Clover will be fine and…'

This story felt all too familiar to me. Here was a young woman whose choices were now limited because of her child, just as mine had been. She seemed to sense my understanding, like she knew my history, and was asking me what I thought she should do. I suddenly felt the weight of responsibility on me, but at the same time she was reaching out to me and I wanted to help her, guide her through this mess.

'Yes, I'm sure Clover would be fine if you got married and took any job. But would *you* be fine?' I asked. 'As soon as we become mums we lose ourselves a little, and that's not how it should be. Our kids come first, but *we* have to have a bite of the cherry too, our lives aren't over the day we give birth – in fact, they're just beginning. I said goodbye to Dan because I had to be with my daughter, Emma, but it wasn't a totally selfless act, it was for my own sake too. I had a dream to follow, a degree to finish and a family to support – and I was determined not to lose sight of that. I got my degree, I'm independent and my family is fine, but I had to put myself into the equation and ask what *I* wanted too.'

She was looking at me with such intent. 'Faye, you're so right, the minute you become a mum everything you want seems selfish… And if we ask for what *we* want, because we're mothers, it can feel so wrong.'

'But it isn't. It's about compromise, yes – but it doesn't have to be about losing yourself in all this.'

She looked at me thoughtfully, then said, 'I really, really want to paint. I'm thirty and I've messed around too long, this is my chance to really build a portfolio, make a career, you know?'

'That's exactly what I mean, we put ourselves and our needs last. Of course our kids have to come first – but be kind to yourself too, Saffron.'

I was surprised at how this had all turned out. I'd envisaged Saffron as this selfish, irresponsible woman, who wanted to ditch her child at every opportunity, but in truth she was just like me, trying to balance her own life against her baby's.

'I really want this…' She looked like a million thoughts were whirling through her head, hope and excitement now dancing in her eyes.

'So go for it, don't hang around taking work you don't want. You'll start with a job in a coffee shop and tell yourself it's "just for now", and twenty years will go by and you'll wonder where yesterday went,' I said, thinking of my own life before I met Dan and broke free.

'But what about Clover? I'm so torn, Faye... Kevin's offering me stability, and I don't know if I want to be a single mum – like my mum was.'

'I understand what you're going through. I was eighteen and pregnant but I chose to marry the father because there was so much pressure at the time. I cared about him, we had our moments, but I made the wrong choice. Marriage is hard enough when you really love someone, but marrying for your child and hoping the love bit will catch up just doesn't work,' I said.

She nodded. 'I think I love Kevin, but...'

'If you say "think" before love, then add "but" straight after you probably don't,' I said gently. I was probably overstepping the mark; I hardly knew this woman and yet we walked the same road. 'Trust me,' I added, 'when you love someone, *thinking* doesn't come into it. You *know*, and there are no buts.'

I looked at her and thought of Emma. What would I advise Emma to do?

'If you were my daughter, I'd tell you to take the residency, put yourself in the driving seat and be with Clover as much as you can. I know Dan will help with Clover and you've agreed to share her so you two will just have to work things out. You can have a rota and you make sure you do your thing and he does his, but Clover must always come first.'

'You make it sound easy, but even this week I couldn't have Clover. Dan had begged me to come back and look after her, said it was make or break for you two, that you needed some time to yourselves. But being an artist isn't nine to five and I got caught up in my work and... I'm sorry you had to take Clover with you.'

'Don't apologise for Clover. She was a joy... even when she filled her nappy and projectile vomited and kept us up all night with colic.' We both laughed at this. 'You know, Saffron, if I'm honest, I'm kind of missing her tonight.'

'That's what I hoped you'd say,' she smiled.

'Why?'

'Because Dan's going to be with Clover for at least half her life – and whatever I decide to do, I want the woman who's with him to be as lovely as you.'

'That's a kind thing to say, but I haven't even made up my mind if I'm staying, or even if he wants me.'

'Oh, he wants you.'

'I sometimes wonder why?'

'Who knows what brings two people together? Do you remember at school those couples where you'd think, how did he get her? And how did she get him, she's punching way above her weight? But it's something between two people, and it can't be put into a box and labelled. I'll be honest, I wondered for a while what the hell a middle-aged hairdresser from England had that I didn't. Was she good in bed? Was it a mother thing?'

I bristled at this. 'I doubt it was "the *mother* thing",' I said. 'And God knows, I'm not Cindy Crawford, but as you say, sometimes people get together and they just work. Hey, is it such a bloody mystery that someone like Dan loved someone like me?' I asked, feigning a laugh.

'No, I can kind of see it now.' She was weighing me up and down and I was waiting for some thinly veiled insult.

'Oh?'

'Yeah, you've got something. I don't know what it is, but you do... and it rocks his world.'

'Thanks... I think.'

She smiled. 'But I'll never understand why you two split in the first place if you both feel the same?'

'My daughter, I had to be there for her and I wouldn't have been happy anywhere else.'

'You must have felt like shit when you got here and found out he had a kid?' she said bluntly.

'Yes, that's exactly how I felt, but the more I think about it, the more I realise that it was a good thing. If Dan and I stayed together, he'd never have Clover in his life, and she's the best thing that's ever happened to him.'

She sighed. 'Ironic, isn't it? I felt that clock ticking and threw away my pills when I was with Kevin. I knew there was a chance I'd get pregnant and I think subconsciously, that's what I wanted. Still, when I saw that line on the test, no one was more surprised than me – except Dan.' She smiled at the memory. 'He was lovely about it, happy at the prospect of being a dad – but we were both doubtful about us being together.'

I poured us both another gin, and we sat and let the silence swallow us up. This hadn't been the cat fight I'd thought it was going to be. This woman was opening up in a way I'd never expected and I felt like she needed me.

She put her face in her hands, slowly moving her fingers along her cheeks, revealing her eyes again. She looked tired, like she'd been wrestling with all this for a long time. And as her face emerged from her hands and I looked at her properly for the first time, I realised I'd seen her before.

'You were supposed to be in Perth, but you were on the beach. I bumped into you and later, in the coffee shop – it was you in the toilets, wasn't it? I saw you leave,' I said, slightly taken aback by this realisation.

She leaned forward, one hand touching my arm. 'Yes... I just hoped you didn't know who I was.'

'I didn't – but I do now, I just realised and... and it's a bit creepy,' I admitted.

'I wasn't sure if you'd seen a photo of me and might know who I was.'

'No, I didn't want to see a photo of you.'

'Well, I didn't have any choice. I was faced with a montage of photos of *you*!' She gave me a look of mock outrage, but she was smiling.

'Sorry!' I pulled an awkward face, and we both laughed.

'You know, my biggest fear in all this has been what will happen to Clover... Not just me taking the job, but moving out and Dan meeting someone else. I know the kind of guy he is and he'd never give Clover up, he wants to be in her life. When he told me you were coming to Sydney, I panicked...'

'Why?'

She sighed. 'As I said, my mum was a single parent, but my dad stayed in touch, sent birthday cards, sometimes called by unannounced, which caused all kinds of rows and shouting – usually around Christmas, which was nice. Then he married this bitch and wanted to play happy families all of a sudden, so I had to stay with them every other weekend. She was vile, really resented me, like she was jealous, and when they went on to have their own kids she was even worse. She judged me, always criticising, always finding mean ways to leave me out,' she said, her voice still holding onto the residue of childhood hurt and anger. 'My stepmother was just jealous and didn't want any reminders of Dad's previous relationships hanging around her house.' She took a sip of gin and came alive again as she remembered something she'd kept hidden: 'Do you know, she once arranged for a family photo shoot and didn't invite me – for years I had to look at this bloody big photo on their wall of her and Dad and their two kids. It said "family" in big letters above and I wanted to punch the glass.'

She stopped talking for a moment and seemed to gather herself together, her eyes were filled with tears.

'Thing is, Faye, I don't want Clover to ever feel like that – like she doesn't belong.'

I reached out and took her hand. 'Oh love, Dan wouldn't let that happen – and if I have anything to do with it, she'll never, ever feel excluded from anything.'

'I know it looks a bit weird, but it was important to me – it's why I wanted to watch you, see how you were with her. You could have put it on for show if you'd known I was there, like my stepmother did for my mum and dad. But you didn't, you were so natural with her, and even in the toilets, when no one was there, not even Dan, you were talking to her like I do, telling her she was loved and beautiful… Faye, I was crying in that cubicle.'

'Oh God! I only realised someone was in there afterwards, and I worried they might think I was crazy, telling a two-month-old she could do anything.'

'My mum used to say that to me. "Saffy, you can do anything, be anything…" She struggled all her life, she wanted the best for me – we all do for our kids, don't we? Mum died a few years back and I miss her every day, but hearing you say those things to Clover just got me.' She put her had into a fist and banged her chest, her gold bracelets tinkled like a wind chime and I saw the tears again, so close to the surface. 'When I saw you with her on the beach, you held her with such tenderness, such care, and you looked at her like you were her mother…'

'I know I never will be, Saffron. I'd never try to… I don't want you to feel that I'd try and take over or…'

She wafted her hand away. 'No, no… I know. But I *want* you to love her like I do. What kind of mother would I be denying her a double dose of mother's love?' she smiled.

'That's lovely of you to say,' I said, thinking that perhaps a life with Dan might not be as difficult or complicated as I'd thought. It was simple really, we all cared for Clover and there were no ill feelings, no resentment or jealousy, all Saffron wanted was to be able to paint and love her kid.

'I don't know what's going to happen with you guys, I know you've both got some stuff to deal with, Faye,' she sighed. 'But I do know that Dan will always be in her life… I just hope and pray you'll always be in Dan's.'

Both of us were crying now and she reached out her hand to me across the table and we held on, both unsure of what would happen next, but with a clearer understanding of each other. And what it means to be a mother. Eventually, we composed ourselves and Saffron told me she'd also been offered the chance to exhibit her art in Europe.

'I don't know when it might be, but it might mean going away for longer than a week,' she said, wiping her eyes, laughing and crying at the same time. 'Honestly, Faye, it freaks me out… I couldn't leave Clover with anyone but you… and Dan, of course.'

I didn't say anything, it wasn't for me to make childcare arrangements at this stage, so I just smiled.

'Dan's told me you're a good mother. He said you're really close to your daughter, that you laugh a lot together.'

'Yes, we do, and I love being with my granddaughter and I miss them like hell, and being with Clover this past week has eased that slightly. She's taught me that I'm one of life's nurturers, and I need to be needed, if that makes sense?'

I now knew the woman sitting across from me wasn't my enemy, or someone to envy, she was just a little girl without her mother. Saff – yes, I think I could call her that now – was a first-time parent who couldn't turn to the woman she needed the most right now. This could have been Emma if I wasn't around, and whereas Emma didn't need me as much anymore, perhaps this woman did?

'I hope I can be a good mum, I hope me and Clover will laugh a lot.'

'I'm sure you will. You have to pick your battles, and I think it's the same as with anyone you love. You also have to let them go.'

'That's the hardest part, right?'

'Oh yes, which is why you need something of your own, something independent from your kids. Don't make the same mistake I did, Saffron. Follow your dream, take the artist-in-residence job, and you'll not only be a good mum, you'll be an example to Clover too. No point telling her she can be anything if her mum isn't even trying,' I said.

'You're right, you're so right. I'm going to do it, Faye, I'm going to go home now, give Clover a big hug, then email my acceptance.'

'You go, girl!' I said as she stood up.

She looked at me for a moment and then reached out and hugged me. We stood there for a while and as she pulled away, I could see she was crying.

'Your daughter's a lucky girl to have you for a mum,' she said, picking up her bag and pulling it onto her shoulder.

'Oh, I'm no saint, Saffron! I've made plenty of mistakes, as you will. We're not perfect, we're human, but we just have to do what we feel is right and if it's wrong, then we don't do it again. It's that simple... and that hard.'

She rolled her eyes. 'Yeah. Hey, I hope you stick around in Sydney – I think you and I could have some fun, go for cocktails, put the world to rights.'

'I'd like that. I don't know yet what I'm going to do. Here's me telling you to chase your dream and mine's all over the place! But whatever I do, it's going to be all about me this time,' I said as we left the kitchen, two empty glasses on the table, two lives shared over gin and Formica.

I walked Saffron down the hall and as we reached the front door she turned. 'Faye, just one thing?' she looked at me. We were both emotional and one kind word away from tears.

'Yes?' I said. I held my breath for what she was about to say.

'If you decide to stay, don't let Dan microwave her food, will you? And don't let him feed her wasabi oysters or parsley fucking foam or whatever he's got on the menu that week? And organic... She'll only eat organic pureed veg, you wouldn't believe the shit that's in jars of baby food.'

I nodded, relieved, almost laughing – we were definitely on the same wavelength. 'If I'm there, she won't be touching that shit... or oysters, or parsley fucking foam!'

Saffron laughed and as I opened the door, she turned to go but not without handing me a parting gift. 'By the way, I moved out of the apartment while you were at the coast – he's there on his own now. I'm staying with my friend, she's looking after Clover while I came to see you. Go to him, tonight, you guys need some time alone... And Faye?'

'Yes?'

'If you stay, he'll be one lucky guy. You bloody rock!'

Chapter Twenty-Eight

A Fairy-Tale Ending or a Fast Ticket Home?

When Saffron left, I felt like my world had been turned upside down, in a good way. I was touched by her parting words and, closing the door, leaned my head against it for a few moments to take everything in and enjoy the calm and the hope now blossoming inside my chest. I'd thought that if I ever met her I'd resent the woman who gave Dan the one thing I couldn't. But people surprise you. She was strong and beautiful and all she wanted was the same as me, to be a good mum to her kid and one day find real love. I'd already found that and I'd wasted time worrying about everyone else and not thinking about myself and my own feelings. At forty-six I'd only just worked out how the narrative of my own life could be – and there was only one person who could provide the happy ending.

I'd come to Sydney hoping to be with Dan, perhaps even live here with him forever and ever, but this had been no fairy tale. Dan's life in Sydney was a very different picture than the one I'd expected, and it had thrown me. I'd assumed time had stood still and he'd still be the free-spirited surfer boy who cooked. But this wasn't going to be a future of romantic sunsets in far-flung places, it was nappies and baby sick, not to mention hard work and long shifts building a business. Having said that, I knew from experience, life is about compromise and nothing worth anything comes easy. Meeting Clover, and becoming close again to Dan the father, I'd discovered something about myself: I was a good mother, I knew how to care for people, share my experience and my wisdom.

I wandered back into the kitchen and rinsed the glasses, wondering if Emma had finished the proposal she was writing, thinking about Rosie's first day at school and if she'd be okay. How I'd have loved to be there for them, but turning off the light and heading into the hall, I heard Emma's voice in my head: 'There you go again, Mum, putting everyone else's needs and wishes before your own.' If those I loved were happy and content, then that meant I could be too. Emma was a big girl now, with her own life, her own family and as much as I missed her and Rosie, I'd loved them enough to let them go. They could visit, I could go and see them, and we talked regularly on Skype, so what the hell was I doing wasting any more time? I stood there, on the crossroads of my life, not knowing if I would walk upstairs to bed, or walk through the front door to Dan.

I had travelled to the other side of the world to find what I was looking for, and that had taken guts. I could have sat in front of the TV with a digestive, a cup of tea and *Downton Abbey* and never left the town I was born in. But instead I'd unlocked my life, opened the windows and breathed in the air and discovered I had so much more to give and so much life to live. I was still that middle-aged hairdresser from the Midlands, and there was nothing wrong with that, it's who I was, along with so many other things: a mum, a graduate, a reader, a lover, and a wannabe scuba diver who spent a day on a yacht with a dashing millionaire. I'd seen Paris and Spain and Italy and Greece and now I was in Sydney, and who knew what adventures awaited me? I just had to open up my heart and say yes.

I slowly walked down the hall. This was my chance to say yes, to seek that happy ending, so I opened the door and ran outside into the night. The stars twinkled above, the road lay in front of me, and Dan's apartment was only two blocks away.

I ran and ran until I reached his place, and tearing up the steps, I banged on the door, calling his name. I waited ages, and just as I was about to turn around and head back, the door opened.

'Faye?' He was looking gorgeous, slightly dishevelled, a little subdued.

I gathered all my courage, took a deep breath and said, 'Dan... I love you, and whatever happens, I know I always will. Thing is, I can't live without you... and after last time when you asked me and I said no... and oh Dan, I'm going on again. Will you marry me?'

His face lit up. 'Oh Faye...'

'What?' I said, pretending to be impatient, but knowing by the look on his face what his answer would be.

'Yes, yes, yes...' He almost shouted this and then lifted me in his arms, carried me into his home and closed the door with his foot as the credits rolled on my happy ending. Just like in the films.

Epilogue

It's a Saturday during a mild Australian spring when we take our vows under the big, purple jacaranda tree in the park. The air is alive with bees and birds and friends and family, a swirling, scented day of love and happiness and sunshine.

Dan and I are pretty perfect as the bride and groom, though I say so myself, but the real stars of our wedding day are two little petal throwers: Rosie, now five, and Clover, eighteen months, both in ballerina pink, both sporting unicorn headbands (naturally!) and both wobbly on their feet. Holding hands, they walk ahead of me, scattering rose petals along the ground, Rosie instructing Clover loudly on where to stand and how to walk. Dan is waiting at the other end to catch them (and me!) if we should fall, as Rosie explains loudly to Clover that 'when Nana marries Dam, we'll be sisters', which causes a ripple of laughter that dances on the breeze. I laugh too, while hoping my granddaughter doesn't go on to inform the wedding guests of more personal family details – like the enormity of 'Nana's *big* pants'. I think she's probably saved that revelation for the reception.

Emma looks proudly on, Richard's arm around her, tears in her eyes, her mother and daughter walking through the grass barefoot, dressed in pastels. As I pass, she nudges Saffron, who hands her a tissue. Both women smile at me through their happy tears. I've become so fond of Saffron, and despite being two different women from the other side of each other's worlds, we're just two mothers caught in the same storm. And here we are now standing together in the sunshine after the rain. Saffron is my friend. She makes me laugh, we share frustrations over life, men, children – and most importantly, she knows where to go to get the best cocktails in Sydney. She's my honorary daughter, along with my other cocktail-guzzling honorary daughter Mandy, who has promised (threatened?) to join us both for a 'girls' night' before she goes back to the UK.

Looking at her now, among all my other family and friends, she lifts her hand discreetly, and we give each other a special, almost secret wave. I'm glad Saffron didn't settle for Kevin, that she's gone from strength to strength following her career, and next month heads to France for the first time, and Dan and I can't wait to look after Clover full-time for a few weeks. I give her a little smile, and just know we'll be there for each other, through thick and thin. And when Saff meets her forever man, I'll cry with happiness at her wedding too.

I see Dan's nephews, his sister-in-law Kimmie, and some of his old friends who are here and their smiles as I walk past tell me that I belong. These are my new friends and family, in my new country. I'm so lucky to be here and the love is overwhelming.

Along with my petal throwers, I also have a very special brides-maid in Mandy. Not the obvious choice, you might think, but she turned up in Sydney with a koala tattoo and a pink lace bridesmaid's dress, so how could I refuse? She even turned up a week early to do my 'makeover', which involved the signature orange skin, surprised eyes and taut smooth forehead from so much Botox I looked like I'd had a stroke. Fortunately it's 'thawed' and with the help of Camilla's herbal calming lotion, I am able to smile again on my wedding day. Camilla is here too, holding onto Sue, whose latest boyfriend hasn't joined her in Sydney as he's apparently been struck down with 'psoriasis' of the liver. She showed me the beautiful ring he's given her, which she insists is 'a purple anarchist stone'. Sue's hopeful of her own proposal soon and I'm looking forward to a visit home and a wedding in Devon in the not too distant future.

Marriage isn't for everyone, but this time feels so much different to my first because I'm with the man I love, and I want this more than anything in the world. Marriage has been good for Emma too, she is positively glowing, and I have a feeling it won't be long before we have another little flower to add to our collection (she refused a glass of Prosecco when she arrived – that's not our Emma!).

Not so long ago, I thought I'd seen the last of any more babies, but now with maybe another grandchild on the way and our own little bundle of joy, Clover, I feel like there's so much to be happy about. I'm glad for Dan that he is finally able to know what being a parent is – the unconditional, all-encompassing love we have for our children is something that just imprints on your heart forever. And I know we don't have them long and when all of the kids have grown up and flown the nest, I'll still have Dan by my side and plenty more adventures to look forward to.

Meanwhile, my Australian adventure is only just beginning. I've started teaching at a nearby uni, and I love it, sharing the knowledge, the passion, the ideas of literature and learning from the students too. I also spend as much time as I can with Clover, and between us, Dan, Saffron and I share the childcare. I learned through Rosie and Clover that I was good at this, that being with my girls made me happy, and that's what life's all about. We shouldn't have to choose between career and family, but so often we are forced to. But I'm one of the lucky ones, and for now I'm having my cake and eating it, in the Sydney sunshine, with the love of my life and I reckon that's a pretty good place to be. I've found a man who gave me the courage to chase my dreams, build a new life from nothing, and become the me I've always known is there.

As the registrar says, 'You may kiss the bride,' I'm swept up into Dan's arms arriving finally at my destination, after our long, rocky road to here. We've travelled continents to be with each other, we spent a year apart and against all the odds we're finally together forever.

Marrying Dan is my second chance, and this time I'm not settling for anything less than the best, it has to be perfect. There will be ups and downs as there are in life, but together we'll get through them. And as we eat the lemon myrtle cake he baked for our wedding, and toast the bride, he tells everyone that he loves me, he's always loved me, and he always will. And I glow, bathed in his sunshine, under the purple jacaranda tree eating lemon wedding cake, *this* is my happy ending.

Dan and Faye's Lemon Myrtle Wedding Cake

Here is Dan's wonderful cake recipe, and you don't have to be getting married to bake it!

For the wedding, Dan made five cakes, placed them at different heights along the wedding table, and scattered them with fresh pink rose petals.

Lemon myrtle is native to Australia (like Dan!) and used in sweet and savoury recipes, but if you don't have any, don't worry – it's optional in this recipe. Just remember to always add an extra sprinkle of love though!

Ingredients

175 g/6 oz softened butter

175 g/6 oz caster (superfine) sugar

3 eggs, beaten

175 g self-raising flour (if you're in the US, use 6 oz all-purpose flour with 2 tsp of baking powder)

2 lemons

2 tsp lemon myrtle (optional)

For the icing

> 200 g/7 oz softened butter
>
> 400 g/14 oz icing (confectioner's) sugar
>
> 1 lemon
>
> 1 tsp lemon myrtle (optional)

Method

1. Preheat the oven to 180°C/350°F/Gas Mark 4. Grease two 20 cm/8-inch round sandwich tins and line with greaseproof paper.

2. Now put the butter and sugar in a bowl and cream together until thick and pale, then add the 3 beaten eggs. Next, sift in the flour and add slowly, then grate the zest from the 2 lemons, squeeze 1 tbsp lemon juice and add this, along with the (optional) lemon myrtle.

3. Beat for about 2 minutes, until everything is combined and the mixture is light and fluffy. Spoon into the 2 tins, spread level and bake for 30-35 minutes or until firm and golden. Leave to cool in the tins for 10 minutes before turning out onto a wire rack, then leave until completely cooled.

4. For the icing, beat the softened butter with the icing sugar until light and fluffy, and squeeze 1 tbsp lemon juice and 1 tsp (optional) lemon myrtle into the mixture.

5. Once the cakes are cooled, spread the icing over the top of each cake using a palette knife. Sandwich together and then using the remainder of the mixture, cover the cake. For their wedding, Dan scattered the cake with fresh rose petals, but tiny pansies or any other edible flowers look pretty and delicious!

A LETTER FROM SUE

Thank you so much for reading *Love, Lies and Wedding Cake*. I loved spending time with Faye and Dan again – I hope you did too!

If you did enjoy it, and want to keep up-to-date with all my latest releases, just sign up at the following link. Your email address will never be shared and you can unsubscribe at any time.

www.bookouture.com/sue-watson

Thanks also to those wonderful readers who made *Love, Lies and Lemon Cake* a bestseller. So many of you have been in touch to say how much Faye's living list inspired you. From jumping out of planes to going on dates after divorce to learning to dive, you've amazed yourselves and everyone else. You rock! And I hope this new book pushes you even further. Just remember Sue's famous words (stolen from Pinterest): *the greatest loss is what dies inside us while we live.* So just keep on keeping on, ladies!

I too will keep on keeping on writing as long as you want to read my books, and if you would like to know when the next one is released, you can sign up by following the link above.

Meanwhile, I'd love to see you on Facebook, become a friend, like my page and please join me for a chat on Twitter. I'd love to know about your own living lists – and your wedding cakes too!

And don't forget, if you want to taste a little more of that Aussie sunshine, I've included Dan's recipe for lemon cake, just like his mum used to make.

So thanks again for reading, and until we 'meet' again, I'll leave you with Mandy's profound advice: 'Life's short – get a vajazzle!'

 www.suewatsonbooks.com

 suewatsonbooks

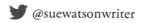 @suewatsonwriter

Acknowledgements

This story has been a labour of love, and writing about weddings is almost as much fun as having one. And like all bridezillas, I had my faithful team by me every step of the way, guiding me down the aisle and helping Faye and Dan achieve their dreams against all the odds.

So a scattering of confetti to the lovely 'wedding planners' at Bookouture – huge thanks to Oliver Rhodes, Claire Bord, Isobel Akenhead, Emily Ruston, Jade Craddock, Lauren Finger, Jane Donovan and all the other wonderful publishing people involved. Fresh rose petals to Kim Nash, publicity queen and maid of honour, for her support, wisdom and friendship always.

Wedding favours to my wonderful friends who are always so understanding when my writing prevents me from attending book club/wine club/cocktail club/coffee club/shopping club/girls' night in club/girls' night out club… and any other 'clubs' we come up with as a blatant excuse to get together.

Wedding bouquets to my mum, who doesn't hear from me for days when I'm 'in edits' but is always on the end of the phone when I need her. A huge slice of wedding cake to my daughter Eve for being fabulous and for showing me the life-changing 'synonyms thingie' on my computer. And a special thank you to my lovely, long-suffering husband, Nick Watson, my groom of many years. He's always in the firing line when I have a book on the go and tells me he often feels like he's living in *The Shining* – and *I'm* Johnny!

But the first dance and final word goes to Kat Everett, my good friend, fellow book lover/blogger, international businesswoman and global nail diva, who has, for several years, demanded a sequel to Faye's story. Here you go, sweet cheeks!

Printed in Great Britain
by Amazon